I0619039

THE GIDORIAN SAGA

THE GOLDEN ACADEMY

ERIC BOWDEN

THE GIDORIAN SAGA - THE GOLDEN ACADEMY

Copyright ©2024 Eric Bowden. All rights reserved.

Published by Park City Publishing
Book Design by Lauren Nadler
Cover Illustration by Andrea Tentori Montalto
Cover Design by Viktorija Elikovi VIKA

The Gidorian Saga: The Golden Academy is a work of fiction.
ISBN: 978-1-7350749-4-8 Paperback

Printed in the USA

PARKCITYPUBLISHING

To Didi and Pop,
thank you for always
believing in me.

TABLE OF CONTENTS

THE GOLDEN ACADEMY

CHAPTER ONE

THE AWAKENING

*B*oom.

Dust fell from the ceiling as my eyes fluttered open.

Boom.

The walls shook, and glass rattled in the window panes.

BOOM.

Closer this time, as if it were coming from right outside my window.

"Mom!" I yelled to her as I leaped out of bed and ran into the living room.

"Kaden! What is happening?" my mom frantically yelled from her bedroom.

BOOM!

The windows of the apartment shattered, sending glass shards onto the floor. I burst through the door and jumped on top of her bed, protecting her from falling debris. A large figure passed outside the destroyed window, lumbering through the streets.

A rogue Golden? I thought to myself.

"Just hang on, Mom. *They'll* take care of it!" I tried to assure her.

I watched helplessly through the open bedroom door as large fingers broke through the living room wall and began to close around it.

"Don't look, Mom!" My hand covered her eyes.

The fingers came downward, crushing the brick, plaster, and drywall. Bits and pieces crumbled off, breaking apart upon impact with the floor. The entire wall was ripped off and thrown into the distance. I extended my arm, covering her head as I pressed my own into the pillow next to hers, trying to drown out the noises that thundered outside.

"Just hang on; we're going to be okay," I said, although I didn't fully believe it myself.

An explosion echoed in the distance, sending a cloud of dark gray smoke and soot into the air. People screamed and yelled from the streets just as a fireball ripped past our window, and then there was…

Silence.

It all stopped at once, and nothing but silence and ash hung in the room. I listened for more explosions, more screams, more destruction, but nothing came.

"I think it's over. Are you alright?" I asked as she adjusted her nasal cannula back into her nose

"I believe so. How bad is the damage?" she responded as I climbed off the bed and dusted myself off.

Parts of the ceiling had fallen in, creating gaping holes into the empty apartment above us. I walked into the living room, and what once used to be our seating area was now nothing more than a giant hole, leading out into the open air.

I carefully made my way to the edge, watching my step as I went. One wrong move, and I would be sent falling ten stories to my death. What was left of our TV and furniture had landed on the street below, along with half of our building.

Then I saw *him*—the one responsible for all of this *and* my ruined morning. He had to have been at least two hundred feet tall, dressed head to toe in some sort of green costume. He was laid out, flat on his back, with a crushed building beneath him. A flying teenager with metallic wings swooped down from the sky and landed on the giant man's chest. Two others—one with black tentacles protruding from his body and one who looked like a humanoid blue crystal—climbed up the side of the giant man. They moved across his body just as the fireball from earlier landed next to them, making it a total of four. Although I didn't know them personally, I recognized them instantly. They were *Heroes* from the Golden Academy.

The humanoid blue crystal made his way to the giant's head.

"That's what you get, asshole!" he yelled, landing a solid punch on his chin.

The punch, although it looked cool, did nothing more than piss him off. With one flick of his finger, the giant man sent the crystal Hero flying through a nearby building. The Hero with black tentacles placed something on the giant's neck, and a faint *beep* sound followed. His body shrank down to normal human size as the others jumped off him.

Suddenly, a pink and purple portal appeared in front of me which provided a pass through onto the street. I watched as people ran across the street, screaming amongst themselves.

"What the hell—" A beautiful girl in a pink, armored suit jumped through the portal and landed in front of me.

I stumbled backward, slipped on the debris, and landed on my tailbone. Her long blonde hair blew in the wind coming from the hole in the side of the building.

"Are you both alright?" she asked. "It appears that your

building sustained heavy damage."

"I noticed," I replied as I looked at the *obvious* damage surrounding us.

"Is anyone hurt?"

"No, I think we're okay. Besides potential emotional—"

"Good. My team has subdued the rogue Golden, and the situation is under control. The Department of Golden Control will be in contact with you for repairs. Have a great day."

And just as quickly as she had appeared, she jumped backward and disappeared into the portal, vanishing as if nothing had ever been there.

I heard the squeaky wheels of my mother's oxygen tank roll across the floor behind me.

"*Happy birthday,* I guess?" she said.

Then it dawned on me, I had forgotten it was my birthday today. Living in a world of Goldens can have that effect on you. Everything seemed secondary to their lives and missions, even ahead of our own.

• • •

That night, my mom and I sat at the kitchen table and tried to enjoy what was left of an otherwise terrible day. I was at least happy that I got to see Heroes up close, even if it meant half of our apartment had to be destroyed for it to happen. The image of the portal girl standing before me never left my mind either. I didn't want to admit it, but she didn't even seem to care about us.

I was pulled out of my thoughts as the blue tarp that the DGC put up on the exterior of our apartment flapped in the wind.

"The big sixteen! Are you excited?" my mom asked.

"I guess," I said hesitantly. "I can't help but see this morning as a bad omen. A rogue Golden smashing through our building… What a gift that was."

My mom took my hand and said, "Don't worry, Kaden, everything is going to be alright, and I have a feeling this is going to be your best year yet. Now, make a wish, and blow out the candles."

I would be lying if I said I didn't wish to be one of the Heroes of the Academy.

How did they get so goddamn lucky? I thought to myself.

Being able to fly around the globe, using their powers to fight Rogues and save the world. Meanwhile, the rest of us useless non-Goldens sit here, helpless, waiting for a building to come down and crush us like ants. It's *their* world; we're merely just existing in it.

"Kaden?" Her words brought me back to the dinner table. "You're not wishing for powers, are you?"

"No?" I responded defensively, but I guess I'm a terrible liar because she looked at me like, *really?*

"I know how hard it is for you, hoping yours would come, but you and I both know that no child has ever received their powers past ten years old. You're *long* overdue. Besides, I'm happy you never got them. You know what happens to those Golden kids when they do."

"They get to go and be Heroes, fighting against Rogues for the Academy," I quickly responded.

"*And* their parents rarely get to see them," she said as I rolled my eyes. "We've been able to stay together as a family without having to worry about all that 'saving the world' stuff."

"What if I want to be out there, Mom? Saving the world! Instead, I'm stuck in this stupid apartment, wasting my life!" I immediately regretted what I said after I saw the heartbroken look on my mom's face. "I'm…" I tried finding the words. "I'm sorry, Mom. I didn't mean it like that. I just feel as if there's got to be more to life than *this*. I just don't think that I'm doing enough with mine."

"You're sixteen, Kaden! You don't need to be doing anything besides eating your birthday cake. A person does not need to be a 'superhero' to be happy. Anyone can be a hero, even us *normal* people, and you know what, Kaden? It's quite alright to just be normal and *not* a Golden. There is absolutely nothing wrong with that. So cheer up; you've got a lot of time to figure everything out. Don't rush it," she said with a reassuring smile.

"I guess."

I tried to believe her, but I just wouldn't accept it. I couldn't help but imagine what it must be like to live life as a Golden Hero.

If only I was one of them.

She placed a piece of cake in front of me, but my stomach felt twisted in knots, still thinking about what happened earlier today. I stuck my fork in it and mushed it on the plate.

"Look, Kaden, I know my condition has not allowed me to be the mother you needed. We also haven't lived the grand life you dream of, but you can't blame yourself for any of it. You've undertaken many responsibilities and taught yourself a lot of things. You should be proud!" She tried to find the right words and finally said, "What I'm trying to say is… This hasn't been easy for either of us. No child should grow up without a father, while also taking care of someone who is unable to take care of herself." A single tear rolled down her face which broke my heart.

My father, I thought to myself.

My ears began to ring, and my face became extremely hot. Thinking about that person, someone I had never known but heard so much about, whom my mother speaks so highly of…

I looked back into her eyes and said, "You've done the best you could, Mom, and I love you for that. Thank you, *truly*. I just—" I choked on my own words, "I just wonder: if Dad had really cared about us—if he was all those things you said he was—then why'd he leave us?"

I couldn't stop it as tears began to fill my eyes. Talking about my father always evoked this reaction. My mom got up from the table, readjusted her oxygen tubes, and came to hug me.

"Your father cared about you more than you could ever know. He didn't tell me where he was going or why he had to go, but I just saw *something* in his eyes—a look I had never seen before. He told me he needed to go for us, to protect us. John never gave me a reason not to believe him, and to this day, I still do," she said.

Suddenly, she covered her mouth and started coughing before collapsing onto the floor.

"Mom!" I yelled as I ran to her side and put an arm around her. "Are you ok?"

She seemed to get her coughing under control before saying, "Thank you, Kaden, I'm OK. It's just all this dust floating in the air." I helped her to her feet. "I think I need to lie down."

I held her up as we walked to her debris covered bedroom, watching our steps as we went. Her oxygen tank bounced and rolled over pieces of the ceiling before finally coming to a halt next to her bed. After tucking her in, she reached out a hand which I took into my own.

"Did he ever say anything about me, Mom?" I said as my voice trembled.

"You weren't born yet, but he already loved you very much. He knew he would do anything for you. You know he even picked out your name, which means *fighter*," she shook her head side to side, "or companion, which I think is a little more fitting for you," she said with a smile on her face.

Her words made me feel better, but I didn't think anything except meeting him would ever heal that wound.

"Goodnight, Mom. Thank you for everything," I said as I squeezed her hand.

She smiled and said, "Happy birthday, Kaden. Now, please, go have some cake. I don't want you to go to bed hungry."

"I will, I promise."

I shut the door and grabbed my plate off the table. My feet moved toward the edge of the opening out into the warm breeze—or at least the closest to it that still felt safe. The blue tarp flapped in the wind, and I had to admit that the breeze did feel nice.

Maybe it wasn't so bad what that giant rogue Golden rampaging through the city did? I thought.

I shoved a piece of cake in my mouth and watched as the DGC continued working, cleaning up the damage caused by the Rogue. As I chewed, the words of my mother ran through my head. It took sixteen years for her to tell me what she said tonight—obviously a hard subject to discuss.

I could tell from the way she talked about my father that she was still in love with him—another reason why she hadn't remarried, aside from her condition. I was afraid that was the last thing I would ever hear about him, not because she wouldn't tell me, but because she didn't *know* anything else. From what I knew, he was only in her life for a short period of time before he vanished, and no one had seen him since.

For the longest time, I thought my life would be better if I were a Golden, and frankly, I still did. Maybe I wouldn't feel so goddamn useless all the time, and maybe the other kids wouldn't pick on me. My Awakening could even give me powers that could help my mother's condition and heal her, so she could get back out into the world again. I didn't know why she was sick, and I didn't think she knew either. She had been this way for as long as I could remember, and none of the doctors could figure out what it was.

Why does the nicest and greatest person I know have to be brought down by an incurable sickness?

The world doesn't make sense to me, but then again, *nothing* does.

Then I thought about what my life would be like at the Golden Academy. Maybe they would let me go out on missions to look for my father. Perhaps I would even have a power that could track people, and I would finally get to meet him after all this time. I could be the *hero* and bring my family together again, just as I always wanted.

I threw the rest of my cake out of the giant opening in frustration and rose to my feet, getting even closer to the edge to the point where I felt the tips of my toes barely hanging over it. My arms rose by my side, and I pictured effortlessly floating into the air and taking off into the sky.

Maybe one day.

• • •

The next morning, I woke up hoping the events of yesterday were just a dream. But as I opened the door to my room, I saw that the hole in the wall was still there.

Great.

My mother was in the kitchen painfully sweeping debris off the floor into a dust bin.

"Don't worry about it, Mom. I'll take care of it when I get home from school," I said as I packed my workbooks into my backpack.

She smiled and said, "I'll help with what I can while I still have the energy so it isn't too much for you when you get back."

"Thanks," I said with a nod as I began to put my shoes on.

"Hey, Kaden?"

"Yeah?"

"Have a good day at school today, OK?"

I hesitated, thinking about what was waiting for me when I get there and finally said, "I will."

I walked toward the door, but she stopped me and said, "And Kaden, you don't need to be a Golden to be a hero. Being a hero is not about having powers or abilities, it's about doing the right thing even in the face of adversity, and for what it's worth, I see one standing right in front of me."

I smiled and said, "Thanks, Mom. I see one *too*."

She gave me a hug, and I headed out the door.

As I walked along the street, I thought about the fact that my mom didn't know I was bullied at school. If she did, I didn't think she'd let me go. She would probably homeschool me the second she found out even though I wouldn't want her to do that. I would probably feel even more trapped than I do now. I just wished I could go to the Golden Academy. But maybe my mom *was* right, and none of that Golden Hero stuff really mattered anyway.

Just then, I saw a little girl in front of me chasing after a ball in the street. To her right, a speeding truck was coming straight at her. Without hesitating, I ran toward her and pushed her out of the way, just as I saw the bright lights of the truck quickly approaching. I braced for the grille of the truck to splatter me, and right before it did, another teenage Hero in a blue, armored suit flew down and dropped his shoulder into the truck. The truck bounced off him and flew off the road, crashing into a lamp post.

"You ok, dude?" he asked as he brushed the metal pieces of the grille off of himself.

I caught my breath and managed to let out, "Yeah, yeah, I'm good."

"I'm glad because you almost got yourself *killed.* Leave this stuff to the Heroes." And with that, he took off into the sky, created a sonic boom, and disappeared into the clouds.

Dick.

After a few blocks, I finally made it to my school in one piece. I would be lying if I said I wasn't a little shaken up, but at the same time it felt *good?* Doing something like that, saving that little girl…

Maybe my mom was right?

By the end of my first period class, I had accumulated at least a dozen spitballs in my hair that came from the bullies who sat behind me. I tried my best to ignore them, focusing on my drawing instead. Seeing that Heroes' suit up close today was inspiring. Although I'd never get to wear one myself, I still drew the suit I pictured wearing *if* I became an Academy Hero.

It was something I had dreamed of ever since I was a little kid. Nothing special, just a black suit with red accents. I loved looking at it and picturing myself in it.

THWIP!

Another spit ball hit the back of my head.

"When did the first Golden appear on Earth?" the teacher asked the class.

"300 years ago," I answered.

"Correct, Kaden." He nodded with a smile and added, "Within The Unity—our one world government—the Department of Golden Control was set up in the 1900's as a means of protecting non-Golden citizens from rogue Goldens."

DING! DING! DING!

The bell sounded as all of the students began getting up from their seats.

"You all will need to know this for tomorrow's test!" the teacher yelled as everyone piled out of the room.

Easy, I thought to myself.

History was the only thing I found interesting in school because we got to learn about Goldens. I had studied them for years, trying to learn everything I could; all their wars, one vs. one battles, famous Heroes and Rogues—virtually anything I could find and get my hands on. Most of it was classified, so I worked with what I could, reading about the events from non-Golden perspectives, which were all *incredibly* limited.

I brought my food over to my usual table in the cafeteria, at the farthest end away from the other students. This was how it always was and would be for the foreseeable future. I didn't mind it too much because I was so used to eating alone at this point. Since I didn't have to talk to anyone, it always gave me plenty of time to read up on Golden history and news or work on my art.

I pulled out my drawing and began to fill in some spots I had missed earlier. A hand slapped down on top of it and ripped it from the table. I turned to see one of my bullies running off with it while laughing.

"Hey!" I shouted. "Give that back!"

"Gotta come get it, Goldilocks!" he yelled as he ran down the hall.

I chased after him before ending up in a bathroom. As soon as I entered, I knew what I had walked into: a trap. Immediately, I felt someone grab me from behind, locking my arms behind my back.

"Please, man, just give it back," I pleaded.

"Oh this stupid thing? What is it anyway? Your little costume that you'll never get to wear? Grow up and face the facts, Kaden: you're just like the rest of *us*," he said as he balled up the drawing and threw it into the toilet. "Not like you're going to be needing it anyway."

The bullies laughed while one of them flushed the toilet. I watched as my suit swirled in a circle and disappeared into the pipes, along with my hopes and dreams of ever wearing it.

"Now that we have that out of the way," the bully said as he wound up a punch, delivering it straight into my gut. It buckled my knees, but the bully behind me held me up.

"Ya know, Kaden? I take it back. You're not like us. You're weaker!" He punched me again. "You're pathetic!" And another. "But there was one thing I was right about… you'll *never* be a Golden, and I know that hurts you more than any of this."

After another punch to my gut, I tried again to drop to

the floor, but the bully behind me suspended me in the air. I coughed, feeling warm blood pooling in my mouth.

"Look! He's coughing like his mom!"

Anger swelled inside me, and blood rushed to my head. He wound up once more and punched me, but this time something *happened*. I felt my body become extremely warm, as if someone dropped me into a hot bath. I started to emit a faint red glow, and sweat poured down my face.

"What the hell?" the bully in front of me said.

The one behind me dropped me onto the cold floor. I looked at my hands as they started to glow bright red.

"No, it's not... *possible*. He's—" they all looked at me in disbelief, "Awakening! Run! Everyone, run!" the bully yelled as he and his goons took off out of the bathroom.

I scrambled to my feet and looked at myself in the mirror. Underneath my brown hair, my eyes flickered from their normal blue color to solid red, and my hands felt as if they were on fire. I shoved them under a running faucet, but it did nothing to alleviate the pain. The entire bathroom glowed bright red like a glow stick in the dark. My body burned, and my legs felt like jello as I stumbled out into the hallway. Immediately, I was met with screams from students who ran away from me after catching a glimpse of the red light pouring off of me. My vision was blurry and red as I attempted to find an exit to get outside. I burst through a door and ended up on the grass of a nearby field.

My legs buckled, and I dropped to my knees, eventually falling flat on the ground. As I lay there, I saw the terrified faces of my classmates who watched me convulse. The entire school had gathered outside, not understanding what they were watching, and neither did I.

"Get the DGC on the phone right now!" a teacher from the crowd yelled. Everyone started to move closer to me as I cried, "Get back…" The words barely slipped from my mouth. "RUN!"

My entire body filled with energy until I reached a breaking point. I screamed as red light *exploded* out of me.

CHAPTER TWO

THE GOLDEN ACADEMY

E VERY TIME I tried to remember what happened after that moment, I drew a blank. The next thing I knew, I was in a cold and unfamiliar place. A bright light shone in my eyes from above, and my blurry vision slowly became more clear. The room was sterile white, and a cardiac monitor next to me beeped along at consistent intervals. An IV led down to my chain bound arm that was attached to the railing of the hospital bed I lay in. Doctors and nurses moved through the room, checking my vitals while making notes on touchscreen devices.

"He's awake," one of the doctors called out to the others as they surrounded me.

"Where am I?" I asked, but none of them answered as they tapped furiously on their devices. "Hello? Someone answer me! Please!"

My heart rate on the monitor began to rise rapidly, but still, no one responded.

"Alright, that's *enough*," a voice came from outside the room. "Zo and I will take it from here."

An elderly looking man with a long white beard walked into the room. His mustache, long and full, had gold beads on it that formed two separate strands that ran down the front of his beard. Two other beads created strands that ran from the top of his head and past his ears. It all flowed to the bottom of his beard which was tied off at his chest with a singular gold bead.

He wore a one-shouldered, white toga with gold accents on it, and although he had an aged face, his physique did not reflect it at *all*. It was as if he had spent the past 500 years eating 10,000 calories a day, swimming across the ocean in the morning, and lifting mountains in the afternoon for exercise.

His arms swung by his sides, creating striations that rippled across his chest and shoulders. Veins protruded from underneath his skin and ran down his biceps, fighting to burst through. His thigh and calf muscles looked like Michelangelo had carved them out of marble for one of his sculptures. I had never seen anyone—let alone someone his age—in such incredible shape in all of my life.

Another *thing* followed him on a futuristic floating lounge chair. His appearance scared me half to death, and I scooted back as far as the chain bound to my arm allowed me.

The thing that I believed to be a horribly deformed person had a brain that was so massive, it made the rest of his body look like that of a toddler. His eyes were two solid white marbles, and I wondered if he could even see out of them. Gold veins glowed and pulsed through his thick skull as if you could see memories and thoughts moving around it in real time.

It seemed that even if he wanted to walk on his own, his legs would be unable to support the massive weight of his head. I supposed that was why he needed the floating chair to get around. He inspected charts and looked at the touchscreen attached to his chair while flashing odd glances at me.

The ripped old man smiled and gripped the side of my hospital bed, and I could hear the metal torque under the massive amount of force that it was subjected to.

This is not *someone you want to fuck with,* I thought to myself.

"I know you have a lot of questions, and I will be sure to answer them soon. Zo, please unstrap our friend. He is no prisoner here," he said, signaling to release the metal clamps around my arm.

Zo pressed a button on his screen, and the clamps released. My body ached and groaned, and I was barely able to sit upward. I wanted to just fall back down and go to sleep again because I felt exhausted. I had no clue why I felt this way with *zero* energy, but then again, nothing about any of this made sense.

"Do you think you can walk?" the older man asked.

I felt weak, but I forced my legs off the bed. My bare feet were immediately stung by the ice cold floor, but I forced through the pain and slowly pressed them further onto it.

"I am Headmaster Fowler," he said while extending a hand to shake.

As mine met his, I felt how weathered and calloused they were, like a carpenter's.

"Kaden Collins," I replied while shaking it. "Where am I?"

"How about we take a walk, shall we?"

I was given a set of new clothes to wear that had the letters TGA on them, and as we left what I assumed to be an infirmary, we made our way to a set of double doors that led outside to an unknown world.

"Kaden, welcome to the *Golden Academy*."

The sun shone brightly into my eyes as he pushed through the double doors, but once they adjusted to the light, the image that was revealed to me was more beautiful than I could have ever imagined.

My eyes danced around the Roman inspired architecture that made up the Academy. There were large temple—like buildings with stone columns that stood tall in front of their entrances. The entire place looked like a college campus with slick stone pathways leading to fountains and grassy areas where young Goldens were lounging about. The center walkway led directly to a dominating edifice with a glass dome for a roof.

"The Golden Academy?" I repeated. "We're really here? I'm not dead, am I?"

The Headmaster chuckled and said, "No, Kaden, no you are not."

I couldn't believe what I was seeing. There weren't any photos of it online because it was probably the most secretive place on the planet, but I had always dreamed of walking through it just as we were now.

"I didn't expect it to be so… Roman?" I said.

"Ah yes, Rome was one of my many inspirations when I was first designing these grounds with Zo. Such inventive and intellectual people. I just couldn't help but model the Academy after their striking architecture."

"Headmaster Fowler, this is incredible and all, but… why am *I* here?"

"Isn't it obvious? You're a Golden, Kaden."

The words sent a shockwave through my body as I remembered seeing red light glowing from my hands before running outside and blacking out, but I had really thought that was all a dream.

"I'm a Golden?" I asked as if the word scared me. "I wasn't dreaming earlier? What happened before was real?"

"Yes, Kaden, *all* of it. The DGC was contacted, and we quickly responded to the scene and found you outside of your school lying unconscious near the soccer field. *Luckily,* no one was hurt during your Awakening."

"But, how is that even possible? I just turned—"

"*Sixteen*," he interrupted. "Yes, we're very much aware, and quite frankly, we're still trying to figure out how. The oldest recorded Awakening in Golden history is sure to raise a lot of questions, but the bottom line is, you're an anomaly, and I've never seen an Awakening quite like yours. Zo, the one you met earlier in the infirmary—"

"The toddler with the giant head?" I said with a chuckle.

"Please do not address him as such; he is quite self conscious about his appearance, and he is *not* someone you would want to make an enemy. To say the least, his looks are quite deceiving, but yes… the one with the giant head. Right now, while we walk through the Academy grounds, he is in his lab analyzing a sample of your blood to figure out what makes you different from all the others who have Awakened before you. We hope we may have some answers soon, and, of course, we will let you know as soon as we do. In the meantime, let me show you around your new *home*."

My eyes grew wide as a new realization set in, *I get to live here!*

We walked across the courtyard, past various Heroes, all of whom gave me odd looks while they whispered among themselves as if I were some kind of freak.

"Ignore them. There are over 1000 Heroes currently

enrolled at the Golden Academy, and they have all been here for a long time. By now, everyone knows each other very well. I assume they are just shocked to see a new student, especially someone your age," he said as he walked with his hands behind his back.

"Is what you said really true? No one in all of Golden history has ever Awakened at my age?" I asked.

"No one, Kaden. Goldens Awaken by ten years old at the latest, before coming here to begin their training as Heroes. You are *not* supposed to exist."

Wow, I guess I really am a freak, I thought to myself.

We made our way to what looked like some sort of mini stadium, perhaps you could even call it a coliseum with a domed roof.

"Speaking of training, this is one of ten Power Domes that we have at the Academy—the only place on campus where your inhibitor chip is disabled," he said, pointing to my neck.

I ran my finger across the spot he was pointing to and felt a small bump underneath my skin.

"Is this why I don't feel any different after my Awakening?" I asked.

"Yes, you should feel like a regular human, because you may very well be one when it is activated. We use them to inhibit all of our Heroes' powers while on campus, except inside the Power Domes, for your safety and everyone else's. Here, I'll show you," he said as I followed him into one.

We walked through a staging area with floating egg chairs and multi-colored glowing lockers, and in front of me stood a blue force field that separated it from a large arena with white squares and gray borders all across the walls.

"Go ahead, walk through it, and see your powers for yourself," the Headmaster said as he ushered me forward toward the force field.

At first, I was hesitant to step through it, only because I didn't know what to expect if I did. I looked at him one last time, and he gave me a reassuring nod to continue on.

My feet carried me along as I stuck out an arm to the force field and seamlessly went through it. There was a cold sensation of the force field on my skin, and once I was fully inside the arena, I heard a *BEEP* emanate from my neck, and I immediately felt a rush of energy surge through my body.

I looked down at my hands and saw the same red glow that had emitted from them in the school bathroom. Then, I saw streaks of red light start to swirl around my forearms and body.

"Whoa," I said as I flipped my arms back and forth, inspecting the light that weaved around them.

"*Here* you will learn how to hone your powers and use them to the best of your ability. You will also learn how to work as a team while successfully executing *all* missions assigned to you."

I was too distracted to focus on what Headmaster Fowler was saying because I saw that my hands had started to glow brighter, while streaks of light swirled around them even faster. I could feel my body wanting to expel energy, so I raised my hand to do just that. I didn't know what I was doing, but it felt *right.* Just before the energy shot out of me, I felt a firm hand come down on my shoulder. The Headmaster's fingers wrapped around it and pressed down hard as if he could easily shatter my bones without much effort.

"We've still got a lot to see before we start doing *that,* Kaden. Let us continue on with the tour," Headmaster Fowler said as he led me back to the force field.

I didn't want to leave, because I wanted to stay and learn what my powers were, but I knew it was time to go, and I had a feeling the Headmaster *wasn't* asking.

We moved across the courtyard once more as he showed me various buildings, but then he stopped. He put a finger to his right ear and focused as if he were listening to a voice that was coming through an earpiece. The happy and calm look on his face quickly changed to one of slight horror.

"I'm on my way," he said as he quickly composed himself, his face returning back to a smile. "Kaden, I hate to leave you before we could finish your grand tour, but it seems as if something else has come up that warrants my attention. See that building straight in front of you? Those are The Villas where your room, number 214, is located. Everything you will need for class will be found there, including your new roommate. You are to report to training tomorrow with Team #22. I am *very* happy you are here, Kaden. Good luck with your first day of training, and I hope you find comfort in your new home. We will be seeing each other again very soon."

"Thanks—" but before I could finish, he was already gone quicker than I would've suspected he could move.

I watched as he hurried down the courtyard, waving to the various Heroes that he passed, all of whom were acting like they had just been greeted by a celebrity.

I turned and looked around the campus as I took it all in. Here I was standing in the middle of the Golden Academy when, earlier today, my day had started in my apartment with my mom.

Then it dawned on me, and a feeling of worry washed over me as I wondered what my mom was thinking right now. She would have definitely gotten a call from my school about her son's Awakening which was promptly followed by him running out of the building and collapsing in the soccer field for everyone to see. I knew that she would've immediately tried to find me, only to find...

Well actually, I didn't even know *what* she would have found. The Headmaster said that they had found me unconscious in the grass before immediately bringing me here, which meant that she would have found *nothing*.

I hoped that he had at least told her what had happened to me and where I was now. I knew she would be worried sick thinking about me, wondering if I was ok. Hopefully we could send messages here, because I wanted to let her know about everything that was going on and how I was completely safe and alright. If anything, I was already doing better than I ever was at my high school where I was bullied most days.

Here, the sun was shining, and things were peaceful. I knew she would love to hear about this place since it was pretty much all I had ever talked about my entire life and now... well now I was *finally* here.

I entered The Villas, not knowing what to expect and what I found was nothing short of incredible. They were, of course, Roman inspired with a tan exterior and an orange tiled roof. The massive building was shaped like a rectangle, and in the center of it sat a long pool and a green area that had trees for shade. Balconies jutted out from the rooms that surrounded and overlooked the center courtyard. Heroes lay in hammocks, some alone, some two in one, and I heard a psychedelic rock song playing while other Heroes did back flips and gainers off the second floor balconies into the water below.

I walked around the place dumbfounded and looked at everything as if it were the coolest thing I had ever seen, which of course it *was*.

I found a staircase that led up to the second floor, and as I walked down the hall, I realized I was being watched by *everyone*. Laughter and conversations came from the opened doors until I walked by, in which case it was replaced by silence and staring. I tried to ignore them and went along counting the numbers above the doors while acting like I belonged, which I wasn't doing a good job of.

211... 212... 213... and finally 214.

I grabbed the door handle and held it, hoping my roommate would be somewhat normal. The last roommate I had was from summer camp years ago, and I didn't even last a week before I became homesick and had my mom come and get me.

The door creaked open, and my new roommate was lying on his bed with his feet kicked up, a pencil tucked behind his ear, and a book resting upright on his abdomen. He was short and stocky but had a nerdy appearance even though he looked tough as nails. He was reading what must've been a 1000 page book that I saw was "The Art of Battle" by *Professor Wayla*.

Perhaps he's working on an assignment?

Scattered across the floor and taped on the walls were pieces of paper with schematics and blueprints which were strange. To me, they looked like attack plans with circles, x's, and lines drawn all across them with a red pen. He slowly lowered his book flat onto his body and squinted his eyes at me.

"Who are you?" he questioned.

"Uh, I'm Kaden Collins... I *guess* your new roommate?" I replied.

He pulled his pencil from his ear and tossed it in his book before closing it. He swung his legs off the bed and stood up, inspecting me intently. He had to stare up as he was a few inches shorter than me.

"*Kaden Collins*, huh. You know, I wasn't expecting a new roommate today."

"I mean, I might've gone to the wrong place? This is my first day here, well, *hour* I should say. I'm a new—."

"Hero of the Academy?" he finished my sentence with a chuckle. "No you're not."

"What do you mean?" I asked with a puzzled look.

"No one your age is 'new here', buddy. You might've been able to use that trick on some of the younger kids, but I'm not buying it. So just tell me the *real* reason why you got relocated from your last room. Let me guess, you set your roommate's pants on fire? Trust me, been there, done that."

"No, no I didn't... light my roommates pants on fire. How did you even manage to—" I cut myself off. "Look man, I really am new here. I know it doesn't make any sense, but trust me, I'm confused too. I *just* had my Awakening even though I'm not exactly sure what I 'Awakened' yet."

"Awakening? You're a little old for an Awakening, wouldn't you say?" He squinted at me harder. "But, you seem to be telling the truth, Collins." He stuck out his hand, and I shook it. "Theo Matthews, nice to meet you."

"What's your power? The ability to know if someone is telling the truth?" I asked. "Like a human lie detector!"

He chuckled and said, "No, no, I'm not a human lie detector. Even if I was, I wouldn't be able to use my powers outside the P Dome," he said as he tapped the inhibitor chip on his neck.

"Ah yeah, that's right."

"What's yours? The ability to look like a teenager when you're really three years old? Did they forget to turn your chip on? I would prefer you stay like that though as I don't have any diapers for you to wear," he said with a smirk.

"Very funny, but I honestly don't know what my powers are yet; my hands can glow! And that's about it…"

"Huh, a human glow stick, nice. What's up with you being so old anyway? Most new Heroes come here in strollers with sippy cups in their hands."

"Seriously, man, I'm not sure. Headmaster Fowler claims he doesn't know either."

Theo's smile quickly faded as he stared at me in disbelief.

"*The* Headmaster Fowler?" he asked. "No, you must have him confused with someone else."

"Is there more than one Headmaster Fowler? Old man, toga, long beard… insanely jacked? If not then, yeah, I guess I did speak with *the* Headmaster Fowler. What's the big deal though?"

He paced back and forth in our small room with his hand on his chin, stepping on the papers on the floor while pondering what I had just said.

"Dude, no one just *talks* to the Headmaster. I've been here since I was ten, and I've never spoken a word to him, and now I'm fifteen. You said you've been here for an hour and already had a conversation with him? Only the top team works with him." He took a seat on his bed and pulled up his book again. "Man, you really must be special then."

I sat down on my bed and was immediately aware of how comfortable and soft it felt—*much* better than the mattress I slept on on the floor of my apartment.

"So… that means you've been here for five years then?" I asked.

"Yep, five years."

"Damn, that's a long time."

"Not nearly as long as some of the other kids around here."

"Really?"

"Yeah, some of them have been here for *much* longer, like they got here when they were three years old. This place and these walls are all they know… poor bastards."

"How many times have you seen your parents since you've been here?" He didn't reply, he only laughed as if I had just asked something completely idiotic.

I thought it was a fair question?

"Really? Come, on man, stop messing with me."

"What do you mean?"

"You know, I forget you're new," Theo said, shaking his head. "I haven't seen them since I came here, not once. We don't see our parents, *no one* does, which now includes you."

His words hurt to hear, but I figured he was telling the truth by the way he said it so naturally. The thought of not seeing my mom for who knows how long worried me greatly.

"Well, what's stopping you from… I don't know, just running away?" I asked.

"Two simple reasons, actually. One: we're surrounded by water. Two: my Awakening gave me the ability to turn into a crystal monster, not really ideal for swimming hundreds of miles across the ocean to shore, you know?"

The ocean? I thought to myself. *Aren't we just outside of some city?*

"What are you talking about? What ocean? That doesn't make any fucking sense," I said in a confused tone.

He let out a long sigh, folded up his book once more, and signaled me to follow him.

CHAPTER THREE

TEAM #22

W E WALKED ACROSS the campus and made our way *behind* the large buildings that surrounded the main courtyard area. That's when I saw *it*: an ocean that completely surrounded us and stretched out as far as the eye could see.

"Holy shit!" I yelled as I ran toward it. "Why are we not rocking like a boat if we're in the middle of the ocean?" I asked.

"Zo—the Headmaster's super genius and right hand toddler—designed an antigravity platform that the Academy sits on. We're not actually *on* the water, we're floating slightly above it," he said just as the wind sprayed water toward us.

Instinctively, my hands shot up to cover myself, but instead of soaking us, the water splashed against an invisible force field of some sort.

"Whoa, how did that—"

"Oh yeah, a third reason why I can't leave: there's an impenetrable force field that surrounds this place. They say it's to protect us and prevent our enemies from attacking here."

"Do you believe that?" I asked, which made Theo shrug.

"Maybe, but who knows? What I do know is that it's

dangerous out there and safe in here, so it's best not to overthink it. Besides, you'll find that out for yourself soon enough," he said with a smirk.

Find what out? I thought to myself.

Even though he sounded nonchalant about it, it still made me feel uneasy.

After he showed me the edge of the platform, we made our way back down the central walkway of the Academy.

"So, why are we in the middle of the ocean?" I asked as I looked around at the incredible architecture that surrounded us.

"The platform constantly moves to different locations across the Pacific, and they claim that it makes it harder for our enemies to find us since we're never in the same spot for too long. Plus, The Unity decided the ocean was probably the safest place for a bunch of super-powered teenagers to be together in case we managed to blow ourselves up while learning how to use our powers. If that were to happen out here, we wouldn't hurt anyone but ourselves and just sink to the bottom of the ocean."

"Like the Titanic."

"Exactly like the Titanic," he replied. "You know a rogue Golden caused that right?"

"What? No way. It was an iceberg… right?"

"An iceberg? Give me a break. Man, you non-Goldens really believe anything they tell you. Well, I guess I should say you *used* to believe anything, since you are now one of us, *Glow Stick.*" He pointed to one of the various Power Domes. "See that over there? It's my favorite place besides the Library of Alexandria, because we—"

"Get to use our powers. Yeah, the Headmaster showed me that," I cut in.

"Wow, you really got the full experience from him, huh? You know, I took down a giant man rampaging through a city yesterday, and I didn't even get a 'nice job' from him! This is bullshit!"

"Wait a second; that was *you?* That guy crashed through my apartment and took out half my wall!"

"Hell yeah that was me," he said, crossing his arms and proudly smiling.

"And *then*, I saw you get thrown through a building."

"Alright, buddy, he caught me off guard. The part you probably *didn't* see was right before that when my teammate launched me at him which took out his legs and sent him crashing down—"

"Onto a building. Yeah, I saw that part too."

"Whatever, it was an accident."

"Didn't look like an—"

Suddenly, a tall, muscular guy pushed past me.

"Sorry you got stuck with the new kid, Theo," he said with a smirk as he walked down the stone path out of earshot.

"What's his problem?" I asked Theo.

He looked as if he was about to burst out of his shirt and walked with his shoulders back and his chin up, like he owned the place.

"Glad you got to meet Ezra Kane! He's one of my older teammates and a hot head—quite literally," Theo said.

"Let me guess, his powers give him the ability to set his pants on fire?" I asked in a joking way.

"Yeah, that's exactly what his powers are. He can set himself on fire and not die while harnessing the flames," Theo said as his stomach growled.

I quickly realized those kinds of jokes don't really fly

here. You could call someone a rat for snitching on you, and then they could actually turn into one.

"You want to grab some food?" he asked.

The thought of eating food never seemed better in my life.

We walked into a large cafeteria with a domed ceiling. A prodigious mural of Goldens battling in the skies and on the ground in a large-scale war stretched across the ceiling like the Creation of Adam in the Sistine Chapel. In the center of the chaos, I saw a man in white and gold armor fighting against someone in spiky black armor with yellow accents.

Next to it, I saw another mural of a Pegasus drawn chariot with a tall, grey being going across the sky while leaving a trail of golden dust behind him. I couldn't quite figure that one out, but, regardless, they were both *mesmerizing*.

I was finally taken out of my trance when Theo yelled from across the cafeteria, "Hey Kaden, are you gonna stare at the murals all day or what? Come on, let's eat!"

I walked over to the table where he was sitting and saw a group of teenage boys and girls around him.

"Kaden Collins, this is Dimitri Erebus and Helio Navarro," Theo said, signaling to the two Heroes next to him.

Dimitri ran his fingers through his jet black hair and said, "Sup." I looked at his black irises, and it felt as if I were staring into a void.

"Nice to meet you," Helio said with a nod as she twisted the end of her long, brown braid.

"And, of course, you met Ezra already."

I immediately got a knot in my stomach.

Great, of course out of a thousand Heroes here, this *guy is sitting with us.*

Then I saw *her*, and that thought left my mind instantly.

She whipped her blonde hair from the front of her face and looked up at me with bright purple and pink eyes. I wondered if she recognized me, but I quickly realized she didn't when she said nothing, looked away, and immediately resumed eating her food.

"And last but not least, we've got Arissa Reed!" he said, pointing to the girl I saw when a giant rogue Golden ruined my birthday.

I tried not to take it personally that she didn't remember me as I told myself that these were Heroes who saved hundreds if not thousands of non-Goldens every time they went out on missions. She probably had to say that same memorized line over and over to every person who was affected by the conflict in the damaged apartment building.

"And that's Team #22!" he said as he threw his arms in the air like, *tada!*

"Wait a second, Team #22? Headmaster Fowler assigned me to this team," I said.

"Sweet!" Theo said as he high fived me.

He waved me over to have a seat across from him which I greatly appreciated. A robot waiter brought out food on a tray and placed it in front of us. No one seemed as blown away by this as I was since this was the first walking humanoid robot I had ever seen. Getting served lunch by robot waiters must have been a daily occurrence for these super-powered kids.

My musings about these things were interrupted when Ezra, with a mouth full of food, asked me, "Why are you so old?"

I was just about to respond when Theo chimed in and said, "We don't know—oldest Awakening in history, there are no answers, and that's it. End of story."

Ezra shrugged and went back to eating.

"So, uh, what powers do you all have?" I asked, trying to strike up a conversation with my new team and break the awkward silence.

None of them responded as they continued to stuff their mouths with food.

Theo finally broke the silence with, "Here, I'll tell you! Arissa can create two portals connecting any location that she can see in front of her. It's honestly pretty cool to witness."

"Actually, I *have* seen it," I responded.

The whole group turned and looked at me as if I were crazy.

"What?" Arissa said with a confused look.

"When that giant guy was rolling through the city the other day, he ended up crashing through my building, and you came by to check and make sure everyone was OK. Once we finished talking, you portaled off somewhere." I knew I should've kept my mouth shut the second I said this because her confused look didn't seem to go away as if she had no idea what I was talking about.

"That's embarrassing," Dimitri said from across the table.

My face became extremely hot, and I felt like burying my face in my tray of food. It also didn't help that she was even cuter sitting across from me, and now I definitely had no chance with her because I was pretty sure I had creeped her out.

"You know what, Kaden... I kinda *do* remember you. It was you and your mom in that apartment, right? It's just tough sometimes to remember the specifics because we see so many people when we're out on our missions," she said, which saved me from the awkwardness of the situation.

"Yeah, yeah, for sure," I said, not knowing if my face was still bright as a tomato.

"Anyway, next we've got Helio's and Dimitri's powers. Helio is a bird," Theo said with a smile toward her.

"Hey, I'm not a bird!" Helio yelled back, flinging a piece of food at him with her spoon.

He dodged it *Matrix-style*, and it splattered on the back of someone behind him. Everyone quickly ducked forward and hid while the person stood up and looked around for the perpetrator.

Eventually, he sat back down, and everyone let out the laughs they were holding in. It dawned on me that this was the first time I had been sitting at a lunch table with other people my age, and I *wasn't* the one getting food flung at me. To say the least, it felt *good*.

"You're a bird, and Dimitri, you're an octopus... but don't throw food at me!" Theo said as he cowered in fear with his hands up.

I stared at them in disbelief, wondering how that could work having a bird and an octopus on our team.

I might've been too obvious because Dimitri picked up on this and said, "Great job, Theo; now he *actually* believes you."

Theo laughed to himself and said, "My fault, my fault."

"No, Kaden, she's not actually a bird, and I'm not actually an octopus. He's just saying that because he's jealous of our badass abilities," Dimitri said, sitting back and crossing his arms.

"Which are octopus powers, right?"

"No! I can summon shadow tentacles..." he said defensively which made Theo and I look at each other.

"*Octopus powers*," we said at the same time, causing us both to laugh.

"That can kick your ass!" Dimitri said as he clutched his fork in anger, his hands red from the pressure of his grip.

"Okay, moving on! You've already met Ezra over there, so yeah! That's everyone!" Theo said as he dove into his food again.

"So… how have the missions been going?" I asked awkwardly.

"Terrible," Ezra said.

"Amazing," Theo said after him, which caused him to glare. "Don't listen to him, Kaden. He's just joking around."

"Why terrible?" I asked as I looked at Ezra.

"Because we fucking suck," Ezra responded from across the table.

"No, that's not true at—"

"Stop lying and just tell him the truth, Theo," Ezra interrupted. "He should know the bullshit he is about to get himself into."

"Alright, fine!" Theo finally yelled, followed by a long sigh. "It's terrible because we are the worst team at the Golden Academy. He *is* telling the truth; however, we've got the most heart! Isn't that right, team?"

Everyone stared at him with annoyed looks on their faces.

"No," Dimitri said unenthusiastically, which finally broke the silence.

Theo slumped forward and put his hands on his face.

"Well, maybe we would be higher on *The Wall* if Ezra was actually a team player!" Theo shouted at him.

"Maybe I'd be a team player if Arissa actually knew how to properly place a portal when we needed her to!" Ezra yelled loudly, slamming his hands on the table.

"If you could actually control your powers and not burn everything to the ground, maybe we wouldn't get points deducted for collateral damage every single mission!" Arissa snapped.

"At least I can do something with my powers! Half of the members of the team are completely and utterly useless!" Ezra said while signaling to the rest of the group.

"Hey! I can do stuff!" Theo responded.

"Oh yeah, Theo? What stuff can you do besides turning into a giant rock?"

"I can punch," he gathered his words, "things…"

"Most of the time, you're the thing that is getting punched!"

"Fair, but I have been working on my slip and jab recently, and I think I'm making some good progress!"

"Pitiful," Ezra replied.

The table went silent, and you could feel the tension in the air.

Maybe I did enjoy sitting alone all those years. At least this never happened.

"Why are you being such a dick, Ezra?" Helio finally asked.

Ezra stared at the table for a minute then said, "Because obviously you all don't take this seriously enough. We're only one year away from graduation, and we are still in the bottom half of the senior class of teams, actually, the *very* bottom of the bottom half. There's no way we're going to make it into the top half before graduation and go to Gidoria to become Warriors. If it isn't painfully obvious to you all, we're on the chopping block, and it doesn't look like we're getting off it anytime soon."

I pondered what he had just said, and virtually none of

it made any sense to me.

Top of the senior class? Graduating and becoming a Warrior? Gidoria?

"Sorry, I'm not really following you here, you mentioned *Jih—Dor—Ree—Ah*?" I sounded out.

"Yes, the Golden Planet," Ezra replied.

My mind was racing at a million miles an hour.

I thought I knew everything about Goldens, yet somehow I had missed an entire planet full of them?

"You *really* don't know; do you?" Ezra said while staring at me.

"Well, it is my first day here, so I don't really know a lot of things right now," I muttered out while scratching the back of my head.

Ezra finally said, "Gidoria is the planet where Heroes go after they graduate. Why do you think you never see any adult Heroes around? It's just all of us teenagers."

That's when it dawned on me: anytime I had seen a Golden out in the real world, it was always someone my age. That was why I fantasized about being one of them. It was so easy to put myself in their shoes and imagine what it would be like to have powers like theirs.

"So what happens if you aren't in the top half of the class when you graduate?" I asked, but everyone remained silent.

"Honestly, we don't really know. No one has ever told us exactly what happens, other than that we wouldn't graduate from Heroes to Warriors. When you get into that top half, they push you to stay there. If you're in the bottom half… well they don't really give a shit about you, almost like they *want* us to stay where we are."

"Well, why don't we just talk to someone who graduated in the bottom half?" I asked, which caused everyone to laugh as if I had said something hilarious.

"We've had friends who have graduated in the bottom half, but just like every Hero who graduates at the top or bottom, you never hear from them again because they're on another planet. So to answer your question, Kaden, we don't know and are afraid to find out, but the way things are looking, I guess it's only a matter of time," Ezra finished with a somber look on his face.

I scanned the rest of the members of the team, and the once cheerful people I saw before were gone—replaced with sad, hollow shells of themselves. It made me wonder if this was how this team always was before I got here.

Maybe Headmaster Fowler really did see me as just a glow stick and expected me to fail?

Placing me on Team #22 probably had something to do with being a late bloomer and having my Awakening much later than everyone else. I guessed that I had just missed the boat in that sense, and there was nothing I could do about it. That was why he didn't even give me a chance to succeed, placing me at the bottom on purpose.

For my entire life, I always dreamed of being here at the Academy—getting assigned to a team, meeting Heroes, having powers of my own; but now that I'm here, I'm starting to regret ever having an Awakening at all.

I sat in silence with the rest of the group, but then I remembered my mother and how there was a big chance— if Theo was telling the truth—that I would never see her again. But, all of this did not need to be for nothing.

This team is not destined for failure. We will turn it around if it's the last goddamn thing we do.

"No," I said as the entire group looked at me with confused looks. "It's not a matter of time before we find out, and we shouldn't worry about that stupid shit since we *won't* be a part of it."

A hopeful look began to appear on their faces as I spoke.

"I'm sixteen, and I shouldn't even be here right now! I don't know what I can do or what I'm capable of, but my late Awakening has to mean *something*. I don't care if Team #22 has previously been the worst team; from this day forward, things are going to change, and thinking we are a terrible team ends right here, right now! We're no longer going to define ourselves by our past failures but instead by our future victories!"

The group looked around at each other as smiles grew on their faces. They moved in closer, as if waiting for another profound speech.

"Now... how do we actually move up?" I asked because I really didn't know anything.

"We complete successful missions—" Ezra said.

"With *minimum* collateral damage. Ezra loves to leave that part out," Arissa added as Ezra scoffed and shook his head.

"They pay attention to our control over our powers—" Dimitri chimed in.

"While also working fully as a team, using our abilities collectively to bring out the best in each other," Helio said with a nod.

"Successful missions using teamwork with minimum collateral damage leads to points gained, which leads to higher placement in the graduating class," Theo said.

"And I'm assuming unsuccessful missions lead to a subtraction of points," I asked Theo.

"Correct," Theo responded as he looked around at the group, "I think it's time we show Kaden The Wall."

• • •

We walked up the steps of a Roman style building with large columns standing tall in front of it. I looked up ahead and saw the rest of the group with smiles on their faces.

"If Kaden thought the cafeteria was cool, his mind is about to be *blown*," Theo said as he pulled open a large door.

We all followed in after him, and the best way I could describe what I saw next was how I always pictured the New York Stock Exchange to look, but instead of charts and numbers being displayed on the various flat screens scattered around the room, the screens displayed teams of Heroes out on missions.

Each screen showed a different battle, showcasing Heroes using their powers to save non-Goldens while fighting Rogues. The videos invigorated me, as I had never seen such raw footage of so many Heroes before. My only source to see anything even close to this was YouTube, and those videos were always heavily edited by The Unity, only ever showing the successful missions with no casualties. Here, I could see all the successes *and* failures in front of me with no edits.

"*Great*, they're showing a rerun of our last mission," Theo said as he looked away from the screen in shame.

The giant Rogue grabbed a piece of a building, and I immediately recognized it as my old apartment. Watching the battle on a screen felt horrifying and surreal at the same time, knowing my mom and I were inside that building, cowering in fear for our lives.

Ezra blasted the giant man with fire, while Dimitri and Helio slashed at him. Theo, in blue crystal form, jumped off of a building and dove through one of Arissa's portals. He exited out of another and flew head first into the giant man's legs which caused him to stumble backward and fall. +10 points appeared on the screen like a video game. As the giant man fell backward, he landed on a building and flattened it beneath him.

I had to look away because I realized that easily could have been *my* building that was destroyed. Many people were now injured or dead because of something completely beyond their control, and my mother and I could've been one of them.

Then, -10,000 points popped up on the screen which made me feel *even* worse. People's lives were reduced to numbers on a screen. Something about that didn't sit right with me, and I felt a hand grab mine as I looked to my right and saw Arissa standing next to me.

"Come on, we didn't come here to show you that," she said with a sad look as she pulled me along. "*This* is what we wanted to show you." She released my hand, and my face returned to a normal temperature.

I looked up and saw The Wall: a giant scoreboard with all 42 teams of the senior class listed. Points were posted on the right side of The Wall next to the team numbers. Team #1 and Team #36 had 15,000 and 10,000 points respectively, and as my eyes tracked down The Wall, I saw good-ol' Team #22 sitting alone at the bottom of the list with a grand total of...*100* points.

"And there we are in all our glory," Ezra said as he put a hand to his face and shook his head.

"Hey, would you look at that? We've got 100 points!" Theo said, his finger pointing at The Wall while jumping up and down.

"Theo, I don't think it updated yet," Dimitri said.

A low pitched *beep* sounded, and the points across the board changed with teams flip flopping, moving up and down spots. I scanned all the way down the board looking for Team #22's points and finally saw... *0.*

"Great," Theo said sarcastically.

I stared at that #1 spot and tried to imagine what it would feel like for our team to be there, but then something *happened:* the teams shifted around, and Team #1 dropped by 50 points.

"There must be a glitch. I've never seen them lose points before? They are always perfect," Theo said as he squinted his eyes, making sure he saw that correctly.

"Well, Team #22, I say it's time to get off the bottom of The Wall and give Team #1 a run for their money! Who's with me?" I called out to them, placing my hand in front of me.

They hesitated, but eventually a hand came down from beside me and landed on top of mine. It was Theo's, and he looked at me while giving me a nod. Three more came in: Arissa's, Dimitri's, and Helio's. The only one missing was Ezra. He stood a few feet away, shaking his head at the group with his arms crossed.

"Fuck it."

He slapped his hand down, and we all threw them up and cheered. I looked at the faces around me and knew that we *could* do this. I noticed a red light on a surveillance camera in the corner of the room that was aimed at us, and I watched as its lens oscilated back and forth.

Glad to know they've got good security, I guess?

Still, for some reason it made me feel uneasy. I shook the idea out of my head and focused on the moment before me with my new team. I saw their smiling faces and heard laughter, and I thought that if there's at least *one* thing that I could bring to this group, it would be hope, and I would try anything and everything I could to accomplish that.

• • •

That night, Theo and I lay in our separate twin beds, and as I looked around the room that also held a small closet at the foot of each bed, a sense of comfort arose. Today, being with my team, I spent more time talking to other people than I had in the past year.

However, I couldn't help but wish that my mom could share these moments and see how happy I was here. In my mind, I could picture the look—the smile on her face, realizing that I was where I *truly* belonged. I knew she was thinking that right now, even though she missed me.

She knew that I would eventually leave the apartment and go and do something like this—going out into the *real* world and becoming my own person. I just wished that she could be here to see it; that's all.

As long as she's ok, then I'm happy, and hey, maybe one day I'll even see her on a mission, just like how Team #22 came right by our apartment!

The possibility of seeing her again eased my racing mind.

"Hey Kaden," Theo called out from the darkness beside me.

"Yeah?" I replied.

"Thank you."

"For what?"

"Today and just… *everything.* My team and I…" he tried to find the words and finally said, "we haven't laughed like that in years."

Neither have I, I thought to myself, but I didn't tell him that.

"I can see it on their faces; they really believe in you, and I know this because I do too," Theo said. "Goodnight, man, I look forward to seeing what the future holds for us."

And with that he rolled over.

No one had ever said anything like that to me, and I honestly didn't know how to take it.

"We can do this... *together*, I know it," I finally said back.

"Me too."

CHAPTER FOUR

THE HIGH LORDS

EADMASTER FOWLER ENTERED his chamber, which was a large room with a domed mosaic glass ceiling. A sleek stone desk sat in the center of the room, flanked by bookshelves on one side and a large window on the other that stretched across the entire length of the chamber, allowing him to peer out to the rest of the Academy.

Headmaster Fowler took his seat, and holographic screens with different teams out on various missions appeared in front of him. One screen showed footage of Kaden's old high school, *decimated* and in ruins. Department of Golden Control vehicles had set up a perimeter around what was left of the school with DGC soldiers inspecting the crater left behind after Kaden's Awakening.

They moved through it, scanning the energy signature with hand held devices. Headmaster Fowler's fingers passed anxiously through his white beard while he silently thought to himself. Zo appeared in the doorway, floating on his antigravity chair. The Headmaster held up a hand and waved away the screens that vanished into nothingness.

His face was tense and stressed as he asked Zo, "You wanted to speak with me?"

"Yes, Headmaster, I did. The lab results have come back for the boy," he said with a flick of his finger, projecting a new hologram screen in front of the Headmaster. "Although we anticipated a high level of Golden cells based on the magnitude of his Awakening event, we couldn't have predicted this."

Headmaster Fowler sat forward and inspected the screen as a worried look grew across his face.

"Have you ever seen anything like this, Zo?" the Headmaster asked while pointing to the screen.

"No sir, never in all my years at the Academy. His Golden cell count is higher than yours, and that makes his power potential well…" His voice trailed off.

The Headmaster stared intently at Zo while he tried to formulate the correct words.

"Tell me, *now*."

There was a long pause.

"I don't want to make irrational assumptions here, but based on the data, his power potential is… *limitless*," Zo finally uttered, nearly choking on the word as if it were wrong to say. "Should you tell the High Lords?"

A shadow swept across the floor of the room behind Zo.

The Headmaster looked at him and said, "They already know."

A figure formed from the shadow and stood before them. She wore a dark gray cloak with black smoke pouring off the bottom hem.

"Headmaster Fowler," she said in a deep voice, "you are requested to appear before the High Lords, *immediately*."

The Headmaster stood up from his chair and moved around the sleek table.

He looked at Zo and said, "Gather Team #1. I will want

to speak with them when I return. I shouldn't be long."

The cloaked woman grabbed the Headmaster as their eyes turned black, and they vanished into the shadow. All that remained in the room was a large puff of black smoke in which Zo floated.

• • •

A collosal stone castle, illuminated by the glow of the moon, jutted out from a cliffside, overlooking a vast valley below. Lightning struck and thunder roared as a torrential downpour soaked the surrounding area.

Inside the castle, the Headmaster and the cloaked woman emerged from the shadow, before he doubled over and caught himself on a cave wall. He looked uneasy and attempted to catch his breath—the dizziness and disorientation being a common side effect from traveling across space within the shadow realm.

"It never gets easier…" he mumbled to himself.

"They are waiting for you inside the throne room, Headmaster. Make haste," she snapped.

"How about getting the door for me?" he asked, but the cloaked woman had already disappeared into the shadow before she heard his snide comment. "Yeah, I thought so."

Once the Headmaster had regained his composure, he looked around the large cavern he had now entered. This was a place Headmaster Fowler unfortunately knew all too well.

The Headmaster sighed and made his way to a set of dominating doors at the end of the cave. They were tall and obviously built for someone much bigger than him, with two gold ring handles that hung far above the Headmaster's head. He laughed to himself as the handles seemed like a cruel joke—as if he'd be able to reach them anyway.

The Headmaster placed his large hands on the cold stone doors and pushed against them, muscles flexing and bare feet digging into the rock below him. They cracked and groaned while the room rumbled with the sound of the doors opening. Once the doors had finally been pushed in, he entered the chamber which was illuminated by lit torches that lined the walls. He made his way to the center of the chamber and bowed before the High Lords: four giants, approximately ten feet tall, who sat in jagged thrones. They each had four solid gold eyes that blinked at different intervals. Their skin was dark gray and wrinkled, and their fingers were long but fat.

The Headmaster said their names in order of their thrones, "High Lords Thedeus, Avan, Orion, and Ristottem. I have been summoned?"

"Fowler Zaelzan of the first blood, Headmaster of the Golden Academy, and... the exiled son, it has been centuries since we last spoke with you. Your victories and work at the Academy do not go unnoticed. *He* has been very pleased with the results so far," High Lord Ristottem said. His voice, deep and powerful, rumbled through the room and shook the cave, sending small pieces of rock down from the ceiling.

"Thank you, High Lord Ristottem. I exist to serve," he responded as a smile grew across the High Lord's face.

"Yes, yes you do. Now, for the matter of the Red Demon. We have been expecting his Awakening for a long time, and now that it is finally here, something new has come upon us. The prophecy we spoke of when we last saw you has *changed*."

"What have you foreseen?" the Headmaster asked.

"Chaos, death, destruction, and victory at the hands of that child… but for the enemy. The Red Demon prophecy is a future that only Orion and Thedeus have foreseen. The victory prophecy Avan and I have foreseen has not changed."

"Which is why the boy has not yet been killed?" The Headmaster guessed as they nodded in unison.

"Now listen closely, it is imperative that the boy does not know what he is capable of nor his *true* nature. Kaden is the final key we need for victory, but he walks along two paths, and it is up to you to keep him on the right one. I hope you know the implications for the war and the Empire that your failure would bring."

"I understand, High Lord Ristottem. I conquered Earth after the Seeding, I can handle a child."

"Don't be so arrogant!" High Lord Thedeus yelled. The cave shook as if it were about to collapse, but it finally settled again.

"I greatly apologize, High Lords. I should not have stepped out of line," Headmaster Fowler said.

"We already know what you are capable of, Fowler, which is why the Emperor has given you another great responsibility that now rests on your shoulders," High Lord Avan said.

"Thank you, High Lords."

"That is all we have for you at this present moment. You are dismissed," High Lord Orion said.

He bowed once more and began to walk out, but something caught his eye for the first time: a carving, etched into the rock above the entrance to the chamber. A being stood with his arms out by his side, floating in the air. Then, Headmaster Fowler noticed red streaks of light coming from his hands that swirled over his arms. As his eyes tracked upward, he saw *them:* two red glowing crystals in place of eyes that were staring back at him. The longer the Headmaster looked at them, the brighter they seemed to glow as if burning a hole through the center of his soul.

"Do not fail him, Headmaster. The fate of Gidoria now rests in your hands."

CHAPTER FIVE

A NEW MISSION

S UDDENLY, IN A puff of black smoke, Headmaster Fowler reappeared in his study. The cloaked woman released him, and he caught himself on his desk as the dizziness lingered. In a fraction of a second, she disappeared into the shadow beneath her and left the Headmaster in solitude.

He pondered everything that was said before: the boy, the visions, the fate of Gidoria. He felt the weight that was now resting upon his shoulders, as one small mistake could result in *catastrophe;* however, none of this was new to him. He had been down this road many times before, and, therefore, he was invigorated to start his new task as a twisted smile grew across his face. And with that, he got to work.

Headmaster Fowler entered the War Room—the futuristic command center for the Academy. The room was made up of dozens of stations that connected into three rings with an aisle to walk through the center of them. Each station had a console of multi-colored buttons and keypads with large curved screens behind them. Operators sat at their stations wearing headsets that allowed them to talk to the Heroes out on missions.

Live feeds of the missions played on multiple screens around the room. Each operator carefully monitored the events that unfolded before them, entering numbers on a keypad adjacent to the consoles. The total number of points awarded to each team that they were observing was being altered based on what was happening on the screens.

On one screen, an operator was watching a team fight a rogue Golden with energy powers. They bombarded the Rogue with different attacks, but the Rogue still managed to let off an energy blast that struck a building, causing it to crumble to the ground. The operator began to type numbers on a keypad which decreased the team's score due to the failure to stop the Rogue and the collateral damage.

On a massive wrap-around screen that surrounded the room like a jumbotron, the overall team leaderboard was shown, where the points were added or subtracted and eventually sent out to The Wall. Team's positions on the leaderboard changed as points were plugged in in real time.

Boom.

Boom.

Boom.

Boom.

An ominous feeling filled the air in the War Room as Headmaster Fowler loudly walked down the aisle to the center of the inner ring of operators. They tried focusing on their work but would occasionally flash a side eye, attempting to get a glimpse of the mysterious Headmaster before returning to their work. He stood next to a sleek black, circular table in the center of the inner ring with a holographic Earth displayed above it. Blinking red lights were seen on the globe, and the Headmaster inspected a group of six of them.

"Headmaster Fowler, they are ready for you," Zo said

through his earpiece.

"I'll be right there," he responded.

Headmaster Fowler walked through a set of double doors into a large auditorium with 1000 seats. Zo floated on his chair at the front of the room while four Goldens sat in the front row of seats.

"Team #1, my unstoppable Team #1! How delighted I am to see you all," he said as he called out to the laid back team.

From left to right: *Chloe*—brutish with a purple mohawk, the obvious "muscle" of the group, sat on the end since she nearly took up two seats. *Mark*, an expert hand to hand combatant and swordsman with a black headband tied in a knot behind his head and dyed orange hair, sat next to her. Next to him sat *Alex*, who had optic blast powers and wore dark green glasses to contain them. Finally sitting on the other end of the group, was *Jayson*—the leader of the team with a muscular physique and bright blonde hair.

"I have gathered you here today as you now have a very specific, very *personal* assignment that is coming directly from me," the Headmaster said to the team.

Their laid back attitudes quickly changed as they sat up onto the edge of their seats to focus better.

"The Rogue leader—Zahavi—the one who threatens the Academy the most—must be found and neutralized. He is *the* rogue Golden, highest on our priority list, and it is time I assign my top team to target him and hunt him down. It is now your job to find the so-called 'Sanctuary' where Zahavi has housed and trained rogue Goldens against the wishes of The Unity and the Golden Academy. This mysterious place has eluded us for far too long."

"I've read about Zahavi, and if he has been a problem for

hundreds of years, why are we just now going after him?" Jayson asked.

"Jayson, Jayson, Jayson, you are much too smart to ask such *stupid* questions."

Jayson shrank into his seat.

"Isn't it clear? Unknown to him, Zahavi has continued to produce world class Rogues for all of you to hone your abilities with, becoming better teammates and Heroes while simultaneously giving you an easy ticket to Gidoria as Warriors. Unfortunately, I now have new orders, and the old ways of the Academy are outdated. Going forward, our biggest priority is to shut him and the Sanctuary down, *once and for all*."

The Heroes started to get antsy in their seats, as if they couldn't wait to get out and do just that.

"Zo, please brief them on their mission. You start tonight. Do not fail me, Team #1." Just as Headmaster Fowler exited the room, he signaled to Jayson and said, "A word, my boy?"

Jayson gulped and followed him.

Headmaster Fowler stood next to the globe in the War Room, inspecting it once more. Jayson walked up beside him and cleared his throat.

"You wanted to talk to me, Headmaster?"

"You are my brightest and favorite Hero at the Academy, Jayson. I always thought you had the most potential of *anyone* here, and you and I have spent a lot of time together; haven't we?"

"Yes sir, we have," he replied.

"I have raised you since the day you were born. You've been here longer than any other student, not because you were a danger to the world but because I knew you were too powerful to be among *them*—the non-Goldens. I trained you in the ways of the Academy, knowing what you could one day accomplish here and that eventually, you could become the Hero of Earth and… Champion of Gidoria."

"Why are you telling me this, Headmaster?"

"Because you have a big responsibility now, Jayson. This mission is the largest, most ambitious mission in the history of the Academy, and I do not say that lightly. We've had our well-known wars and battles, powerful and infamous Rogues who have leveled cities and led armies that have all been neutralized, but no Hero before you has *ever* led something of this scale. If you succeed, we shall build a statue for you," he said with a smile.

Jayson's eyes lit up at the sound of this.

"I'm giving you this mission because I trust you more than any other Hero here… but you already know that. Show me."

Jayson held up the palm of his hand, and blue electricity crackled within it.

"*Exactly*. I don't give that privilege away to just anyone, but there's no one here that I would rather have to lead and protect the Academy than you. You are a smart boy, Jayson, and I know you are aware of these things already, but I just thought I would remind you of what is at stake once more. Now go, join your team again, and make me proud."

"Thank you, Headmaster. I will not let you down," he said as he hurried off.

Headmaster Fowler watched him leave, shaking his head in disappointment.

"No, no you will not."

• • •

Team #1 entered the ship hangar of the Academy. Hundreds of futuristic aircraft were floating throughout it and landing in their designated spots. The ships were not shaped like conventional aircraft with wings and propulsion systems, instead, they were propelled with an antigravity drive and had no need for such ancient and arbitrary things. This was all thanks to Zo's groundbreaking technology which he reverse-engineered from the Empire and used on his chair to move freely without any restraints.

A drop hatch with stairs opened on the bottom of one of the ships, and they all climbed inside. Jayson situated himself in the cockpit and began operating the controls.

"Everyone strapped in?" he called back to the team.

"We're good! Let's do this!" Chloe responded.

Jayson rolled the throttle slightly forward, lifting the ship silently into the air. It floated out of the hangar and emerged from the side of the Academy platform, hovering over the ocean. Inside the cockpit, small bubble shields formed around them, allowing them to be unaffected by G—force.

"Here we go," Jayson said as he rolled the throttle all the way forward and applied full power. They took off into the night, and the Earth zipped by underneath them as the ship carried Team #1 toward their destination.

CHAPTER SIX

POWER DOME #1

"TEAM #22, REPORT to Power Dome #1 immediately. Team #22, report to Power Dome #1 immediately."

The second I heard that message over the intercom, I shot straight out of bed. It felt like Christmas morning, and I couldn't wait to get to the Power Dome and find out what my powers were.

I couldn't remember the last time I was this excited for well... *anything*. I had never been excited to go to school because of the bullying, and I always had to put on a happy face in front of my mom before I left the apartment.

The truth was: I hated school, but I knew *this* would be different. This was a different type of school where instead of learning math and English, you learned how to be a hero and save the world. This was the moment I had been waiting for my entire life.

"What time is it?" Theo said as he rolled out of bed with a long yawn.

"Who knows, but the sun is out, the non-existent birds are chirping, and the intercom just yelled at us, so let's get a move on!" I responded.

Theo wiped his eyes and stretched his arms above him.

"Hey man, don't get your hopes up too high. I know you're excited and all, but you could seriously just be a human glow stick. Trust me, I've seen it happen before. There have been plenty of kids who had Awakenings, and then their Golden abilities turned out to be nothing powerful. Like that one kid who turned into a hamster."

"Were any of them sent back?" I asked. "To the *real* world?"

"Honestly, I'm not sure. Probably? All I know is we never saw them again since they served no purpose at the Academy."

"Damn, that would suck. Let's just hope that doesn't happen to me," I said, opening my closet.

Inside were dozens of the same blue, skin tight, athletic shirts with white TGA lettering and black shorts. I grabbed one and threw it over me, the hexagonal pattern stretching across my body.

Theo did the same and asked, "I mean, do you even remember anything about your Awakening? Anything that could tell us what we might see today?"

"Nothing. I just saw my hands glowing, and then I ran outside. Next thing I knew, I was laying in a hospital bed with an elderly body builder standing over me," I said, which made Theo laugh.

"You know, I thought the same thing the first time I saw him, and just think about how weird that was for a ten year old kid to see. Some Goldens come here even younger than I was and have a really hard time adjusting," he said as he finished getting his clothes on.

"What happens to those kids?"

"They turn out like Ezra. Now, let's roll!"

• • •

After breakfast with the team, we made our way down the center walkway of the Academy. The sun was shining, and a warm beach-like breeze passed through the campus, which was surprising considering the giant force field dome that surrounded us.

Perhaps Zo had made modifications that allowed wind to pass through?

"Well, Kaden, this is your big day. I can't wait to see you and your powers turn out to be useless and for you to get sent home!" Ezra said as he punched my arm.

"What are you going to do when he's more powerful than you and takes over as leader of the team, Ezra?" Helio chimed in.

"Never gonna happen, but go ahead, keep dreaming," he responded.

"I know *I* would love to start taking orders from someone else besides you," Dimitri added.

"Shut it, Octopus," Ezra snapped back.

"Alright guys, let's not get ahead of ourselves here. Why don't we see what he can do first?" Arissa said, calming the group down.

Theo ran to the front of the group and started walking backward.

"Or, plot twist, he has the exact same powers as one of us!" he exclaimed

"For Kaden's sake, he should *hope* he doesn't get your powers," Dimitri chirped back which made Theo roll his eyes.

"Anything can happen, I guess. I just really don't want to get sent home," I sheepishly admitted.

"That won't happen no matter what. We all like you too much to let them take you back," Arissa said, which felt reassuring to hear.

Although I was excited to find out what my powers

were, I was secretly pretty nervous. I did talk up a huge game with nothing much to support it, and I promised my team a lot and had some pretty big expectations to live up to. I wasn't sure if I even believed everything I had told them.

We entered Power Dome #1, and I immediately heard noises rumbling from the other Power Domes next door, realizing they were also practicing. The walls were white, sleek, and curved, and the entire room looked so futuristic, it felt as if we were in a spacecraft. Then, I saw the blue, transparent force field in front of me with the massive coliseum behind it.

My arms and legs were littered with goosebumps, and I could barely contain my excitement. I reached forward and felt my hand easily pass through the force field, but *something* grabbed me, pulling me backward.

I said "something" because I actually didn't know what had grabbed me. The hand was huge and furry, and I turned around to see a large silverback gorilla wearing a white lab coat and glasses staring back at me.

"What the hell!" I said as I jumped back, brushing up against the forcefield.

"Whoa, slow down there Freshman!" the gorilla said to me.

"You're... a *gorilla?*"

"Indeed I am, but we're both Goldens just the same. Is there a problem with that?"

"No, um, not at all, I've just never seen a gorilla *talk* before, that's all."

"Good, because I am your powers and abilities instructor, Professor Guano," he said, sticking out his hand to shake.

"Kaden Collins, nice to meet you," I said as I shook it.

I joined back up with the rest of the class who were all holding in their laughter.

"You should've seen your face," Theo whispered.

"How was I supposed to react? He's a goddamn gorilla," I whispered back.

"Now Kaden, I know everything here is new to you, but we never enter the Power Dome without first putting on our suits," Professor Guano said.

Suits? I thought to myself.

"Like *superhero suits?*" I asked.

"Indeed, would you like one?"

I quickly nodded *yes*.

"Follow me."

We followed Professor Guano over to another room in the Power Dome.

"Welcome, Team #22, to the design studio," a disembodied voice said from an overhead speaker.

Six circular platforms sat in the middle of the room, and each member of the team stepped forward and stood on one, except for Theo and I.

A tinted cylindrical tube came down and covered them completely. A few seconds later, the tubes rose from the plates, and my teammates looked completely different. Ezra's suit caught my eye first: it was skin tight with black and orange dots that went across his body in a wave pattern, starting with black dots by his neck, that blended into orange dots that covered the rest of him.

I looked at Arissa's, immediately recognizing her suit from the morning she portaled into my apartment, and I now noticed that it was much more armored than Ezra's. She was unlike Ezra, whose body flames could melt any object that came near him, hence her need for more protection. Her suit was a mismatch of pink and gray with small circular accents that glowed white.

The next suit I saw was Dimitri's. His face was covered by a skull mask hidden under a hood that was connected to a long black cloak, and at the bottom, it looked like a six-year-old had cut it up like you would with a paper snowflake. I never asked when Dimitri first arrived at the Academy, so maybe he had actually done that as a "stylized" choice. But the more I stared at him, the more he reminded me of the Grim Reaper.

Finally, I saw Helio's which was a gold and black armored suit—easily the biggest and bulkiest of them all. The shoulder pieces and helmet were shaped into eagle heads, which I thought was pretty damn cool, and a sword in a sheath sat on her back. She obviously had an artistic vision and knew what she was doing when she designed it.

I looked over at Theo and asked, "So, where's yours?"

"I don't need a suit because I *am* the suit," he said with a smirk.

"What does that even mean?"

"*Kaden Collins, it is now time for you to design and fabricate your suit,*" the disembodied voice said from above.

I gulped and walked toward a large touchscreen that sat in the center of the platforms. A robotic arm descended from the ceiling and scanned me head to toe with a blue laser.

"*Scan complete,*" the voice said as the arm quickly retracted back into the ceiling. A blue hologram of my body was now hovering and rotating in circles in front of the touchscreen.

I looked down at the screen and saw a color wheel and a large selection of different-shaped armor pieces. I placed my finger on a piece of armor and swiped upward, throwing it onto my holographic body as the rest of my team gathered around me.

"Oh, do that one!" Arissa said as she slid a piece up.

"No, this one!" Helio said, as she added another.

"What! No, not that one! That shit is ugly!" Theo said as he took over and removed all of them while adding more.

"Guys!" I yelled over the chaos. "I think I got this."

They all took a step back with embarrassed looks on their faces. I closed my eyes and thought back to the drawing of my suit that ended up flushed down a toilet. I found the most similar armor pieces to what I had imagined and began throwing them up to the hologram. I added a large chest plate, bulky shoulder and knee guards, a thick collar, intimidating gauntlets, and red lights all over it. I moved my finger across the color wheel, selecting the perfect shade of red and also adding black to make it two-toned. Finally, I threw on just a bit more armor plating over the entire suit.

Better to be safe than sorry, I thought to myself.

I took a deep breath and raised a finger over the complete button on the screen.

"Is your design final?" the disembodied voice asked. *"This process can only be done once."*

"Wait, what? Maybe there is something I want to change," but before I could do anything else, Arissa leaned over and pressed confirm on the touch screen.

"Confirmed. Please step onto the platform to begin the fabrication process."

I heard Arissa laughing behind me as I shook my head.

That girl is a piece of work.

I stepped onto the platform but didn't know what would happen once I was inside the tube. It shot down on top of me quicker than I could blink, and, thankfully, I didn't have my toes sticking out over the edge because I would've definitely lost them.

Lasers cut off my clothes before they were sucked into a hole on the floor, leaving me naked in the tinted tube, which I *hoped* my teammates couldn't see into. Nanobots filled the tube and formed into hexagonal pieces that swirled around me. They finally landed on my skin, connecting into a neoprene-like base layer as if I were wearing a thin wetsuit. Then, armor pieces came down on robotic arms, riveting and bolting together like LEGO pieces that extended and connected with audible clicks as they were situated into place. I was completely amazed by this otherworldly and futuristic technology, and it was incredible to see the things we had inside the Academy that were not available to the rest of the world.

"Process complete."

The tube lifted up, and I saw my teammates' faces again, staring open-mouthed at my new suit.

"How do I look?" I asked.

"Damn," Arissa replied, looking me up and down.

"Yeah, way to show all of us up, Kaden. How did you just throw that together? Did you spend years planning that thing?" Ezra asked which made me smile.

If only he knew.

I walked over to a mirror and saw my full suit for the first time. It turned out exactly how I envisioned it, and it felt surreal finally getting to wear it. To my surprise, the armor allowed for completely resistance free and effortless movement, but at the same time had a hefty and strong feel to it. Every time I moved my arms or legs, the motors and servos whirred, allowing my weak and skinny frame to move such a heavy suit. Only two days ago, the same suit was flushed down the toilet, and here I was standing in it.

I looked up at the group once more and said, "I think I'm ready to find out my powers."

We followed Professor Guano in a single file line into the power dome. Entering one by one, I watched each of my teammates' powers activate.

BEEP!

Helio's inhibitor chip was disabled, and her wings re-grew and extended from the back of her suit, covered in shiny gold metal armor.

Smart, I thought to myself.

Next, Dimitri passed through.

BEEP!

Dark smoke poured off of him, and black tentacles shot out from the folds of his cloak, creating four other arms which dropped to the floor and lifted him up into the air. The tentacles seemed to work independently from one another and could be used for various things such as lifting, carrying, or attacking. He was currently using them to walk across the Power Dome without using his legs which seemed like a really nice ability to have.

BEEP!

Arissa threw a portal onto the floor and another one onto the wall. She dove into the first one and launched out of the second one. She soared through the air, throwing another two down as she made her way across the floor, diving dolphin-like as if in and out of water.

Whoa.

I also noticed that she could only place two at a time which must've been a limitation of her powers, since it looked like she could only control one portal with each hand.

BEEP!

Ezra walked inside and flexed his body, bursting into flames. He launched into the air and began flying around in circles, propelled by his own fire, before landing back on the floor.

BEEP!

Theo walked inside and tore off the sleeves to his shirt, revealing a decently muscular frame—at least for a fifteen year old.

"Welcome to the gun show," Theo said as he flexed his arm.

It became a solid blue crystal with a sharp point at the end. Underneath the point, I could see his crystal-covered fingers moving freely. He flexed more of his body, and other limbs grew the same crystals until he had formed a full blue crystal suit around him.

"See? I don't need a stupid knock-off suit, I've got my own!" Theo's voice was muffled by the crystal mask that now covered his face, except for two eye holes that peered out to the world.

My turn, I thought to myself as I walked through the force field.

BEEP!

Nothing happened.

Theo laughed and said, "Well, at least you didn't turn into a hamster. Perhaps we should kill the lights and see if he—"

Suddenly, my hands glowed bright red. Light trails began to swirl around my forearms, and I could feel an overwhelming energy flowing through me, almost like the inhibitor chip hadn't actually shut off my powers but instead dammed them up with no release valve. I felt

supercharged, with so much energy just waiting to be—
   BOOM!
   A beam of red energy shot out of my hands and collided with Theo. His body was sent flying across the room, smashing into the wall of the Power Dome.
   "Holy shit!" Ezra yelled.
   I tried to stop the beam that was still shooting from my hands but nothing was working. It was like a waterfall going off the edge of a cliff, flowing out of me with no end in sight. I directed the blast all around the dome, striking the walls and narrowly avoiding my other teammates.
   "I'm sorry! I can't control it!" I yelled.
   Arissa dove out of the way at the last second before the beam nearly took her head off. Now, it was moving in a beeline straight for Professor Guano, and just before it reached him, Arissa threw out a portal and redirected it.
   Where's the other...
   BAM!
   The blast shot straight into me and sent me flying backward, skidding across the floor and colliding with the wall. I lay in a mess of red energy and smoke as it dissipated into the air.
   "I'm sorry, Kaden, but I had to take that risk before you killed someone!" she yelled, as she portaled over to check on me.
   I regained my composure and shook my head, finally checking my body to make sure I was still in one piece. To my surprise, I was completely injury free.
   "Well, at least we found out I'm immune to my *own* energy," I said, still smoking from the blast.
   Theo came over to me and extended a hand, helping me up.

"Thanks, man. I'm really sorry about…you know… *blasting* you with a beam of energy. Are you good?" I asked.

"Yeah, I'm fine. Good thing I'm made of nearly indestructible crystal! And I'm sorry to tell you, but your beams don't hit for shit," he joked.

The rest of the group came over, including Professor Guano.

"I'm sorry, everyone. I feel terrible about that. I just couldn't stop it," I said as I hung my head in shame.

"You're fine, Kaden," Ezra said. "If I had known your powers were energy based, I could've let you know what to expect, but none of us could've predicted it. That's how these inhibitor chips react to energy wielding Goldens like you and me. The energy doesn't just *disappear* inside of us; instead, it gets bottled up, compounding over time until we finally get to release it. And, sometimes, it comes out in ways we don't expect. Think of it like a side effect of the chip," he said, but then something grabbed his immediate attention. "Uh, I'll be right back."

He ignited with flames and flew straight up into the center of the Dome. We covered our eyes as he released a massive amount of blinding fire into the room, eventually flying back down.

"*Ah*, much better. It's kind of like a sneeze, you know? You either have to fight the urge or wait to safely release it," Ezra said.

All of that made perfect sense to me, and I realized when that urge came, I had done nothing to hold it back.

"Don't feel bad, Kaden," Dimitri interjected. "What Ezra is *not* telling you is that the first time he came in here, he almost went supernova and nearly burned down the whole Academy. Shit happens, and that's what we're here for: to learn how to best use and control these powers."

A smile grew across Professor Guano's face as he looked around at the group in front of him.

He finally said, "Well put, Dimitri. Now, shall we get started with today's lesson?"

• • •

Everyone was doing their own thing in the Power Dome: Ezra was inside a box testing how hot he could get, and I swore I saw a hint of white inside there amidst his usual orange flames.

A human-shaped dummy was being thrown around, and Arissa was using her portals to guide it through the air in order to get it to land safely on the other side of the Dome. A few times the dummy would eject from a portal and slam hard into a wall or accidentally fall from ten stories high, causing it to crash onto the floor and break into hundreds of pieces. She looked around, hoping no one saw what had happened, but I did, and it didn't make me feel too good knowing we would be relying on her and her portals in the future.

Theo was throwing crystals from his body at bullseyes on targets that were set up across the room. Occasionally, he would run over and smash through them with ease. It seemed as if he was much stronger than he usually was when he was in his crystal form, almost as if *everything* was reinforced—even his bones and muscles.

Dimitri was being riddled with bullets from a sentry minigun, which I thought was incredibly dangerous, but he used his tentacles to form a black shield to block them.

Definitely not his first time practicing that, I thought to myself, as a tentacle shot out from beside him and sliced the turret in half.

And, finally, I saw Helio flying through the air with a silver sword. She sliced apart drones while passing through a training course consisting of different colored rings that floated in the Dome.

Ezra offered to help me with my powers, which surprised me because I really thought he would be the *last* person on the team to do that for me, but since our powers were so similar, it was only the natural thing to do.

He showed me how to extend my arm and imagine that I was forcing the energy out of my open hand. When I was ready to make it stop, he told me to bring a closed fist back toward me. I tried this new method, and it worked like a charm... but only after a few close calls with the other teammates.

"Sorry!" I yelled, as an energy beam nearly blasted Helio out of the air.

Yeah, this was going to take a little getting used to.

I watched as the energy shot out of my hand in a small burst and took out a target in front of me.

"Not bad for a first timer," Ezra said with a reassuring pat on the back.

Professor Guano watched intently and made notes on a handheld touchscreen device.

"Now try a flying drone," Ezra said, pointing to a row of them that had appeared from the wall of the Power Dome, taking off into the air.

I aimed at one and opened my hand, releasing another short burst of energy, but I completely missed. I tried again—this time with my other hand—but I missed a second time. I started getting frustrated, so I released energy from both of my hands which sent out a massive blast, obliterating the drone.

Total overkill, I know, but I was getting pissed off.

I nearly doubled over, breathing heavily while trying to catch my breath. The last time I exerted myself this hard must've been when I ran the mile in 7th grade P.E. class, and half way through, I had given up and had to take a rest under a tree next to the track.

"Whoa! Easy there, Glow Stick. How about we slow it down?" Ezra said as he raised his own hand. "The goal is to use the least amount of energy as possible to get the job done. You just saw what can happen if you use too much at the wrong time, and if you do that out in the field, let's just say... you *won't* have time to catch your breath."

I watched as Ezra took a deep breath, tracking the flying drone with his hand, and finally shooting out a small fireball that took it right out of the air. He made it look effortless, as if he were a trained sniper. I quickly realized he knew what he was talking about and that I had *a lot* to learn from him.

"Try again, but this time focus on your breathing, and track the object until the right moment," he said, signaling me to go.

I did as he said, following the flying object with my hand like a sight on a rifle. I took a deep breath and slowly opened my fist. The energy shot out in a quick burst and precisely struck the object. I quickly closed my open hand, remembering what he said about the conservation of my energy.

"There you go, newbie! That's how it's done," he said, holding up his hand to high five.

We clapped hands, and without realizing it, I let out a small amount of energy that sent us both flying backward.

I slammed into the wall, and he skidded to a stop on the other side of the Dome.

My bad.

"Well, Kaden. You have proved to be quite the quick learner. I am sure Headmaster Fowler will be pleased to hear the results of today's power lesson," Professor Guano said as I got to my feet once again. Ezra flew over and landed next to me.

"Thank you, Professor Guano. I've obviously still got a lot to learn, but I'm just glad I'm not getting sent home."

"Well," Professor Guano said while repositioning his glasses, "we will see about that. I've got another class to teach today, so feel free to stay here and continue to train until another team kicks you out. See you all next time!" He hurried out of the Dome and disappeared through the force field.

"He's joking, right? *Right?*" I asked Ezra, but he only laughed and shook his head.

"Come on, I want to show you one more thing."

Next thing I knew, the team was standing ten stories high in the air on floating platforms. The top of the Dome was only a few feet above my head, and looking over the edge of the platform made my stomach turn.

"Alright, Ezra, what are we doing up here?" I asked, trying to stay steady on my feet.

My other teammates were standing behind me with crossed arms and smug faces.

"Seeing if you can fly," Ezra responded.

"*Fly?* What! I barely learned how to shoot a drone out of the sky, and now you want me to fly? Can't we at least start a little lower?" I asked, but all he did was shake his head *no*.

"Sometimes you have to run before you can walk, Kaden. Most Heroes here with energy-based powers can fly, so I have no reason to believe you can't."

"And on the off chance you're wrong?"

"Then you have no reason to be on our team."

My stomach did a backflip, and my legs felt unsteady. Everyone was watching, so I knew it was time to face the music.

Heed my warning: this is what happens when you promise to take your team from the bottom to the top of The Wall.

I made my way over to the edge, taking each step carefully as I went. I had already heard enough laughter from my team behind me to know that no one thought I could actually fly, but I knew I still had to try.

I love you, Mom!

I jumped off the edge of the platform, putting my hands down by my side while opening my fists. Energy sputtered out of my hands in a sad burst of red smoke and then... *nothing.*

Oh shit.

I was in free fall, screaming the whole way down. The wind tore past my face, and I knew my armor wouldn't save me from a fall this high. I raised my arms in front of my face, bracing for impact...

Wait. What happened? I'm not dead?

I fell through a portal and landed back up on the floating platform again. My armor skidded across it as sparks flew, getting closer and closer to the edge until my legs fell off the side and hung over the ten story drop below. Eventually, my legs pulled the rest of my body off with them, and at the last second, I managed to grab hold of the edge with all of my strength. The servos in my gauntlets worked hard to keep my grip from slipping, but I felt the tremendous weight of the suit pulling me down.

One by one, each of my fingers plucked off like strings popping from a violin, until I was only holding on with one finger. It finally slipped, but a crystal covered arm extended at the last second and grabbed me by the forearm, hoisting me up. My body flew into the air, over Theo, and crashed down hard onto the platform again. The laughter picked up once more.

"OK, OK, enough with the laughing," I said, calling out to the team, but they couldn't stop.

Theo reenacted the fall *and* the screams to the group which got them laughing even harder. I shook my head and was just glad I wasn't splattered on the floor. I wondered if Professor Guano would have let us stay if he had known they would try to kill me.

"Thanks for the help on that one, Arissa," Ezra said as he pulled me to my feet. "Flying is complicated, Kaden. You're not gonna get it on your first day, but don't give up. I saw a little bit of lift somewhere in those flailing arms."

"Food time?" Theo interjected.

"Last one down has to eat the mystery meat!" Helio yelled as she dove off the platform and glided toward the force field.

"Oh no you don't!" Dimitri said as he jumped off the platform and fell toward the ground. His tentacles formed into wings, slowing his descent.

"Oh, you little—" Ezra turned into a ball of fire and blasted off toward the force field.

"That's not fair! I can't fly!" Theo yelled back.

"Come on, you giant rock," Arissa said as she threw down a portal that led to the ground and walked through it.

"*Crystal,* not rock! How many times do I have to tell you people! There's a big difference!" he yelled to her as he went through the portal.

Arissa looked back and gave me a wave to come on.

"You coming? Trust me; you *don't* want to eat the mystery meat," she said as I took one last look at my hands and the Power Dome and ran through the portal.

CHAPTER SEVEN

MISSION PREP

I WOULD BE LYING if I said I wasn't a little overwhelmed during my first days at the Academy. It hadn't been easy catching up on years of combat and mission knowledge that I was obviously lacking. It didn't seem fair to be thrown into a graduating class since some Heroes at the Academy had been here since they were four years old, so by the time they were assigned to teams at thirteen, they were already well versed in this world. Those were usually the Heroes who made up the top teams on The Wall.

As Theo and I made our way down the center walkway of campus, I realized how nervous I had become for my first class.

He must've seen that because he said, "You got this! It's only mission prep, Kaden. It's just like regular school where if you memorize what you're supposed to, you'll be just fine. The worst thing that can happen is that you go totally blank during a mission, forget everything you learned, and get us all killed!" He patted me on the back. "Nothing to worry about!"

"That's not reassuring at all," I responded.

"Ah, I'm just pulling your leg. The good news is you'd most likely only get *yourself* killed."

The thought of messing up a mission terrified me, but I was still set on bringing this team up from the bottom and making it to Gidoria, and nothing was going to stand in my way.

"See that over there?" Theo said, pointing into the distance at the domed building I saw on my tour. "That's the Pantheon where Headmaster Fowler's chamber is. I've never been in it, but it looks cool. Next to it is the Library of Alexandria, one of my favorite spots on campus. And finally, we've got the Basilica. Come on, we're right in here for mission prep."

I looked up at the Basilica and saw hundreds of floor-to-ceiling windows with students milling about behind them. We made our way up smooth stone steps and past tall columns before ducking inside. I thought the classes would be something similar to what I was used to from my "normal" school, but nothing could have prepared me for this.

Once inside, I saw just how expansive the building really was. It was built in the shape of a square, and there were at least eight floors made of glass and marble. All the walkways and classrooms surrounded a central area which had a statue of Headmaster Fowler with his arms crossed in the center of it.

Inside the various classrooms, Heroes were learning first aid, building gadgets, running battle simulations with VR headsets on, steering ships in high tech flight simulators, and drawing out combat strategies on large touch screens.

I looked through the glass wall of one of the classrooms and noticed a large table with a blue hologram floating above it. The hologram had 3-D mountains, trees, and clouds, and I could see a simulation of an aircraft that I didn't recognize flying above the map.

Suddenly, the hologram ship stopped in mid air, and six hologram Heroes were lowered down by cables into the forest below. The Heroes surrounding the table were pointing at different objects and using their hands in sweeping motions, acting out different approach angles and attacks for the mission. Another student would make an adjustment on a touchscreen, and the aircraft would follow a different flight path and redo the same simulation.

A massive explosion erupted within the hologram map, and the Heroes put their hands to their faces. Negative point deductions started appearing all over the table, and the Heroes began blaming each other for the mission failure.

"Who would have thought *that* would happen?" one Hero sarcastically said to the other.

"I didn't hear you come up with any other strategies, dickhead! At least I actually tried to complete the mission. All I hear from you is complaining!" he yelled back.

"Alright, that does it!" the Hero said, before tackling the other onto the table and rolling around through the hologram, eventually falling off of it and crashing onto the floor.

"Come on! Class is this way, and we do not want to be late. Professor Wayla would not be happy," Theo said, running down the atrium.

I got one last look at the fight and laughed to myself as I chased after him.

We entered the classroom with Helio and Dimitri already inside, waiting for class to begin. There were six seats facing a wall of screens and another one of those hologram tables.

"You managed to not be late on your first day. I'm impressed," Helio said with her feet kicked up on the seat in front of her.

"I would've been late if it weren't for Theo pulling me along," I said while looking around. "This place is insane. What *don't* we have in here? The coolest thing my old school ever had was a pet frog."

"Good snacks," Dimitri said. "All we have are stupid protein shakes and energy bars. It's almost as if they think we're high performance athletes or something!"

"Uh, we kind of are, Dimitri," Theo responded.

"Whatever, still doesn't mean we can't have something good for once."

Professor Wayla finally came through the door, and I nearly jumped out of my seat. One would've thought a talking gorilla for a professor was enough for me to realize that this place wouldn't be normal, but this lady had purple skin and *six* arms. She wore a long, sleeveless gray athletic shirt with yellow accents across it.

I wondered when I would get used to seeing all this weird shit around here, but I guess it would take a few more weeks because she made me feel *very* uneasy. You go your entire life living among regular old non-Golden humans, barely ever interacting with Goldens—except when they're destroying your city—to being taught mission prep by one with purple skin and more arms than I had fingers on one hand.

"Sorry I'm late!" Arissa said as she came running into the class. "If they would actually let me use my portals instead of running up eight flights of stairs, I might have a better chance of getting here on time."

"Exercise is great for you, Arissa! You need good cardio,

probably more than anything else for when you're out in the field," Professor Wayla said.

Ezra finally came through the door with a sour look on his face as if he didn't want to be here.

"Ah, Ezra, thank you for showing up today!"

Ezra took a seat and said, "Yeah, yeah, whatever. I'm only here because it's the new kid's first day, and I couldn't miss seeing his face by the end of it."

"Fair enough. Now, class, let's get *started*," she said, bringing all six of her hands together in a triple clap.

• • •

The next three hours of mission prep were a blur—so much information, yet I couldn't get enough of it, and I never wanted class to end. Collateral damage was a big point that Professor Wayla continued to emphasize.

"Let's say Theo here is being pinned down by a rogue Golden with super strength," Professor Wayla said, pointing to the hologram table with four of her arms. It had a 3-D model of a city with all of us in our full suits simulated on it. I had to say, mine looked pretty cool from this angle.

"Impossible, no one could pin me down even if they tried," Theo said while crossing his arms and smirking.

"I was afraid you were going to say that. Why must you force me to embarrass you in front of your other teammates?" she said with two hands on her hips, two on her face which was shaking back and forth, and another two holding a remote.

She pressed a button, and a compilation of clips of Theo being pinned down by Rogues while screaming for help played on one of the screens. The whole class laughed, and Theo slumped lower in his seat, trying to hide.

"How did you have all of those clips ready to go like that?" he asked.

"You are as predictable as you are arrogant. Now, *Mr. Collins.*"

I quickly contained my laughter and replied, "Yes, Professor Wayla?"

"What shall you do to rescue your friend?"

"A well-placed energy blast about medium power from *this* direction would send the Rogue flying off him."

A simulation of a beam attached itself to the tip of my finger, and I was able to drag out a dotted line, tracing the trajectory of the beam directly to the Rogue.

"Let's see if you are correct," she said as the hologram began moving. "Kaden uses an energy blast with medium power as his attack. It makes contact with the Rogue at a twenty degree angle, striking him in the back."

My hologram released an energy blast straight at the Rogue, sending him flying off Theo.

I smiled and said, "Almost like I'm a natural at this."

"Not quite," Professor Wayla said, pointing at the hologram with one of her arms.

"The rogue Golden went flying into a building, and if we do an x-ray scan and see the inside of it," I watched as the hologram zoomed into the bottom floor of the skyscraper, "we can see the rogue Golden that you blasted away is now on a direct collision course with 10,000 containers of potassium nitrate, sulfur and charcoal. When the remnants of your energy interact with these materials…"

BOOM!

The entire bottom floor of the skyscraper detonated, causing the rest of the structure to collapse and crumble into the city. The explosion caused a chain reaction taking out other buildings like dominoes falling in a row. Screams and more explosions were heard as our team's holograms tried to run into Arissa's portal but were crushed by the falling debris before they could escape.

"Oh, come on!" I exclaimed as I slammed my hands through the hologram and onto the table. "That is *completely* unrealistic. I've seen action movies more believable than that!"

"Is it, Kaden? That was a building that housed fireworks. Not unrealistic at all. Real life is often more unrealistic than you could even imagine. Anything that can go wrong *will* go wrong in any number of ways." She pressed a button on her remote, and a video appeared on one of the screens. "Take Team #43 from fifteen years ago for example. They decided the best way to subdue a rogue Golden was to cause an earthquake. One of the members of the team had seismic abilities, and although he successfully completed the mission on paper, the earthquake he caused destroyed a dam, flooding a nearby city, killing thousands of civilians, his entire team, and himself. *That* is why we teach you situational awareness and put such an emphasis on collateral damage. You always need to be aware of the people and places around you, no matter the mission."

I looked over at Ezra with a side eye.

"OK, piss off," he snapped back.

"Collateral damage has been the biggest reason your team has been so unsuccessful in the past. It is the easiest and quickest way to lose points. I hope that if I hammer this into your brain now, you can lead by example, and the rest of your teammates will follow," Professor Wayla said with a smile.

I looked over and saw all my other teammates slumped over, sleeping on each other's shoulders.

"At least *you* were awake for that, Ezra," she said.

"Oh, don't kid yourself, Professor, I just woke up after I heard Kaden cry out in anguish and knew I couldn't miss what was going to follow," Ezra said with a wink.

"Well, Team #22, that's about it for today's mission prep. Expect a mission assignment within the next few months. Headmaster Fowler wants Kaden to have ample time to get used to things around here before you are sent out into the field," Professor Wayla said. "Go have a wonderful day." And with that, she exited the classroom.

"Don't expect to see me here," Ezra said as he got up from his chair.

I gave him a confused look and asked, "Like after class or—"

"Like ever again, but hey, I'm glad you're learning! You've got *a lot* to catch up on." Ezra gave me a salute and walked out the door.

Thanks, I thought to myself.

"Hey, wake up," I said as I tried nudging Theo awake.

He let out a big yawn and asked, "Geez, what time is it?"

"Come on, dude; class is over. Let's go!"

"Already? Man, that was quick!"

"Yeah, that's what happens when you sleep through the whole thing."

Theo stood up, stretched like a cat, and said, "Not like I'm missing anything. I've been in these classes for years. This is all for you. Professor Guano just told us to come support our new teammate since he doesn't think that we have an ounce of teamwork among us," he said, rolling his eyes.

"Said by a Golden on the worst team at the Academy," I

said mockingly. "Maybe if you *did* pay attention during these, we would have a better chance of turning this ship around."

"That's a good point," he pondered, "but I'm good."

"Should I wake them up?" I asked, signaling to the rest of the team that was still asleep.

"Nah, leave 'em be. They need it anyway. I sure know I did."

"Yeah, you're probably right," I said as we started for the exit.

Theo noticed something at the door and stopped before leaving.

"I think those are for you?" Theo said, pointing at a large stack of books, leather bound journals, papers, and scrolls all tied together with a brown string and a sticky note on top.

I picked it up and read:

For Kaden,
Enjoy.
H.F.

"Who is H.F.?" I asked.

"I can't believe it," Theo said, ripping the note from my hand before flipping it over and back a few times while inspecting it. "Man, he must really like you."

He handed it back to me, and then it clicked. The books came from *Headmaster Fowler.*

• • •

Once I finally went inside the Library of Alexandria, I practically lived in it. It was Roman in design, as was everything here, and it had breathtaking arched ceilings with windows that let natural light into the massive room. The walls were lined with floor to ceiling bookshelves, filled from the bottom to the top with books, manuscripts, and scrolls dating back hundreds of years.

As I explored the library, I found a cozy nook in the back corner of the second floor with a desk that overlooked the campus through large windows. It also had a skylight through which I could see the galaxy at night.

Have I ever mentioned that the stars look incredible out here in the open ocean with no light pollution for hundreds of miles?

Although it was very easy to forget I was living on a floating city in the middle of the ocean, Theo had said I would occasionally feel it move late at night, and when I heard the faint groaning of the walls that signaled its departure to a new location, it always reminded me of where I was.

Over the course of the months leading up to the first mission, I barely slept. Instead, I stayed up all night, nearly every night, in that nook, reading everything that the Headmaster had assigned to me.

The first time I opened one of the books, the pages were a little blurry, and I couldn't quite make out what they said, but as I blinked my eyes a few times, the letters seemed to rearrange themselves and become clear, and I quickly found myself completely enthralled by the stories that they held.

There were a lot of books about a Golden in the past who was titled the *Hero of Earth*, which was *also* the highest rank a Hero of the Academy could achieve. It was bestowed upon the best Hero in every graduating class.

The Hero of Earth that I read about brought order and balance to the planet during a time when Goldens roamed freely, causing chaos everywhere they went. There were a lot of wars during this time, most notably the Earth Civil War, a war that was fought between humans and Goldens, and the First Golden War, a war fought entirely between Goldens. One side was led by the Hero of Earth, and the other by a mysterious enemy named Zahavi.

The writer of the books came off as too much of a fanboy for the Hero of Earth, but I still think I got the message. Everything that was discussed happened during a time *long* before the Academy, and it was eventually founded to keep the peace that the Hero of Earth had brought about.

After reading through the books, I couldn't be more thankful that this place existed. Giving Goldens like me a place to train and learn for a chance to one day graduate to Gidoria as a Warrior was the greatest gift of all.

Speaking of Gidoria, I wanted to learn more about it after my conversation with my team in the dining hall, but I couldn't find any books in the library talking about the planet or what happened there. The only things I really knew about it were from the Headmaster's assigned texts, and from everything I gathered, it seemed like a utopia that I couldn't wait to get to one day, even if getting there meant I had to leave Earth behind.

I wasn't too bummed about that part since I never really felt like I belonged on Earth anyway. I knew my mom would be sad to hear that I was going to be leaving, but she would understand that I was doing it because I was serving a greater purpose—making something of myself and becoming the hero I've always wanted to be.

Maybe Gidoria would even be the place where I would

finally feel at home.

I also read through a number of journals from previous Heroes before their trips to Gidoria, many of whom had energy powers like me. Reading what they had learned about their own powers helped me tremendously with mine, and I started applying their knowledge to my training when I wasn't studying.

I spent countless hours in the Power Dome, sometimes with the team and sometimes alone—which was the best time to test the things I had learned from the journals. The most important thing I had figured out was that my powers were an extension of myself because I *was* the energy. I realized that it didn't come from my hands but instead came from within me, and I could create nearly anything I imagined.

I called these creations my *projections*: objects that I could form out of my energy—mainly different types of shields that could block just about anything. The first time I had the sentry guns shoot me while I projected a shield was a terrifying experience, but once I realized I was unharmed, I felt even *more* powerful.

Believe it or not, my flying had also improved. Ezra continued to walk me through the process of sticking my arms out and propelling myself through the air, using the energy coming from my hands to hold myself airborne. I had only been able to glide for short distances before my arms gave out, but I would get to "real" flying eventually— hopefully not falling out of the air every two minutes. It only took about a dozen times of smashing my face on the edge of a platform and falling through hundreds of Arissa's portals to finally get the actual gliding part figured out.

Speaking of Arissa, what a trooper!

She had been nothing but supportive of me throughout all of my training. One night after dinner, she came by the room and knocked on my door.

"Hey, Kaden, want to see something cool?" she asked.

Before I even got a chance to respond, she grabbed my hand and pulled me out of bed. She brought me to the top floor of the Villas and opened a window. She climbed outside and stood on the edge of a stone ledge.

"Come on! Don't be scared," she said as she signaled to follow her. "It's perfectly safe, I promise."

I didn't believe her, but I took a deep breath and thought that if I was afraid of this, then I wouldn't last a second in the field.

I followed her out and walked along the ledge trying not to look down as I went. She grabbed the top of the roof and hoisted herself up before I did the same. When I finally managed to claw my way up, I saw why she wanted to bring me here. The stars were *beautiful*—much better than looking at them through the library skylight above my nook.

We laid on that roof for hours and talked about our dreams, favorite movies, food, music, and eventually our pasts, which was sad because the more I learned of hers, the more I realized she didn't really have one. She was brought here at the age of seven after her Awakening, and all she had ever known was the Academy which was hard to imagine. After some more time had passed, we played a game where we would ask each other things we've experienced.

"Concerts?" I asked.

"No," she quickly responded.

"What! Concerts were the best!"

"I've always wanted to, but I just never went."

"Roller coasters?" I asked again.

"Yes."

"Me too! I loved those!"

"What about... Have you ever been on a boat?" she asked.

"Yes," I responded.

"Lucky! I never got to go on one."

"Really? No boats either? Dang your childhood really sucked."

"Hey, don't be mean."

"Sorry, that was a bad joke, but it's just crazy to me. There are so many things that I took for granted before I came here. I guess you don't really know what you have until it's gone."

"Yeah... if you even had it to begin with."

I saw a sad look grow across her face.

"Hey, we're kind of on a boat right now! It's pretty much the same thing, they're both just vessels that take you across the water," I said, trying to cheer her up.

She laughed, but it didn't last long.

"You know what I miss the most?" she asked.

"What?"

"Christmas morning with my family. I only have faint memories of two Christmas mornings, but when I do think back to them, I can't help but smile, and a warm feeling of comfort rolls over me."

"Christmas was the best. Opening presents with my mom, eating cookies, and watching Christmas movies."

"That *was* the best."

"You ever miss your parents?"

"All the time, even though I don't have that many memories of them. I was only with my family for seven years, but every day I wish I could see them again," she said while looking up at the stars. "That's one thing about being at the Academy that never changes: no matter how long you've been here, you never truly stop missing them, even though you know they're not really a part of your life anymore… and never will be again."

A long silence hung in the air as I thought about what she had said. The idea of not seeing my mother again made me incredibly sad, and I attempted getting those thoughts out of my head by looking up at the Big Dipper and the rest of the galaxy in the night sky, trying to picture Gidoria somewhere out there among them.

"What about you? I know you've only been here for a few months, but have you missed them at all?" she asked, finally breaking the silence.

"I definitely miss my mom, a lot, and I just wish I could at least hear from her and tell her that I'm doing OK; you know?"

"I feel the same way. Ten years and not a single word from them. I almost wonder if they've forgotten about me… What about your dad? Do you wish you could talk to him too?"

"My dad…" I paused, trying to find the words to talk about him. "I didn't know him. My mom always said he was a good person who loved me, but he left before I was born, so I never met him. I hope I can one day."

"I'm sorry to hear that, but you know what? I bet one day you will."

"Thanks." A shooting star ripped past our view, and I secretly made a wish.

Soon after, I felt her scoot closer to me, and I decided to put my arm around her. It was pretty cold up there, and we needed to stay warm, or at least that's what I told her, but she seemed to agree since she scooted in even closer and wrapped herself around me.

"Kaden, I had one more thing I was going to ask you."

"Throw it at me."

"Have you ever kissed anyone?"

My face instantly felt hot, and my stomach did a backflip.

"Oh, uh, yeah… plenty of times," I said, lying through my teeth.

"Oh," she hesitated like it hurt to hear, "well, I haven't so, I don't know… maybe you could show me how?"

Now I was *really* in some deep shit. I ignored my inner voice screaming at me to abort the mission before I embarrassed myself beyond repair and went for it anyway.

I knew I wasn't that good at it, but hey, I'm learning a lot of new things. That's why I'm here, right?

• • •

By the time I made it back to the Library of Alexandria to study more, I was zapped. I found another nook with a sleeping mat and a bunch of pillows next to a small kindling fire, where I set up camp each night since Theo had kicked me out of our room for staying up too late with the light on to study. He claimed it was annoying him even with an eye mask and headphones on, but I actually didn't mind getting kicked out at all since I found myself spending so many late nights in the library anyway.

I would eventually pass out covered in papers or with a book open on my face, and that's the scene that Zo floated in on when he eventually found me the next morning and woke me up. I wiped the gunk from my eyes and focused on the giant head in front of me.

"Headmaster Fowler has requested to speak with you. Follow me at once to his chamber," Zo said without giving me much of a choice to say no.

"Can I at least take a shower first?" I asked.

He took a sniff of me and zoomed backward.

"Please do. I assume the Headmaster will understand and *appreciate* the delay."

• • •

I entered the Headmaster's chamber and looked around in amazement.

"Hello? Headmaster Fowler?" I called out but received no answer.

Then, I heard the sound of a creaking door and saw a section of the bookshelf slowly opening. I ran behind the door I came through and peered in between the crack. Headmaster Fowler and Zo came out from a secret room behind the bookshelf and made their way over to his desk.

"The boy is making considerable progress with his training in the Power Dome. I have been personally watching him through the cameras, and he is excelling more quickly than I predicted. He seems to be finally getting a grasp on his powers," Zo said.

"That is *very* good news. I think that is all the more reason to give him his first mission. He is more than ready, but do not tell him what you have just told me. Just as the High Lords demanded, it is imperative he does not know his true—"

Creak!

I leaned on the door too hard, and the sound echoed across the room. I had to play it off the best I could and decided to knock twice, hoping they thought I was just pushing through the door.

"Headmaster Fowler, you were expecting me?" I asked, my voice echoing off the tall walls. "I hope I'm not interrupting anything, and I'm really sorry if I did."

"Ah, yes, Kaden, I was, and no, you were not interrupting *anything*. Zo was just telling me about a mission report from Team #1. Come in, come in." He signaled for me to walk to his desk as he waved off Zo. "Leave us." Zo nodded and floated away. "Kaden, my *favorite* student," he said, which made me smile. "How have the assigned texts been treating you these past few months? I know it was a lot but—"

"Actually, Headmaster Fowler, I have already finished them," I interrupted.

"Which one?"

"*All of them.*"

The Headmaster shook his head and chuckled, "I never assigned texts to any of my other Heroes since knowledge can be... how do I put this—a *burden*; however, it seems to me that you have handled it just as I had anticipated."

"Thank you, Headmaster Fowler. I truly appreciate your trust in me with those books."

"They are from my *personal* collection, after all," he said, signaling to the many bookshelves in his library.

"I really enjoyed reading them, but I had a question, Headmaster, well actually a few."

"My favorite student is allowed to ask any and all questions that he so pleases."

"First, is my mother OK? Would I be able to talk to her?"

His face twitched, and he said, "Rest assured, Kaden, your mother is fine and well."

"OK, thank God," I said with a sigh of relief. "That is

good to hear."

"As for talking to her… well, that is a different matter entirely. *No* Heroes are allowed to speak to their families."

"But why not!" I asked as I quickly realized I had raised my voice. I regretted it as soon as the words slipped from my mouth.

Headmaster Fowler dropped his head and pursed his lips.

"Kaden, my boy, the outside world doesn't understand what we're doing here. We're saving lives—saving the world! These things are not easily comprehended by people who are not like *us,* and some families cannot put their egos aside and let us do what needs to be done for the greater good of the planet! They complicate things, to put it frankly. We tried open communication in the past, and our Heroes were too distracted by it. It is better this way, I promise you that, and you know I would never lie to you, right, Kaden?"

"Of course." I tried not to think about what I had heard earlier when they didn't know I was listening. It was something I was obviously *not* supposed to hear.

"It distracts you from things such as your first mission, which I am assigning you as soon as possible, only once, of course, a proper threat arises that needs your abilities to handle."

I sat up to the edge of my seat.

"Really? You think I'm ready for my first mission?"

"You've *been* ready, Kaden—since the day you first got here. Everything else has just proven to me that I have been right to think that. Now, it is time that you inform your teammates of the good news."

Headmaster Fowler stood up from his desk and walked

over to my side.

"Headmaster Fowler?" I asked.

"Yes, my boy," he responded.

"Can I—" but before I even finished my question, I hugged him. Headmaster Fowler slowly put his arms around me and then hugged me back tightly. "Thank you."

"Of course, Kaden," he said before releasing me. I headed toward the door, excited to tell my team about the good news.

"Oh wait, Headmaster? I had one last question." He raised his chin to me as if to say *go on*. "Those books you gave me about the Earth Civil and Golden Wars that took place hundreds of years ago… were you the first Hero of Earth?"

The Headmaster smiled and said, "I thought if I was learning so much about you, it was only right for you to learn a little bit about me. Now go, your teammates are waiting for you."

CHAPTER EIGHT

THE FIRST MISSION

W E ALL STEPPED onto our platforms, except Theo, of course, since he didn't need a suit. The tinted tubes came down from the ceiling, and I watched as the nanobots swarmed around me, connecting themselves together to form the neoprene base layer.

The armor pieces came next, bolting together and securing into place with audible clicks and pops. It sounded like a mix between a NASCAR pit stop and a welder fabricating pieces of metal together. The tinted cylinders finally lifted, revealing our fully formed suits.

I looked at the team around me, thinking about how lucky I was that *these* were the people who would accompany me on my first mission. After getting to know them for the past few months, I really couldn't have asked for a better group of people to march into battle with.

A robot brought out earpieces, and we each slid them into place. I tapped mine a few times to make sure it was working and heard a soft static noise.

"Is this thing on?" I asked as the static faded and became clear, almost like putting on noise-canceling headphones for the first time.

"Yes, we can all hear your annoying voice loud and clear, Kaden," Ezra said with a thumbs up.

"Attention, Team #22! It is time to depart for your mission. Godspeed, and good luck. Your aircraft is waiting for you in the hangar," Professor Guano called out with a salute.

The hangar? I thought to myself.

I knew it existed from learning about it in mission prep, but I had never actually been in it, and before I could think about it any longer, we were on our way, running through a tunnel under the Academy. My suit made a clanging metal noise that echoed down the tunnel, and I looked to my left and saw Arissa.

"Are you nervous?" she asked me as we ran.

"Not at all," I responded, and I was telling the truth. I had never been more excited for anything in my life.

We entered the hangar which was filled to the brim with these alien, otherworldly-looking, metallic silver ships. They didn't resemble any traditional aircraft that I could name, and they didn't appear to have a propulsion system, so I wasn't exactly sure how they were hovering around the hangar without making any noise other than a faint *whoosh* sound. I guessed that they used the same antigravity technology that held the Academy above the water and Zo's big head on his chair.

No one else on my team looked as starstruck as I was, and they just followed the directional signal that one of the hangar operators gave them with a glowing orange stick. After all, it was only *my* first mission, and to the rest of them, this was just business as usual. I wasn't even sure how many missions they had completed in past years, but the way they calmly walked across the hangar toward the ship told me everything I needed to know.

A drop hatch opened from the underbelly of the ship,

and stairs were lowered down to the floor. As we climbed up them, our metal suits clanked and whirred. Once I was inside, I could see perfectly out of all sides of the ship, which was surprising because, from the outside, it appeared to have no windows, just sleek silver plating. The hull must have been made of some type of transparent material that, again, was not available to the rest of the world.

Large seats were situated throughout the cabin, with one for the pilot at the front facing the controls, then two rows of double seats behind it, and one single seat in the rear. I sat in the seat behind the pilot with Arissa sitting to my right.

"Alright, everyone, buckle up!" Ezra yelled back to us.

We strapped into our seats with a five-point harness like those in race cars. I clicked the buckles together, gripped the edges of my seat, and put my head back while closing my eyes. I had been on a commercial plane once in my life when I was younger, but I didn't really enjoy it.

This couldn't be much different, right? I hoped.

"Not nervous at all, huh?" Arissa said with a giggle, staring down at my hands which were pale white from gripping the edges so hard.

I shot one eye open at her and said, "Nope, not at all."

Then, the aircraft lifted into the air, and that confidence quickly dissolved. The ship crept out of the hangar and hovered above the ocean. The nose began to angle upward until we were nearly vertical.

"Team #22, you are cleared for takeoff."

"Copy that, hangar control. Engaging full power," Ezra replied as he rolled the throttle forward.

A transparent blue canopy came over the top of our seats like a miniature force field. I instinctively gripped

Arissa's hand and braced as the ship shot into the sky and tore through the clouds at a tremendous speed, but my head didn't snap back from G-force as I was expecting. It didn't make any sense because I knew we were moving fast, very fast—probably at a greater speed than anything non-Goldens had ever achieved.

I turned to Arissa with a confused look on my face and mouthed, *What the hell?*

She saw my confusion and replied, "The canopy protects us from G-force; otherwise, we would all be a big puddle of goo right now."

Her comment reassured me as I was finally able to relax my grip on the seat.

"That's an image I didn't want to picture," I said, which caused her to laugh.

"Team #22, listen very carefully," a War Room operator at the Academy said through our earpieces. "Here is your mission report: we have a bank robbery in progress, and DGC soldiers who arrived at the scene have confirmed the presence of three Rogues."

I remembered learning about the War Room in one of my classes a few months ago, and it was essentially a giant room where operators observed our missions, made sure we're alright, and added or subtracted our points in real time. We toured the War Room one random afternoon, and I thought it had to have been the coolest thing at the Academy, except maybe the Library of Alexandria.

"What's the power assessment?" I asked in a stern tone, which surprised even me as well as my teammates.

It was a question I had also learned in class—one you always asked during the mission report to find out exactly what you're going up against.

"One of them is a Class 2 with water manipulation abilities; the second is a Class 1 with the ability to cover himself in an impenetrable, armored skin," the operator replied.

"Looks like we've got a copycat, Theo!" Ezra said while laughing to himself.

"Yeah, we will see about that, hot head. He's got nothing on my graphene shell," he answered, slapping his chest.

"The third is a Class 3 with shockwave abilities," the operator finished.

"A *Class 3?* For Kaden's first mission? Damn. They're really trying to show you what this is all about, huh," Ezra said while shaking his head.

Hearing this information made me more nervous than I let on because there were five classes of Goldens that the Academy categorized. Class 1 Goldens had non-lethal abilities like Arissa and Helio. Class 2 Goldens had lethal abilities that could cause *some* damage but not city wide destruction; think Theo, Dimitri, Ezra and me. A Class 3 could cause serious damage such as taking down buildings in a single blow, and a Class 4 could level a city, obviously making them extremely dangerous. Based on the books I read about the First Golden War, I would classify Headmaster Fowler as a Class 4 which was a scary thought.

As for Class 5, the records were incomplete as the Academy had never identified one since it was founded a hundred years ago. I didn't even want to imagine what kind of power a Class 5 could possess, but the fact that the Academy recognized that there even was a Class 5 meant that there probably was one out there, *somewhere*.

"Alright, we're approaching the mission zone!" Ezra

yelled as he brought the ship to a hover over a city.

"That was quick," I said to Arissa. "Didn't we just cross the entire North American Division?"

"We have to move fast in order to get to the Rogues in time since we only have a short window before they try to escape into hiding again," she said. "Ready?"

I nodded as two hatches opened underneath the ship, revealing a city I *instantly* recognized.

"Powers on!" Ezra yelled.

"Copy that," came the operator's reply.

BEEP!

My hands and body started glowing, and I finally felt the incredible power within me once again. I looked at Arissa and smiled.

"Let's get to the top of The Wall," I said as I dove out of the ship.

I fell through the air with the New York City skyline in front of me. My arms and legs were spread out, and wind flew across my face, whipping my hair. Surveillance orbs deployed from the ship and zoomed past me toward the ground.

Ezra appeared next to me doing front flips and spins through the air until he finally flexed his muscles and ignited into flames. He shot straight down toward street level and flew out of sight. I realized I was quickly approaching the ground, so I thought it was a good time to slow my descent.

"I hope this works!" I yelled over the noise of the deafening wind.

I shot energy from my hands and immediately felt my body become weightless as I started to rise. I tried steering down to the street, avoiding cars, light poles and pedestrians, knowing that any mistake could cost us points. I saw the perimeter the DGC had already set up outside of The Unity National Bank and tried to land in the center of it.

"Shit!" I yelled as my metal boots made contact with the ground, skidding and sparking across it. I was still going too fast to stop, and before I knew it, my foot caught traction, flipping me over and sending me rolling across the ground before finally sliding to a stop in front of the bank.

"Ow…" I let out.

My body ached, and my suit whirred as I got to my feet and brushed off my scratched armor.

Man, I gotta work on that.

"Look out below!" Theo yelled.

I looked up and saw Helio carrying him by holding onto his hand with one arm. He let go of her, turning into his blue crystal form and landing hard on the street, cracking it and forming a small crater under his feet.

"The muscle has arrived!" Theo yelled before thrusting a fist into the air.

"Theo! Collateral damage!" I yelled back at him.

"Oh…" He tried brushing away the rubble with his crystal foot. "Sorry."

I rolled my eyes and then heard the ear piercing sound of glass breaking coming from above as it rained down next to me. My head whipped toward the source of the noise, and I saw Dimitri sliding down the windows of a skyscraper with his tentacles, shattering each one he touched along the way. He jumped to another building and took out six more windows before finally dropping three stories down onto the ground, using his tentacles to absorb the impact of his fall.

"Dimitri! Come on, man!" I said as I pointed up to the trail of shattered windows that he had created during his grand entrance. "Are you guys even *trying?*"

"My bad," he replied.

I shook my head in frustration just as a fusion of purple and pink light formed into a portal in the street in front of me. Arissa rose out of it, and it closed below her just before she landed.

"How'd we do?" she asked as she looked around at the immense damage. She pursed her lips and shrugged. "*Not bad.*"

I put my armored hand to my face.

"Ezra, how's the situation looking?" I asked.

"The Rogues are still inside; let's move in!" he shouted, as he swooped down from the sky in a blaze of fire.

"Ezra, wait! Look at you, man! You're literally made of fire. If you go into that enclosed space, you would torch every non-Golden hostage alive! We have to wait for them to come to us."

"Fine."

And so, we *waited.*

Twenty painstakingly long minutes had passed, and by that time, my team had fully set up camp. Ezra wasn't on fire anymore and was instead stretched out on the front windshield of a DGC cruiser. He accidentally cracked through it and looked around hoping no one would notice, but I think the DGC could understand his use of their hood as a bed while we killed time.

Dimitri was playing rock-paper-scissors with two of his tentacles. The right tentacle lost and started fighting the other. He snapped at them which quickly got them under control.

Helio sat on the curb, sharpening her sword over and over again. She brought it to her face and inspected it, but a dissatisfied look grew.

"Stupid piece of steel shit," she said, bringing it back down to continue sharpening it.

Theo had formed two sharp points for arms and was acting as if he were stabbing imaginary foes with different punches and kicks.

"Take that, Rogue scum!" He spat onto the ground where the imaginary person was supposed to be. "Oh yeah? You really want a piece of this? Come and get it!" he yelled as he stabbed in the air.

Arissa floated in and out of a portal like a trampoline, appearing right side up from one, and upside down from the other.

I formed a ring of energy around me and watched it spin in a circle. I would change the direction of the ring every few seconds, spinning it back and forth while sending it up and down my body like a hula hoop.

Suddenly, a barrage of loud footsteps came from the entrance of the bank.

"Alright! Let's get out of here!" the metal Rogue yelled as he and the other Rogues ran out of the building while carrying dozens of gold bars and stacks of money in duffle bags. They were dressed in bullet-proof vests, camo pants, and had tattoos on their faces.

"Wait! Who are *they?*" the Rogue with water abilities questioned as they caught a glimpse of us while we were all quickly getting to our feet.

"Your worst nightmare!" Theo yelled back.

There was a long pause as the goons stared at us in disbelief. Then... they burst out *laughing.*

"Oye! I see, you're the little children from the Academy, aren't ya?" the shockwave Rogue said.

"Little children? Alright, that does it!" Theo ran straight toward them, extending his arms into sharp points.

"Theo, stop!" I yelled as he broke formation. The shockwave Rogue merely flicked his finger, releasing a small blast that sent Theo flying into the distance and out of sight, cursing the whole way.

"Kaden, what's the play?" Ezra said as he engulfed himself in flames once more.

"Me? How am I supposed to know what to do? It's my first mission!" I yelled back.

"Kaden! You *know* what to do, now trust yourself and tell us!" Arissa cried out.

I closed my eyes and took a deep breath as I thought back to all of my reading and training.

"Alright, playtime is over. I've about had it with these clowns," the water Rogue said, unleashing a massive torrent of water from the sewers, sending it straight at us.

"Arissa! Redirect!" I yelled.

Arissa threw out a portal in front of us and placed another above the Rogue. The water passed through the first and came down on top of him through the other, crushing him hard into the ground.

"Helio, find Theo and bring him back here. Now!"

She nodded and took off into the sky.

"Dimitri, keep the water Rogue busy while we take care of the others."

Dimitri launched toward him as he was getting up and wrapped his tentacles around him. He picked him up and slammed him into the street over and over again.

"Ezra, see if you can find the melting point of that metal

Rogue."

Ezra exploded toward him and shot fire out of his hands, dousing the metal man in flames.

"Arissa, I need you to help me close the gap with the shockwave Rogue. Keep redirecting his attacks safely into the sky while avoiding damaging any structures. Don't let him destroy anything else, OK?"

"Got it!" she replied, while readying herself.

I propelled myself into the air with energy and focused more into my fists as the shockwave Rogue let out a blast toward me, but before it could hit me, Arissa placed a portal in front of it, sending the blast flying away above us. I closed the distance and punched my fist hard into his stomach, sending him skidding down the street.

He struggled to get to his feet, and as I flew toward him, he sent another shockwave at me, but again, Arissa redirected it into the sky. I let out an energy beam with both of my hands, but he dodged it by diving out of the way. As he dove through the air, he returned a shockwave at me before Arissa could redirect it. I tried to project a shield in front of me, but the shockwave came too quickly and struck me, sending me flying into the air toward a building.

I projected a shield behind me and used it to absorb the impact of the collision with the glass windows. I crashed through one and skidded to a stop, finding myself lying on the floor of an office building. Non-Goldens screamed at the sight of me and ran for their lives.

I shook my head, trying to regain my composure. My suit had been banged up, and so was I, but I pushed through the pain and managed to get to my feet. I started running toward the hole I had come through and launched myself out of it. Suddenly, I found myself falling from ten stories high. I slowed myself with an energy blast, landing hard on the street again with my fist and knee pressed into the concrete.

I looked up and saw Arissa defending herself with portals from the many shockwaves the Rogue was throwing at her.

Dimitri fought with his tentacles, and the water Rogue fought with transparent ones, slashing and slicing at each other. Helio and Theo arrived back inside the perimeter and landed in the street, while Ezra doused the metal man in flames.

"Ezra, help out Dimitri and focus your fire on the water Rogue!" I yelled before pointing at Helio and Theo. "You two, take care of the metal Rogue!" They nodded and moved toward him.

Ezra stopped his fire, and the metal Rogue glowed bright orange. Theo formed a large crystal fist and hit him, ripping the metal coating off his body like melting wax.

"There's his weakness!" I yelled.

"Boss! I need to cool off!" the metal Rogue said frantically.

The water Rogue attempted to send a torrent of water in his direction, but Ezra blocked it with his fire, turning it to steam. Dimitri used the distraction to his advantage and slashed at the water Rogue with a tentacle, sending him careening into the stone wall of a building.

Helio and Theo kept attacking the metal Rogue, dealing out vicious blows left and right, and with each hit, another chunk of metal flew off his body. He attempted to protect himself by moving the only melted metal he had left to different areas of his body, but more and more of him became exposed as bare skin and clothing shone through.

I turned my attention back to Arissa who was still redirecting the shockwaves with portals while trying to keep them from causing any more damage.

"You stupid little bitch!" the shockwave Rogue yelled, while trying to hit her.

"Hey, asshole!" I yelled to him, and before he could react, I delivered an energy beam to the side of his body, sending him tumbling down the street.

He came to a stop and wiped the blood dripping from his nose with his forearm before spitting more out of his mouth.

"Fuck this shit," he said as he took off into the sky, using shockwaves from his hands to propel himself.

"He's getting away! Throw a portal in front of him!"

Arissa threw out a portal above him that he flew straight into, redirecting him out of another, and causing him to collide head first into the street. He cried out in pain and barely managed to get up again.

"That's it! Time to choose."

He held out both hands, one aiming toward me and one at Arissa.

"Arissa, don't!" I yelled just as he released a shockwave from each hand.

I knew she could only protect one of us, and I hoped she wouldn't pick me, but before I could say anything else, a flash of pink and purple light appeared in front of me, and the shockwave passed through it. She took the full force of the other, sending her flying backward. A helmet deployed from her armor, which surrounded her head and protected it as she bounced and skidded across the pavement. Her body finally came to a stop when she collided with a parked taxi.

"Wrong choice," the shockwave Rogue said with a crooked grin on his face.

He launched another shockwave as I ran at him with a projected shield in front of me, but with no one to redirect his blasts, the shockwave hit me like a freight train. My feet slid across the ground as I tried to gain any sort of traction while slowly being pushed backward.

"Give up, 'hero'. The Academy made a mistake sending you children out here to try and stop someone as powerful as me," he said over the loud scream of the shockwave.

He laughed as he unleashed more of his power, shattering all of the windows of the buildings around us.

I looked around at the damage in horror and yelled, "NO!" just as my knees buckled and my shield projection broke, blasting me straight into the concrete. I lay helplessly in the street as he took his time walking toward me.

"You stupid, stupid child! Let this be a lesson for you, this is what happens when you try to be a hero."

He brought both arms backward, then extended them forward, releasing a shockwave bigger than any of the previous ones.

BOOOOMMMM!!!!

When my vision finally cleared, I found myself lying in the dark, gasping for air. A faint light glowed in the far distance above me, and I tried to extend my arm to reach for it, but I was completely pinned by the rocks and dirt around me. My suit was torn to pieces, and I could tell I was *badly* injured. Blood trickled from the top of my head and ran down the front of my face. My ribs felt broken, and every breath hurt. In the distance, I heard a faint cry for help.

"*Kaden!*" I could barely make it out, but I knew it was Arissa's voice.

Then, I heard her *screaming* which echoed deep into the

underground tomb where I found myself. She was about to die, and it was all my fault. I should have fought harder, used better strategy, and not let that dickhead get the best of me, but I was stupid and charged him head on.

Her screams got louder and louder, until I lost all control. I was filled with rage, and an immense feeling of unlimited energy rushed over me. I yelled as the entire tunnel lit up bright red. I could feel myself healing and getting stronger. My cracked ribs began reforming, and the cut on my head sealed itself. I yelled louder as I brought my arms up from my side, breaking free from the dirt and rock.

I began scrambling-clawing my way through the tunnel before energy shot out of my feet like a rocket. I flew toward the light, breaking through the rock around me, until I exploded out of the Earth in a flash of red, and floated ten feet above the street. I saw Arissa below me, screaming in pain as the Rogue smiled and laughed while torturing her with his shockwaves. She held her ears in pain, tears streaking down her face.

"Get away from her! *NOW!*" I yelled as something *else* took full control of me. The shockwave Rogue turned toward me and laughed.

"Look who decided to come back to the land of the—" I cut off his words by releasing a beam of energy from my hands.

He shot out his own, and the two met in the middle of the street sending a sonic boom out to the surrounding buildings, damaging them and shattering more windows. He tried to fight off my energy by sending out more of his, but it was of no use as I was too powerful for him.

I closed in, my beams overpowering his more and more, until I was finally face to face with him, staring directly into his terrified eyes. I grabbed his forearms and began to squeeze, feeling his weak, brittle bones crunching and cracking under my grip. He screamed in pain as I squeezed even harder, watching his forearms splinter and shatter, bones tearing through fragile skin, spraying blood all over both of us.

"Kaden, stop!" Arissa yelled, blood trickling from her ears.

Seeing her like that caused something in my mind to click, and I immediately snapped out of the trance I was in. I saw my reflection in a window and noticed my body was glowing bright red. Smoke and energy poured from my eyes and floated upward into the air.

"Don't kill him, *please*," she said while tears ran down her face.

I slowly lowered to the ground until my feet met the pavement, and I looked at her and saw fear in her eyes. My hands released the Rogue's pathetic, bloody arms, and he crumpled to the ground with a *thud*. I looked down and saw that his arms now looked like an accordion—broken and bent. Sharp bones protruded from where his hands used to be, bleeding and oozing onto the street where he lay. I didn't know it in the moment, but I now realized that my energized hands seared his completely off. I doubled over next to Arissa, trying to stay awake. The rest of my team ran over to me to see what had happened, and their eyes tracked down to the crumpled and bleeding Rogue lying before them.

"Kaden, we subdued the other two Rogues. We've placed inhibitor chips on their necks, muzzled them, and put them in power cuffs," Ezra said.

"G... g—" I had no energy to even speak.

"Are you okay, man?" Theo asked.

My head was spinning, and I felt numb and lightheaded with my vision fading in and out. My whole body was drained as if my life force had been expelled from me in the red smoke that continued to pour from my eyes. I fully collapsed to the ground and nearly passed out.

"Your mission is *not* finished, Team #22. Bring the Class 1 and 2 Rogues back to the Academy for lockup," Headmaster Fowler said in a demanding tone.

The entire team froze in shock. They looked at each other, wondering as if they had all heard the same thing. A surveillance orb swooped in very close to us, the lens oscillating back and forth trying to focus in on our faces.

"What... What about the Class 3 Rogue, Headmaster Fowler? He is badly injured and needs medical—"

"He's too dangerous to be kept alive!" Headmaster Fowler interrupted. There was a long pause. "You know what to do, Ezra... neutralize him."

Ezra looked at the Rogue's crumpled and mangled body once more. He was still alive but barely conscious.

"But Headmaster—"

"That is an *order*, or you fail the mission."

Ezra looked around at the rest of us. No one, not even Arissa, objected.

"Yes sir, neutralizing the Class 3 Rogue now."

Ezra grabbed his barely identifiable arm and dragged him down the road, away from the rest of the group. The other Rogues stared at him with horror, their screams muffled by their muzzles.

"No! Please! I... I promise, I'll never rob another bank again. We just needed a little bit of money, that's all." Ezra tossed him aside. "I'll wear an inhibitor chip for the rest of my life! I'll give up my powers, and I'll never hurt anyone else again!" Fear filled his eyes as he attempted to crawl away. "Please! Listen to me! You don't have to—"

His gut wrenching screams and cries were the last things I heard as I passed out.

CHAPTER NINE

RETURN OF THE ENEMY

A LONE, CLOAKED FIGURE walked along a dirt road through a forest. He followed the path, looking over his shoulder and checking his surroundings as he went.

Unknown to him, Department of Golden Control soldiers stalked him from the bushes and trees, following him as he moved. The soldiers wore all-black armored suits with glowing green accents and held high-powered assault rifles in their hands. One soldier aimed his weapon and looked down the scope. Through it, he could see the cloaked figure illuminated with a golden glow.

"I'm detecting a positive heat signature for Golden cells," the soldier whispered into his ear piece.

"Confirmed. The DGC does not have any record of Heroes in the area. He is a rogue Golden, I repeat, a rogue Golden," a War Room operator responded. "Sending in Team #1 for interception now."

He signaled to his fellow soldiers to fall back, and they disappeared into the darkness of the night.

Inside Team #1's ship, Jayson manned the controls with his three other teammates sitting behind him. Jayson brought the ship down from the clouds and descended toward the Rogue. He looked at a map on the console and saw a Golden dot flashing on it.

"The target's location is confirmed. Team #1 to War Room, do we have a power assessment?" Jayson asked.

In the War Room, an operator manning the Team #1 station watched a live feed of the soldiers on one screen and the inside of the ship on another.

"Power Class: unknown. He hasn't used any abilities yet," she responded.

"Permission to engage the Rogue?"

"Team #1, you have a green light. Release the surveillance drones, and engage the target with the goal of subduing the rogue Golden and bringing him back to the Academy alive."

"Affirmative," Jayson said as he pressed a button on the control panel.

Multiple surveillance orbs were released from the ship, silently descending and surrounding the Rogue. They sent a live feed of the situation back to the War Room that all of the operators were watching intently.

"Alright, Team #1, we're dropping! Let's move!" Jayson, dressed in a blue armored suit, yelled to his teammates as they stood up from their seats and made their way to the drop hooks resting on the interior walls of the aircraft.

Alex and Mark attached their cables to their green and black suits respectively, and Jayson followed suit, as they all braced for the drop. Chloe, who wore a silver chest plate, held her hook within her hand. A red light illuminated the cabin before changing to green. The floor dropped from beneath them, and they fell to the Earth, only to be slowed by the cables moments before impact with the ground. The team disconnected the cables and approached the cloaked figure.

He stopped his gait and turned his head slightly at the sound of their footsteps. His face remained hidden behind the dark cloak as he turned back, continuing on his way.

"Stop!" Jayson yelled, but the man ignored him. "You are operating as a rogue Golden outside of the jurisdiction of the Golden Academy, a violation of the Treaty of The Unity. I order you to surrender now!"

The man continued to ignore him, and a visibly angered Jayson shot a barrage of lightning that struck the cloaked figure in the back, sending him skidding down the dirt road.

His cloak, tattered and ruined, smoked in the distance as Team #1 cautiously approached him. Just as they got within arms reach, he ripped it off to reveal a body entirely covered in scales. He shot out a sharp scale from his forearm toward Jayson, but Alex took it straight out of the air with a flash of green light from his eyes. He cut off the laser beam, and the green glow faded, returning his eyes to normal.

"Thanks for that," Jayson said to Alex, who nodded back. "Chloe, Mark! You're up!"

They charged at the cloaked figure, engaging him in hand-to-hand combat. Chloe tried punching him, but his scales were too thick. The blows seemed to do relatively nothing. Mark unsheathed one of his swords and slashed at him, but the blade was deflected, unable to penetrate the scales. Chloe wound up a huge punch and connected it directly with one of his scales, causing it to slightly crack. Mark saw the opening and jammed his sword into the crack which made the Rogue yell out in pain. He swiped Mark away with his forearm and sent him crashing into a tree. The Rogue pulled the sword from his body and swiped it at Chloe. She caught it in her bare hands, but the blade was unable to cut through her thick skin.

"Bastard!" she yelled, pulling the sword from his grip before snapping it in half.

He stepped back, and a sharp scale grew from his forearm into a point over his fist. He stabbed it toward her face, but she caught it in her hands.

"He's too damn strong! I can't…"

She lost her footing, and he slammed her body into the dirt road. He drove the scale further as it slowly pierced through her chest plate, inching toward her heart.

"Alex, hit him with everything you've got! Now!" Jayson yelled.

Simultaneously, Jayson and Alex unleashed a barrage of electricity and laser beams toward the Rogue. He pulled the scale from Chloe's chest plate and used it to redirect the attacks, cutting down trees in the process.

Chloe took advantage of the Rogue's distraction and extended a punch into his chin, uppercutting him and sending him flying into the air with a spray of blood from his mouth.

"Alex, again!" Jayson yelled.

They blasted him again, hitting him square in the chest and sending him flying into a boulder. The boulder exploded into a million pieces, and the Rogue lay there, smoking and unmoving.

"Stand down, *now*. We have direct orders from the Golden Academy to bring you in. You are unauthorized to freely operate as a Class 2 Rogue," Jayson said as electricity snapped and crackled in his palm.

"What makes you kids the goddamn police?" he

managed to muster out.

"We are going to put you in power cuffs and take you back to the Academy where you will await further trial by The Unity," Jayson said.

Mark handed over a set of power cuffs to Chloe, who went behind the Rogue, pulling his arms back and fastening them on as the Rogue hung his head in defeat.

A scream was heard in the forest behind them, and everyone quickly turned to see where it came from. Yellow light flashed through the forest, bullets fired, and a DGC soldier was sent flying over them, crashing into the trees in the distance.

"Alert! Team #1, someone has broken the perimeter. Be advised!" the War Room operator warned them through their earpieces.

The team scanned their surroundings, forming a defensive circle around the Rogue to see who was approaching. A hooded man wrapped in black and yellow robes with a glowing yellow aura around his body stood in the middle of the road, staring them down.

"Let him *go*," he said in a deep and threatening voice.

Chloe cracked her knuckles and approached him.

"We have another Rogue in the area. Permission to—" Chloe was grabbed by the throat and sent flying down the road, tumbling across the dirt.

Alex unleashed a blast of optic beams, but the man put a glowing yellow hand up, blocking them. He pushed forward toward Alex, unfazed, until he was face-to-face with him, grabbing Alex's glasses and crushing them in the palm of his hand. Glass and metal pieces dropped to the ground, falling between the mysterious Rogue's fingers. Alex screamed in horror as the Rogue backhanded him across the face, the tremendous force sending him ragdolling down the road.

Mark yelled, unsheathing another one of his swords as he raced toward the Rogue. He jumped into the air and stabbed it into the Rogue's glowing yellow aura, but the blade was caught in some type of force field, and the tip of the sword began to melt as he tried pushing it deeper into him. The Rogue hit away what was left of the sword and uppercut Mark into the air. He did a spinning kick that connected with Mark's body and sent him flying off into the darkness.

Jayson stared at the man with burning rage.

"I would run if I were you," the handcuffed Rogue said with a smirk.

"Die!" Jayson yelled as he unleashed as much electricity as he could at the glowing yellow Rogue.

The electricity connected with him and sent the glowing man backward, his feet dragging across the dirt until he managed to gain traction again. Jayson gritted his teeth, not letting up on his attack, thinking he was hurting him, but *something* within the palm of the Rogue's hands seemed to be forming. He wasn't being hit; instead, he was absorbing the energy into a ball that was growing bigger and bigger.

Fear swept across Jayson's face as the glowing Rogue unleashed the energy back toward him in the form of a yellow beam, launching him far off into the forest. Jayson's body crashed through dozens of trees, breaking them in half, until he was finally stopped when a tree landed on top of him, pinning him underneath it. His armored suit sparked and creaked as he tried lifting up his head, before his face finally dropped into the dirt.

Back inside the War Room, chaos had erupted. Operators were frantically talking into their headsets and were pressing a myriad of buttons on their control panels. All screens in the War Room had switched to the live feed of the beaten Team #1 that was coming in from the surveillance orbs.

"Deploy Team's #14, #69, #87, #5, and #45 immediately! We need any DGC soldiers in the area to report to Team #1's position with weapons hot! Medical personnel are en route," an operator yelled into his headset.

An alarm blared through the War Room. Negative points were appearing across the screens while Team #1's score plummeted in real time.

Then, silence filled the room as Headmaster Fowler entered with Zo floating behind him. The Headmaster stormed down the middle of the command stations, each step shaking the room, before he finally stopped and faced the large display of screens in front of him.

Team #1's operator looked at him and said, "Sir, we have a—" The Headmaster held up a hand and cut her off before she could finish as he closely watched the screens. One of the surveillance orbs zoomed in on the glowing man causing Headmaster Fowler's eyes to grow wide.

Back on the road, the scaled Rogue sat with his arms behind his back staring up at the glowing Rogue before him. The glowing Rogue walked behind him and put a solid yellow hand on the handcuffs. Yellow light was pumped into them, and they began melting piece by piece into the dirt. The scaled Rogue pulled the handcuffs apart as the glowing Rogue offered a hand and helped him to his feet.

"We need to get to the ship *now*," the glowing Rogue said.

They sprinted toward the trees, but just before they disappeared into them, the glowing Rogue stopped and looked back, seeing the surveillance orbs floating above him.

Back inside the War Room, Headmaster Fowler stared at the glowing figure on the screen. He unclenched his fist before his finger reached down and pressed a button on one of the stations.

"It has been a long time, *old friend*," the Headmaster said, transmitting through the orb. "It is good to finally see you again... Zahavi."

Zahavi smiled as a flash of yellow filled the screen, cutting out the camera feed, leaving Headmaster Fowler in the dark.

CHAPTER TEN

THE SANCTUARY

ZAHAVI AND THE scaled Rogue broke through a clearing in the forest where a silver ship sat—much like the ones the Academy used. A drop hatch on the underside opened, and they climbed aboard. Zahavi quickly sat down in the pilot's seat and took control. He activated the ship's cloaking feature, making it invisible to anyone trying to follow or track them. The outside of the ship turned into a mirror, reflecting the sky around them as they launched into the night.

He looked at the reflection of himself on the transparent wall, seeing his tired face underneath a head of dark brown hair. He brought his hand to his face and rubbed his stubble in contemplation.

"What the hell were you doing out there, Silas?" Zahavi asked.

"I was following a lead on my daughter. I'm sure you, of all people, can understand," Silas responded.

Zahavi pondered this for a moment while staring out of the front windshield at the endless rolling clouds.

"They were tracking you. I'm not sure for how long or far, but that wasn't a random attack. They've been watching you, and they knew you had a connection to the Sanctuary—"

"How do you know!" Silas shouted.

"Because you didn't do anything wrong!"

"And has that ever stopped them from killing us before?"

Besides the low hum of the ship flying through the sky, silence filled the cabin once again.

Finally, Zahavi said, "That was Team #1 that he sent after you. His best team isn't sent for just anyone, Silas. You and I both know that to be true."

"That doesn't make any sense. I must've just been spotted in the nearby town, and someone called the sighting in," Silas responded.

"No."

"Why do you act like you know everything!" he yelled, slamming a fist into the wall of the ship.

"I don't... but I know that's not true because you're still *alive.*" Silas turned and looked at Zahavi. "He was trying to get to me, Silas. He knows that you have the location of the Sanctuary, and it's why you were in cuffs instead of a body bag. If they had managed to take you back to the Academy..." he paused mid sentence as if it hurt to think about the possibility of Silas going to that godforsaken place.

Silas thought about this for a moment and added, "Why did you come and rescue me?"

"Because we've already lost too many. For far too long, I've hidden in the Sanctuary while you all go out and fight my battles for me, no matter how many times I've tried to convince you not to."

"You made a choice, Zahavi, and it has kept our community alive and safe for many years, but *I* didn't, and I'm tired of hiding as long as I know she is still out there alone," Silas said as he stared out at the passing views.

"You can't just be walking around out there searching for

her, Silas, no matter the reason. You're young, you want to find your daughter, and I understand that, but it's getting too dangerous. The Academy is becoming ruthless—"

"I know," Silas interrupted. "Things are changing… and I'm afraid we're losing this war."

There was a long pause with neither saying a word.

Still staring out the forward facing windshield, Zahavi finally said, "*Me too.*"

The faint glow of the screens and buttons on the console lit up their faces. Silas looked at Zahavi and saw fear, something he had not seen in a long, long time.

• • •

Later that day, the ship—barely seen except for a faint shimmer of light in the sky—appeared over an ocean and flew straight for a jungle on a cliff side. It looked like it was about to crash into it, but it passed through an invisible force field, revealing the *Sanctuary*: a village suspended in the trees with wooden and canvas huts that were connected by hanging walkways and zip lines.

The ship flew by one of the huts, and a child ran out and waved to it as it made its way to a landing pad filled with dozens of other ships. People of all ages, men and women, came out of the trees and huts and met Zahavi and Silas as they landed and exited the ship. Noel, a woman Zahavi's age with glowing golden irises, ziplined down from a hut and hugged Zahavi.

"He's back! He's back!" a young child called out, surrounded by other children.

Noel looked at Zahavi with wide eyes, as if expecting him to have returned with something, but he *only* had Silas. Zahavi shook his head, and she gave an understanding nod.

"I'm just glad you made it back safely, Zahavi. It's been a while since I've had to worry about you," Noel said.

"Thank you… Me too," and there was a hint of pain in Zahavi's voice as he said those words. "Noel, Silas, gather the others of the council for an *emergency* meeting."

• • •

Zahavi stood on the porch of his hut that overlooked the ocean. He watched as Golden children ran around the Sanctuary, turning into animals and chasing the others who had super speed or agility. One child swung on a low hanging branch and launched into the air, coming down on top of another and tackling him into the dirt. They wrestled and laughed with each other as more children joined in on the fun.

In another area, teenagers were practicing their combat skills against wooden dummies, while others dueled each other with weapons. Arbor, the strong and intimidating combat specialist at the Sanctuary, led a sword class with young male and female Goldens taking part in it. He wore bulky silver armor at all times since he believed war could come at any moment, and one must always be prepared.

"Goldens! Eyes on me and follow exactly what I do," Arbor said as he raised a great sword into the air, signaling the group to join him in copying the moves he was about to perform. "High parry!" He lurched the sword above him as if blocking an incoming attack. "Slash, slash." He swung it back and forth, cutting through more imaginary foes. The blade effortlessly sliced through the air and reflected in the sunlight. "Dodge into a quick parry!" He rolled to the side and immediately held his sword above his head, ready to block a slice that would have come down on him if he had been fighting anything but the air. "It is imperative that you ready yourself after the dodge as your enemy will be coming down upon you with a quick strike. Now begin!"

The young Goldens began mimicking his moves. "Higher, Athena! Higher!" he yelled to one of the Goldens with orange skin and horns. "Train as if your life depends on it! One day what you learn here may save it, so practice these moves with ferocity, purpose, and vigilance!"

Zahavi turned to another scene and saw adults washing clothes in the streams that ran through the Sanctuary and off the cliffs as waterfalls. Others had large fires going where they were cooking food. A roasting pig slowly rolled over, skewered on a long rod of metal. Zahavi took a deep sniff, and the smells coming from the searing meat made him hungry.

He looked over at another group of Goldens who were relaxing, hanging out in hammocks, reading books, and listening to music while enjoying the warm Costa Rican air. A feeling of peace and tranquility rolled over him as he looked out across his Sanctuary.

Seeing these things every day reminded Zahavi why he created it in the first place. It was a place of safety and security that "rogue" Goldens, as the Academy called his peaceful people here, could seek refuge—*if* they were lucky enough not to be found by the Academy first. Of course, Zahavi did not call these men, women, and children *Rogues*, but instead, he called them his brothers, sisters, and family. But most importantly, over all else, the Sanctuary reminded Zahavi of *home*—a place he once knew that he had not returned to in a long, long time and may *never* be able to again.

A loud horn blew, and he knew that it meant the Council of the Sanctuary had been called to gather. He took one last look over the cliffs that led out to the vast ocean and hurried inside.

The Council of the Sanctuary was now gathered in a large room with a canvas roof and a view overlooking the ocean. It was connected to the other huts by bridges and zip lines leading down to the training areas and mess hall. Five chairs formed a half-circle facing one throne-like seat.

"The Council is now in session," Zahavi said as all of the members took their seats.

From left to right: Noel, Silas, Arbor, Leona, and Donatao made up the Council. Noel had long blonde hair that hung far down her back. She wore a silky dress that fluttered gently in the wind. Her gold eyes were mesmerizing, accentuating her innocent face.

Leona, on the other hand, had short dark hair, and a weathered face and hands. Taking care of Goldens in the Sanctuary—especially the children—was no easy task and it showed. Arbor leaned on a large greatsword in front of him and stared intently at Zahavi. Silas sat next to him, nursing his wounds from the fight in the woods.

Donatao rounded out the group, wearing a dark gray armored suit that was scratched, scuffed, and dented from years of use in the field. He rested his arm on top of a black, tinted helmet sitting in his lap.

"Arbor, how has the training been going since I've been gone? It looks successful from what I saw moments ago," Zahavi said.

"It has been good, Zahavi. The children are learning quickly, and they would be able to defend themselves if they needed to."

"Good. I want to increase their training sessions to three times a day from here on out."

"Are you expecting something?"

Zahavi paused, finally saying, "You can never be too prepared, can you?"

"I understand," he said with a nod.

"Leona, is everything under control at the Sanctuary? How are the non-combatants and children?" Zahavi asked.

"Everything is under control with nothing new to report. Everyone is happy and healthy," she responded.

"I'm glad to hear some good news. Donatao, how are things looking with *our* heroes?"

"I am not happy to report that we lost another five today," Donatao said.

"That makes thirty in this past week alone, more than we lost in the last year," Zahavi added.

"They're now hunting Goldens like *animals*. The teams are getting stronger and faster. I am not sure what is going on at the Academy, but they're different—better than they've ever been before. Apparently, their training has improved. The Unity is also able to identify Goldens faster with some sort of new detection and tracking technology, making it harder for us to move openly in public. I believe this technology has been added to a robust surveillance network that has been implemented in every major city across the world.

"The Unity has also increased their DGC forces ten fold, now having them patrol 24/7. The moment a Golden has an Awakening, they find them quicker than we can, even with the help of Noel. Lately, we've been struggling to rescue them before the DGC finds them, and the Academy's numbers continue to grow," Donatao said with a defeated and tired look on his face.

Zahavi pondered this information for a long time as the rest of the Council glanced uneasily at one another.

"Keep me updated if we incur any more casualties. There have been a large number of natural disasters across the globe that we can assist in *without* creating more violence. Remain out of sight, move in the darkness of night, and try your best to continue to rescue Goldens after their Awakenings... which is still our top priority," Zahavi finally said.

Donatao sighed, hung his head, and took a deep breath.

"Sir, I know you have not agreed with me in the past on this, but I believe it is finally time we make a counter attack against the Academy."

"No, we will not sink to their level," Zahavi answered sternly.

"How many more Golden lives are you willing to lose before we finally do something—until we finally fight back against these savages?"

"My decision is final, Donatao. I still believe that those *children* at the Academy, no matter how many vile and horrific acts they have committed thus far, are innocent. If we attack now, all we are doing is taking more innocent Golden lives from this planet."

"But Donatao is right, Zahavi. I've seen it with my own eyes!" Silas added. "I've been out in the field more than anyone here, and the Academy isn't even capturing them like they used to; they're just killing them on sight! We must act now before we lose too many of our own and don't have a choice but to fight back!"

"We would lose!" Zahavi yelled. "We would lose..." He gathered his composure once more. "Is that what you wanted to hear?"

Somber looks grew on the Council member's faces.

"But Zahavi, look how easily you beat their *best* team?" Silas said.

"It is not the children I am afraid of, Silas," Zahavi paused, looking out at the setting sun, "I cannot face Fowler, not again."

"What about the *boy*?" Noel asked.

"I inspected the crater, and I've never seen anything like it. That much power and energy from someone who just had an Awakening... Only a Class 4 Golden could be capable of such a feat. He vaporized his school..."

"Do you think he is the one *she—*"

"No, as he unfortunately matters nothing to us now. He was taken to the Academy faster than Silas or I could get to him. He is not the one." Zahavi stared off blankly into the distance, still thinking about the Golden boy he almost saved.

Had I gotten there sooner...

"If there are no further matters to discuss, the Council is dismissed," Zahavi finally said.

All of the Council members disbanded, except Silas.

"Zahavi, I know facing him again would cause the death of thousands of innocent Goldens and potentially *millions* of innocent non-Goldens, but if we do not act soon, the Academy will only grow stronger. With this new technology, how long do you think it will take until they find the Sanctuary?" he said, before he turned and exited the Council room, leaving Zahavi alone with his thoughts.

• • •

Later that night, Zahavi knocked on the door of Noel's

chamber.

"Come in," she said, as Zahavi entered and looked around.

Books were stacked around the room and across the floor. A large, spinning, holographic globe of the Earth sat in the center of it. Noel was sitting cross legged on the floor with a touchscreen device in her lap, entering the locations of newly awakened Goldens.

"I see them, Zahavi, Goldens, spread out across the globe, and I feel more Awakening every day," she said as she entered one last location into the touchscreen device and set it aside.

"How many of them does the Academy find before we do?" he asked.

"Nearly *all* of them."

Zahavi rubbed his face and took a seat on a chair next to her.

"I wasn't lying when I told you that boy was different, Zahavi. I've never felt anything like his Awakening before. It was palpable."

"It just doesn't make any sense. Gora told me—*promised* me at the Infinity Tree that when he Awakened, he would come to me, but the Academy already took that boy away. It must be a different Golden; it *has* to be. We will have to keep waiting, and I can only hope that he will Awaken before it is too late."

She reached out and held his hand.

"You already know the answer, Zahavi, you're just afraid of what he will bring with him."

The sun finally set on the Sanctuary, casting it in a beautiful golden glow.

CHAPTER ELEVEN

THE GOLDEN ANSWER

EVERYTHING FELT *different* after the first mission. When we finally returned to the Academy, Ezra and I took the two Rogues that we had secured on our mission to the Lock Up—a massive holding area that was spread out underneath the Academy, an area that I didn't even know existed until this day.

Inside the Lock Up were hundreds of cells that held some of the most dangerous Rogues on the planet that had been secured on previous missions, waiting to face trial. Once The Unity had decided their punishment, they would be relocated to different holding facilities around the world, never to use their Golden powers again.

As we walked through the Lock Up, I thought about how lucky we were that these Rogues were in cages and not out causing mayhem. They beat on the walls and yelled at us, but we couldn't hear anything. Their cells were completely soundproof which was probably for the best. If a Hero with a wavering will had come down here while transporting an enemy of the The Unity, one of the Rogues might have tried to convince that person to let them out, and I was sure they would have been able to convince at least one person here to do it.

We finally made our way to the holding cells for *our* captured Rogues and pulled off their muzzles and threw them in.

As the doors were closing, the metal Rogue yelled, "You may not know it yet, but you're not the—" the doors sealed shut.

I couldn't guess what he was going to say, but at the same time, I didn't care. Our job was done, and we *successfully* accomplished our mission, giving our team more points and allowing us to slowly claw our way up from the bottom of The Wall.

The one thing I couldn't quite get out of my head, however, were the persistent screams from the shockwave Rogue. I also wasn't able to shake the look I saw on Arissa's face while I was holding him within my grip. She looked at me as if I were a *monster.*

"Well, what did you think of your first mission?" Ezra asked as we walked back toward the exit.

"It was..." I hesitated because I wasn't really sure how to tell him how I truly felt, "incredible," I said, lying through my teeth.

The truth was that I felt sick to my stomach, no matter how much I tried to deny it. Watching Ezra torch that Rogue alive was an image that I would never be able to get out of my head. Everything about the mission was going great up until that moment, but I now knew that neutralizing was just part of it, and it was what *had* to be done to complete the mission.

"How did you neutralize your first Rogue?" I asked.

"The exact same way I did today," Ezra responded.

"No, *how* did you do it? What I guess I'm trying to ask

is: how did you bring yourself to do it that first time? I just can't picture myself being able to do that yet, and I know I will need to if I have any chance of going to Gidoria, but still, that was really hard to watch."

"Neutralizing didn't happen very often before you arrived, but when it did, I think it made the most sense for me to be the one in the group to do it with my fire powers, and since I was the oldest, I stepped up to the task with no hesitation. Besides, I don't think anyone else was really up for it anyway. Theo did it once with a quick slice to the neck with his crystal arm. Dimitri strangled a Rogue with his tentacle until we watched his last breath slip from his mouth. Helio dropped a girl from ten stories high straight onto the pavement, and Arissa placed a portal above and below another causing him to endlessly fall until she removed the one underneath him and… I assume you know what happened to him after that."

She didn't mention that part on the roof.

"After their first neutralization, which proved themselves worthy of staying at the Academy, they've never done it again."

"I don't blame them."

"Me neither, but someone has to do it, otherwise we'd fail the missions that require it."

There was a long pause after that, and I finally broke the silence by saying, "Ezra, I still hear the—"

"Screams?" he interrupted.

"Yeah, the *screams.* Do they ever stop?" I asked as we emerged from underneath the base.

Ezra pondered this question for a moment.

"No, no they do not. Now, let's forget about all that and go check out our place on The Wall."

As we approached the building where The Wall was

held, we joined our fellow teammates, except for Arissa who was still in the infirmary after the injury to her ears.

If only I had been stronger, I wouldn't have been sent down so far underground, and if I had flown faster, I could've reached her before she got hurt. Instead, I sat deep underground while she screamed, and I promised myself that I would *never* let something like that happen again.

"How are you holding up?" Theo asked, pulling me out of my negative thoughts.

"Oh, me? I'm good, man," I replied.

"I'm glad to hear that. First missions are always tough for everyone, and I'll admit, that was one hell of a first mission, but you did well."

The second we turned the corner that led to the front steps of the building, we saw a huge group of Heroes who had gathered outside. As soon as they caught a glimpse of us, they ran up and bombarded us, yelling and asking questions as if we were celebrities, and it kind of felt like we were.

"We all watched your mission! That shit was insane!" one said.

"Your teamwork was incredible!" another shouted from the front row of Heroes.

"Kaden, when the hell did you become such a good leader!" another from the back said. "You can't teach that in classes. He's a natural for sure."

"Ezra even got to neutralize one! Goddamn, he's so *lucky!*"
There they were again, the screams.

The crowd started to chant, "Gi-do-ri-a! Gi-do-ri-a! Gi-do-ri-a" breaking the word into four syllables.

We high fived them as the sea of Heroes parted allowing

us to make our way into the building that held The Wall.

Inside, crowds of kids watched replays of our mission on the various flat screens throughout the room. A standout moment that kept playing over and over was the moment I emerged from underground to save Arissa, with energy swirling and pouring off me like a waterfall.

Besides what I saw in the reflection of the window, I got my first full glimpse of myself when *I* wasn't really there. All I knew was that it felt like a trance—like something else took over the controls in my mind. Someone else had the keys, and I was just along for the ride, observing from the backseat.

I watched as I got closer and closer to the shockwave Rogue, eventually grabbing his forearms.

Crunch.

Blood splattered on the camera lens; the crowd roared, cheering and chanting.

The audio of Ezra neutralizing the Rogue had been replaced with a recording of the Academy's Alma Mater:

"High above the sea lies a Golden Hero's dream!
Together and forever, we stand as one team!
One team!
We fight for the Academy!
Never in battle shall we fall,
for we rise and crush them all!
Warriors unite!
Warriors unite!
To Gidoria, we go and fight!"

Even with the Alma Mater, I could still hear what should've been playing, but then a loud *Oooooooh!* arose from around the room as if anticipating the points to update.

BEEP!

The Wall changed: 1500 points for good ol' Team #22. The crowd of Heroes erupted, pushing us around and cheering. It got us off the very bottom, but still not high enough to be in the top half of the graduating class; that was going to take *a lot* more work. I looked down at my tattered armored suit, suddenly remembering that I was still wearing it. Then, I looked up and saw the faces of cheering Heroes, chanting my name, and in that moment, I knew—no matter what—I was going to get us to Gidoria.

• • •

Once I got out of my suit, I made sure to visit Arissa in the infirmary where I found her lying in a hospital bed with bandages around her ears that wrapped over her eyes.

"Knock, knock," I said as I entered the room.

"*Kaden?*" she called out really loudly.

"Yes, I'm right here, Arissa. How are you doing?" I said as I kissed her forehead, slightly raising the bandage up so she could see me.

She smiled and said, "I'm doing OK. Now you see what this whole 'hero' gig is about."

I laughed which made her giggle, but she quickly showed pain again.

"I'm not exactly sure what I expected the missions to be, but I never thought it would be like that. When I was growing up, I remember watching movies and TV shows that followed fictional stories of what the Heroes of the Academy did to protect the world... I guess I just thought we would be saving cats out of trees," I said, which made her smile.

"Me too. Even with all the preparation we got, I don't think any number of books, training, or lectures can prepare you for your first mission. I know it didn't help me at least."

"You can say that again."

I rubbed her hand for a minute and then asked, "Why'd no one mention the neutralization part of it or how *brutal* it would be—not Professor Guano, Wayla, Headmaster Fowler, or... *you.* I guess I thought things would be different."

She took a deep breath and sighed.

"It's the dirty but necessary part of our job that no one wants to talk about," she finally said.

"Why didn't you let me do it then?" I asked.

"I just..." her voice cracked, and she seemed to be crying underneath the bandage, "I looked at you floating above me, and I didn't recognize the person I saw. I didn't see that same boy I kissed on the roof. I saw someone I didn't know. It scared me, and I just didn't think that could be *you,* holding him like that—crushing him." She tried to hold back the tears but couldn't. "I guess I had hoped to spare you from that, just for a little longer. I know you'll have to do it one day, but I hope I don't have to watch it when you do. Ever since the day I..." Her voice trailed off.

I comforted her and said, "It's OK, I'm right here."

"Ever since the day I neutralized my first Rogue, nothing was the same."

Her words tore through me like a bullet, and I held her as she cried endlessly in my arms.

I stayed with her for the rest of the night, talking about everything that had happened that day. She thanked me for being such a great leader and said I was a "natural." I thanked her for believing in me and told her that what she said to me about already *knowing* how to lead was the only reason I had the courage to take control. She said they probably would've failed the mission, and someone would have died if I hadn't been there to lead them.

By the end of my time with her, I even got her laughing and smiling again which made me feel good. The doctors said she would most likely need hearing aids for the rest of her life, but I was just glad she was alive and still here with me.

Eventually, she was discharged from the infirmary, and we were finally able to lie on the roof again and watch the stars all night. She kept asking if I could see her hearing aids, and I genuinely couldn't. All I could see was a beautiful girl lying next to me, and that's all that mattered. Despite the screams that echoed in my ears, we fell asleep up there, and—trust me when I say this—I never slept more soundly in my life.

We were greeted by an early sunrise over the ocean, and I could've sat up there with her forever, but I knew our break from the "real" world and our moment of peace was over, and we would sadly need to resume our duties and return to reality.

• • •

We didn't have another mission for two months, which I was actually thankful for, because getting called for a mission felt like being drafted for war. After a while, however, I actually started to miss the field combat.

I kept busy by filling my time with more reading of old texts and scrolls that I had found in the library. The more dusty and yellowed ones that I found on the top shelf, the better. One scroll that covered the uprisings after the First Golden War was so long that I had to roll it all the way out across the floor. Then, the librarian with three eyes and four arms eventually showed me how to properly read it without having to roll it all the way out, and after that, I felt like an idiot. I wondered why she didn't tell me sooner, but I guessed I gave her a form of entertainment that she didn't get very often.

During this period, I also spent a lot of time in the Power Dome with my team running through different scenarios.

"Arissa, portal Theo over the enemy! Helio, more swooping attacks! Dimitri, we need to take out that turret!"

"On it!" he yelled back, extending his tentacles before latching onto it, and tearing it in half.

"Watch your flank!" Professor Guano yelled over the chaos.

"Ezra, back to back!"

We collided our backs with each other and let out a volley of fire and red energy from our hands into the Power Dome, taking out any drones and dummies in front of us.

Ezra and I had started off on the wrong foot, but over time, we began growing closer to each other. He was like the older brother I never had nor recognized I needed, and with our powers being so much alike, he had a lot to teach me.

Late at night, we would go into the Power Dome together, and Ezra would show me how to charge up my energy into a ball by my abdomen and release it all at once in a giant beam, vaporizing a dummy instantly, leaving nothing but a small pile of ash. He called them neutralizing moves and told me to only use them if I really meant to kill someone since there was no undoing what would follow.

I also learned how to hold a dummy and overload it with energy, making it explode. That ability scared me a little, and I told myself I would only use that on very rare occasions. I remembered that, during my trance, I had floated above the street without propelling myself at all from my hands—as if I were weightless. I tried focusing on using energy to surround my body and pull myself up off the ground again, but nothing worked. It just seemed to be something that I'd only be able to do during that whole red eyes thing.

After a while, I did end up getting better at flying and eventually was able to move more like Ezra. The key to the improved flight was learning to use my hands *and* feet simultaneously to propel myself, something I had previously failed to do.

One day, Ezra and I talked Zo into letting us fly out of the shield that surrounded the Academy and into the sky, but only with a little help from Professor Guano.

"It's a training exercise. How are they supposed to successfully perform in the field, if you don't let them practice now?" Professor Guano said, turning around and giving us a wink.

"Fine, but if the Headmaster hears about this, it is *all* on you, not me. If you even think about flying away, I won't hesitate to enable your inhibitor chips and let you fall to your death and drown in the ocean. Is that understood?" he said while squinting his white eyes which were hard to look at since his massive, veiny head was right there.

"Yes, we promise!" I said.

"Good, now go while the Headmaster is in a Unity

meeting and pray he does not see you."

Ezra and I high-fived creating a puff of smoke before running out of the room.

• • •

We floated in the clouds on our backs, high above the school, and it felt as amazing and liberating as you could imagine. We chased each other, diving in and out of the clouds while seeing who was faster. He obviously was because his whole body was propelling him. I, on the other hand, was only able to use my feet and hands to push me along, which wasn't all that fair, but I didn't really care. Secretly, I could go faster if I really wanted to, but I didn't feel like hurting his ego today. Plus, he was giving me some awesome tips on how to make sharp turns by eliminating the propulsion of energy from my hands and feet, floating for a few seconds and giving it hell again in a different direction.

"You have to picture you're in a car with a gas pedal," he yelled to me. "Wait, did you ever learn how to drive?"

"I mean, I drove once. Did you?"

"No."

I laughed, and he got embarrassed.

"Well the point still stands. I've done simulations, alright!"

I laughed even harder.

"Shut up, asshole. I'm trying to help you here."

"Okay, okay, sorry, I'm listening."

"Imagine you are wanting to make a sharp turn. First, you let off the gas, and you start your turn. Maybe you even brake a little bit before the turn, and once you've made it, you accelerate out of it. Same principle applies to the way we fly."

He blasted off, decelerated, repositioned his body in a different direction, and took off again into the distance. He emerged from a cloud and stopped in front of me.

"Your turn."

I flew further into the air, let off my energy, did a backflip and half way through my rotation, I blasted energy from my hands and feet and shot back down in the opposite direction.

"Show off!" he called out.

I kept doing that in various directions, spinning and flipping, making sharp and aggressive turns, and during all of that, I learned that I must have been immune to dizziness because I didn't feel nauseous at all and could've flown like that all day.

"Ready to head back?" Ezra called out.

I was starving, but I still had one last thing to do before we turned in for the day. I flew straight up, cut off the energy from my hands and feet, spread my arms out, and floated in the sunshine.

• • •

As time passed, I got better at creating different projections besides shields. I was able to make many more useful weapons, like sharp sword projections that I could cut through things with. They weren't very strong and would often shatter in my hands if I hit them against something too hard, but they were cool nonetheless.

I could also centralize my energy in my fist or leg, feeling twice as strong, and take a dummy's head off with one strike, which I thought would be useful in the field.

I started testing the strength of my shields more and more, since Ezra told me they would save my life one day.

With every practice, they became stronger and stronger, but no matter what, the shields were still breaking under tremendous force. Eventually, I learned that the weak point for the projection was not the shield itself but instead my legs, so we started hitting the Academy's gym and eating more protein to fuel the recovery and muscle growth. After a month went by, I had put on a *little* muscle, which made me proud.

"Have you been lifting weights?" Arissa asked me as I passed her on campus.

"Does it look like I have?" I asked with a smirk.

"Oh no, you're still skin and bones," she said as she walked away from me. "But don't stop. Maybe it'll work eventually."

During training, I even figured out I could expel energy from one finger like a blow torch and cut through things like walls.

One day, Ezra told the team that he had a surprise for us and to meet him on the platform at the top of the Power Dome. Helio carried Theo, Dimitri climbed, Arissa portaled, and I flew up. We all sat on the edge of the platform until we finally saw Ezra flying toward us, landing and sitting down. He pulled out a cigar from his waistband—at least I *thought* it was a cigar, but I wasn't really sure. He told us he had smuggled it in from a previous mission before I got here and was waiting for the right time to finally smoke it.

"You can do the honors, Glow Stick," he said, signaling to light it. I stuck out a finger, focused, and bright red energy formed at the tip of my finger, casting outward like a torch.

"You 'gotta puff it while you light it, or it won't work," Ezra called out.

I placed the cigar between my thumb and index finger and lit it while I fully inhaled the smoke deep into my lungs. I coughed hard and accidentally dropped the cigar, and we all watched as it fell.

"Buddy sold," Theo said while shaking his head. Arissa threw out a portal below it and one next to us as it passed through and reappeared coming up in front of Ezra. He grabbed it before it could fall again and started laughing hysterically.

He patted me on my back as I kept coughing and said, "You're not supposed to inhale it, dip shit! But don't worry, that'll put some hairs on your chest."

"Give me that damn thing, and stop trying to scare us. Kaden couldn't handle the smoke." Theo took a long drag and coughed up a lung himself, producing laughter from the rest of the group.

A black tentacle reached across the platform and lifted the cigar from Theo's fingers before he too could drop it. He took a drag into his mouth *only*, and passed it onward. Arissa, Helio, and Ezra all handled it like champs. Theo and I looked at each other with disappointment but then patted each other on the back.

We sat up there for hours, telling stories and laughing our asses off. Theo brought up a previous mission where he had accidentally released a herd of rampaging cows through a city square, destroying it and costing their team 1000 points in the process, which I thought was pretty funny.

Ezra burned the Mona Lisa while pursuing a Rogue through the Louvre; Dimitri got chased by a pack of wild hyenas in the African Division; Helio flew too close to the sun one time—literally—and nearly got hit by a plane. And

Arissa accidentally portaled the whale shark out of its tank at the Georgia Aquarium.

Professor Guano lumbered into the Power Dome and saw us, adjusting his glasses to check if he was seeing right.

"Hey! What the hell are you kids doing up there! This whole place smells *weird*," he yelled.

"Just a little team bonding!" Ezra called back.

He quickly burned up the rest of the evidence in the palm of his hand, and we flew down, laughing the whole way.

• • •

After another month went by, I realized I didn't actually *need* sleep like my other teammates did. Sleep was just an old habit that I was easily able to get rid of, and that realization dawned on me after I was pulling more all-nighters than I was sleeping, staying awake for weeks at a time because I never got tired. My hunger for more knowledge kept me awake, and every time I felt tiredness creeping in, I would focus hard and pull out a small amount of energy that was stored deep within me. Although it felt like it was locked inside a box, I could still *feel* that it was there.

When I did this little trick, I immediately felt energized, as if I had just downed five espresso shots, which allowed me to keep going with no sleep. It gave me double the time everyone else had for training and studying, enabling me to catch up a lot faster than anyone had anticipated.

The energizing trick had something to do with what Ezra mentioned about our energy storing up over time because it was blocked by our inhibitor chips without us being able to release it. I was able to tap into that well and pull a little bit out at a time—of course, not enough to materialize anything in my hands but just enough to cure my tiredness.

I wanted to teach Ezra my instant energy trick, but I didn't think his powers worked quite the same way mine did, and I also didn't think he cared to try it either.

Every time I attempted to show him how to do it, he shooed me off and told me, "I like my sleep and so should you. You'll understand what I mean one day."

I could only do the trick for a month straight before the tap seemed to finally run dry, causing me to suddenly pass out from exhaustion.

"Kaden, wake up. You have been asleep for three days," a deep voice said while poking me.

"Mom, stop, I don't want to go to school today," I said, still half asleep.

"You have been summoned by the Headmaster," Zo said, nudging me harder with a robotic arm that extended from his chair. I was face down in a book and definitely drooling onto the pages.

Sorry to whomever has to use this after me.

As I lifted my head to look at him, a page stuck to my face, and I peeled it off and wiped the morning gunk from my eyes.

"Again?" I asked. "Didn't I *just* speak to him?"

"That was *months* ago, Kaden. When the Headmaster summons you, you must appear before him—" he sniffed, "after a shower."

• • •

Every time I walked into the Headmaster's chamber, I was amazed. The glass dome roof above his desk cast a beautiful display of light across the room, and the windows along the wall allowed for a perfect view of the campus. I could see my teammates tossing a football in the grass and wished I could be down there with them.

Of course Headmaster Fowler wasn't there again, and the secret bookshelf door called to me, begging me to open it. I sorted through the books on the shelf, pulled one, and *Voila!* The door lurched open. I saw a winding stone staircase leading down into a dark abyss, and I knew I shouldn't have, but I just couldn't help myself. I *had* to know what was down there. I shut the bookshelf behind me and descended into the unknown.

My feet carried me down the steps as I went further into the darkness. Glowing purple crystals appeared next to me, illuminating the path. I finally entered a secret study and saw more multi-colored crystals coating the walls and ceiling. Even though I knew it was artificial since we were on a floating platform above the ocean, I couldn't deny how much it resembled an *actual* cave.

I must admit, the Headmaster has very good taste.

I looked around and saw a pristine white armor set propped up on a piece of wood. Gold engravings flowed across the armor in a beautiful, stylized design. The lights from the glowing crystals bounced off the face of the chest plate as I looked at my reflection on the mirrored surface.

On one of the walls, crystals of different sizes and colors hung on pieces of string as if they were necklaces. I couldn't figure out what they were supposed to signify, but then I saw *it:* a badly damaged white and gold chest plate with a massive hole in the center. I wondered if the person who had originally worn the armor survived the attack that created the damage.

I moved past it and saw a scroll spread out on a sleek

marble desk that read:

To the Champion of Gidoria and General of the Great War, the best this planet has ever seen. The greatest of your race, your brothers, and uncles… The High Lords and the Zaelzan Empire bestow this tremendous honor upon you.

—Emperor Ozul

What the hell does any of that mean? I thought to myself. I hadn't read anything about that stuff in the scrolls or books in the Library of Alexandria and decided not to fry my brain trying to make any sense of it, but a part of me *really* wanted to know who or what it was talking about.

I saw a green crystal on a broken leather cord above the scroll, and then I made the connection: they were medals of honor from the Great War. The hunger to learn more about it burned inside of me once again, and the answer to my questions was sitting right in front of me. I saw a large scroll protruding from a shelf which now belonged to Kaden Collins.

• • •

I slowly crept out from behind the bookshelf and looked both ways, making sure the coast was clear before I fully reentered Headmaster Fowler's chamber. I saw his chair in the center of the room, tempting me to sit in it. I had to know what it felt like, so, I sat in it.

What was he going to do? Not let his favorite Hero sit in his chair?

Especially after my first mission performance, I felt like I could do *anything* and get away with it.

My body sank into the huge, leather chair, and I became

absorbed in it.

Ahhhhh.

I nearly fell asleep before I heard an *eh-hem* sounding cough. I looked up and saw Headmaster Fowler staring at me from across the room.

Shit.

"Sorry to keep you waiting, but it seems that you have already made yourself comfortable in the meantime," he said with a smile.

"Headmaster Fowler, I greatly apologize," I pleaded as I shot up from the chair.

"Nonsense. What's mine is yours."

Good to know, I thought to myself. The scroll that was hidden in my pocket felt as if it weighed a hundred pounds.

I got up from his chair and sat in mine.

"It is great to see you, my boy. How have you been?" he asked as he took his rightful seat in front of me.

"I'm good. Just been doing the usual: studying and training," I responded.

"Wonderful. I wouldn't expect anything different from my favorite Hero. I'm sorry we could not discuss it sooner, but as you know, I am very busy with many Heroes to worry about and manage, but tell me, how was your first mission?" he asked.

There they were again.

I shook my head and replied, "It was great, Headmaster. Thank you for assigning my team that mission. We definitely learned a lot."

I pictured Arissa hiding her hearing aids in shame from me.

"Ah, just what I wanted to hear. Zo thought I was crazy, assigning you your first mission against a Class 3 Rogue, but I told him he just didn't believe in you the way I did."

"Really?" I asked.

"Of course. No one here believes in you the way *I* do, Kaden. I hope you know that." He looked at me closely. "Being a true hero, not just one of the Academy, is more than just successfully completing the mission—which of course you did flawlessly. I believe what makes a true hero is doing the right thing even in the face of adversity."

Those words made my ears ring since the last person I had heard say that was my mom.

"And I think you exemplify that, Kaden." Headmaster Fowler eyed me up and down. "You even look like you have put on a little muscle as well."

"I've been lifting… a bit," I said with a chuckle.

"Professor Guano tells me you are becoming stronger every day—discovering things about yourself that you didn't even know were possible."

"I'm trying to at least, but I must give credit to Ezra, who has taught me a lot and continues to push me to be the best Hero of the Academy that I can be. We even flew—" I stopped myself the second I said it.

Headmaster Fowler's eyebrow twitched.

"Flew?"

"In the Power Dome… I'm sorry I got distracted by something else," I said, trying to play it off. "Ezra has been a huge help, and combined with your readings, I have been making a ton of progress."

"Well, that is great to hear," he said, smiling back at me. "Now, there was a specific matter that I wanted to discuss with you regarding your first mission. I truly apologize that I failed to inform you sooner of the practice of neutralizing Rogues. That was my honest mistake. Things have been very busy at the Academy lately, and that completely slipped my mind."

I tried shutting out the screams, and as I took a deep breath, a feeling of extreme lightheadedness rolled over me.

"Are you alright, my boy?"

"Yes, I'm fine, just got dizzy there for a second."

"It is perfectly normal to be shaken up by what happened on your first mission. It can be traumatizing witnessing such things without the proper context for why we do it. Every new Hero feels the same way until the second or third mission, and then they understand."

"Why do we do it, Headmaster? He offered to willingly wear an inhibitor chip, his hands were—" I hesitated. "Why couldn't we have just brought him back with us as we did with the others?"

"He was a Class 3 Rogue, my dear Kaden. Just because his hands were gone doesn't mean he was unable to still use his powers. Rogues like him are far too dangerous to be kept here under the Academy. What would happen if his chip were to malfunction? He would unleash devastation and destruction on this entire Academy, and that is only *one* Class 3. What if we kept multiple Class 3 Rogues here and experienced a system wide failure. They would destroy everything we've built, and a thousand innocent Golden children—you, your friends—would perish and sink to the bottom of the ocean, dying before you ever saw your true potential as Heroes."

"But there *has* to be another way!"

"THERE IS NO OTHER WAY!" he yelled as he slammed his fist on his desk, cracking it in the middle. I shot backward, and he saw the horrified look on my face.

"I…" he gathered his thoughts and words, "I am truly sorry, my dear boy. I apologize for that outburst, but as you can see, this is a very hard subject for me to discuss. When you raised your voice at me, I just…" His fists relaxed on the table. "There truly is *no* other way. Class 3 and 4 Rogues are just too dangerous to be freely roaming this planet without any guidance. Their very existence endangers the lives of everyone else on it. Every day, hundreds of thousands of lives are lost because of the actions of a few reckless individuals. They had their chance to come here, just like the choice you made to join the Academy and commit yourself to the greater good of the Earth, and eventually, the greater good of Gidoria. Rogues have no place in The Unity, and I have only recently begun to realize that this fight will never end unless they are eradicated from the face of the planet."

There was a long pause, but the more I thought about it, the more I realized he was *right*.

"What he did to Arissa… how badly he hurt her for no reason… They were robbing a bank; we had to stop them, but…" I paused, "he *tortured* her." The words were barely out of my mouth when I saw her again, lying on the street with blood dripping from her ears. "When I watched Ezra burn him, I wished it had been *me* torching him alive… Is that wrong to say?"

The Headmaster stared at me, his jaw hung wide open. He breathed in and let out a long breath, eventually standing up and towering over me.

"No, Kaden," he said as he moved around his desk. "That is quite possibly the greatest thing any Hero has ever said to me in all of my years as Headmaster of the Academy."

He put his hands on my shoulders, and I could feel his

immense strength. I knew that if he wanted to, he could instantly tear me in half, and based on the stories I read, I knew he could too.

"Listen to me very carefully, my boy. You will get your chance to *kill* every Rogue on this planet. Together, we will hunt every last one of them down and save this world, bringing peace to it, once and for all."

He drew me in for a hug, and as I held onto him, I realized Ezra was *wrong*. Everything I heard in my head— the screams—they stopped and never came back.

CHAPTER TWELVE
THE HUNT

AFTER THAT CONVERSATION, my team was quickly assigned more and more missions. As I sat in my seat watching the clouds pass by outside the transparent walls of the ship, I thought back to that first one. I didn't tell anyone then, but truthfully, I was shaken up afterwards, and rightfully so. Seeing Arissa bleeding from her ears, watching my first neutralization—both of those things took a lot of time to get over.

But now? These missions had become second nature to me.

We rarely brought any Rogues back since the Lock Up was at maximum capacity. The Unity wasn't able to process them fast enough, so it didn't matter if they were a Class 1, 2, 3, or 4, we had direct orders to neutralize any and all Rogues on sight.

The more of them we neutralized, the harder they became to find. They were much less bold and didn't commit nearly as many crimes as before—unless the potential reward was worthwhile. Most of their time was spent hiding in fear from us, but it didn't matter if they weren't causing as much mayhem as before, the only thing that mattered was that the Headmaster's answer to the rogue Golden problem was working, and we couldn't let up now.

The Rogues were an infection—a blight on this planet—who refused to play by the rules. They could have used their powers for the greater good, protecting the world, but no, they used them for their own personal gain. Even the ones who cowered in fear doing nothing at all were just wasting their gifts.

The Headmaster saw any and all Rogues who didn't report themselves to the Academy, no matter how "peaceful" they were, as our *enemies*. They couldn't be left to their own devices as everything they did eventually led to death and destruction. One day they may be peaceful, not hurting anyone; the next they could be leveling a city just because they woke up on the wrong side of the bed.

Even if some Rogues are truly good, why won't they turn themselves in?

They could get the proper guidance and training from the Headmaster and learn how to save the world, because that's what the Heroes of the Academy were doing: *saving the world.*

The Headmaster told us that, currently, the Earth had never seen a longer period of uninterrupted peace, and the citizens of The Unity thanked us greatly for it. Although our duties kept us from attending them, cities across the world held parades for the Heroes of the Academy. With every Rogue I neutralized, I pictured crowds of people in the streets cheering me on.

"We're approaching a Rogue hideout in the Eastern Eurasia Division. Move to drop positions," Ezra called out to the rear of the ship.

My teammates and I moved to our positions, and instead of feeling fear, I now felt butterflies growing in my stomach, as this was now my favorite part of the day.

"The DGC has confirmed multiple Rogues of unknown classes inside the hideout, so stay alert," the operator said through our earpieces.

"Powers on!" Ezra responded to the operator.

BEEP!

Our inhibitor chips were disabled, and I looked down at my hands, seeing red energy swirl and grow upon my command. I brought my hands together, as in prayer, and pulled outward, forming a ball of pure energy between them. A light show of pulsating red streaks glowed brilliantly, illuminating my face in the dark cabin. I slammed my hands together, and the energy was absorbed back into me.

"Dropping in three… two… ONE!"

The floor fell out from underneath me, and my body plummeted toward the ground. Cold air and snowflakes hit my face as I focused and used my energy to keep warm. As I fell through the sky, I did spins and flips before eventually blasting energy from my hands and feet, thus, slowing myself as I approached the snow covered ground. I landed and looked into the distance and saw vast mountain ranges with sharp, snowy peaks towering above us.

Arissa appeared next to me as a portal closed behind her. Helio dropped off Theo, who cracked the concrete under the snow upon the hard landing. Dimitri formed black goo wings, which allowed him to glide effortlessly toward the ground. He eventually sucked the wings back into his body and formed tentacles to absorb the impact of the fall. Finally, Ezra landed next to me in a ball of fire before extinguishing his flames. The surveillance orbs descended, surrounding us while focusing on the coming action.

"Everyone ready?" I asked.

They all nodded in agreement, and we crept toward the warehouse hideout. It was mostly made of sheet metal and looked as if it were about to collapse in on itself if the wind blew in the wrong direction.

"Arissa, can you get us inside?" I asked.

She nodded, as there was a small hole in the exterior of the hideout that she could see through. She tossed out one portal with her right hand and another with her left, and we got our first glimpse inside, revealing six Rogues, all putting on armor and gear while trying to stay warm next to a fire in a rusted barrel. Unseen, we walked through the portal, entering the hideout and standing behind them. Eventually, one turned around and noticed us.

"Holy shit! How did they find—" I blasted him with an energy beam, sending him flying into a small TV. The other Rogues got into attack positions, one by one unveiling their powers.

One grew to a massive size until his head scraped the ceiling. His muscles bulged as he flexed and pounded his fists together.

Vines erupted from the ground and wrapped themselves around another Rogue's arms. He broke the vines from the floor and aimed them toward us as they slithered up and down his arms like snakes.

Two daggers slipped out of another Rogue's sleeves just as he levitated off the ground and pointed them at us.

The room got even colder as another's body started to become coated in ice until he was fully covered in it.

The last one jammed his hands together, then separated

them which projected out two spinning gold energy shields. Symbols danced off the shields which immediately made me realize I was dealing with a magic user.

I had read about them in some of the ancient scrolls in the library, and although they were still Goldens, they didn't have any innate abilities. Instead, they had a cognitive ability that allowed them to learn how to wield the Overforce—an invisible magical energy that surrounded us at all times.

"Well, I think we all know by now how to match up. Team #22, attack!" I yelled as Helio swooped down toward the dagger wielding Rogue with her sword.

Their weapons collided, sending sparks dancing through the room. They swung back and forth, jabbing and parrying each other's blows. Helio grabbed the Rogue and threw him straight through the roof. She flew after him, disappearing into the dark gray sky.

Theo charged forward and tackled the oversized man, crashing through the sheet metal wall of the warehouse and causing it to violently shake.

The vine wielding Rogue shot two vines toward Dimitri who sliced them apart with his tentacles that he had formed into sharp blades. He then created a large hammer and swung it, sending the vine man flying through another wall.

"This whole place is gonna come down! Arissa, portal out of here, now!" I yelled as she threw a portal and dove into it.

I created a hole in the roof with an energy blast, and Ezra and I took off through it just as the warehouse came crumbling down behind us. We floated above the destroyed building watching our other teammates duke it out.

A massive ice blast shot out from the debris and knocked Ezra backward out of the air. I didn't have time to check if he was OK because large pieces of sheet metal were levitating and sailing past my body, coming from the magic Rogue. I barely dodged them as I attempted to project shields in front of me to block them. One finally hit me and knocked me out of the sky, throwing me into a snow bank next to the now destroyed warehouse. I was covered in snow with only my head sticking out of the pile.

That hurt.

I had no time to focus on the pain, because I felt something wrap around my leg like a rope. The magic Rogue yanked me out of the snow bank, pulling me toward him with a golden lasso. An energy sword formed in my hand, and I sliced the lasso in half which caused it to disintegrate. I dissolved the sword and extended both of my hands outward, unleashing a beam of energy toward the Rogue. Just before it struck him, he formed a gold shield and blocked it, but I watched as it shattered into pieces.

He was a strong magic user, but raw power beats magic every time. I charged up my fist to deliver the final blow, but a boulder came careening toward me. I projected a shield in front of me, but the impact of the boulder sent me flying.

I covered myself in a weak projection—since it was all I had time to create—just as I crashed and skidded across the snow covered landscape, clawing at the ground as I slid toward a steep cliff. My hands filled with snow and dirt, trying desperately to get a grip. My suit was working overtime, the servos whirring and crunching as they tried to mechanically force my hands closed. I sent energy out from my feet, attempting to slow my slide. I stopped right at the edge, my feet dangling freely off the cliff.

Suddenly, the ground began to shake violently as I saw the magic Rogue floating in the air above me with his hands raised in front of him. Two symbols of an unknown language appeared in the palms of his hands that faced the earth while he pulled upward, fingers clenched and straining. The cliff I was lying on began to lift up in front of me, detaching from the rest of the mountain in one solid piece. He rolled his hands forward, flipping the cliff upside down and sending it careening toward a ravine. There wasn't an opening for me to escape, so I held on and did my best to channel all of my energy into a shield to protect myself from the falling rocks and boulders as I was crushed and buried alive in the rubble.

When the dust finally settled, I found myself in total darkness. The shield projection around my body had shattered from the enormous weight of the cliff side. I created a ball of red light in my hand, illuminating the small pocket of air in which I was trapped. I started to hyperventilate, gasping for air, but the more I breathed the more lightheaded I became. My vision blurred, and my hands felt numb.

"Come on, Kaden! Come on!" I yelled as I tried to gather energy from within me. "You're not dying here! They need you, Kaden! They need you! Now, *come on!*"

In a last ditch effort, I compressed my energy into my hands. It was unstable and hard to contain as I gathered more and more of it, until I finally released it, sending energy exploding outwards.

BOOOMMM!!!

Rocks erupted into the air, freeing me, and I found myself at the bottom of a ravine with a river running through it. I remained on my hands and knees, trying to muster the strength to get up and help my friends, but the second I tried, I doubled over in pain and exhaustion. I heard rocks falling behind me, and before I could react, I was flipped over with two hands at my throat, pinning me down.

"All you Heroes of the Academy are the same. You think you're so worthy of this power, yet you don't even know how to use it! Everything I'm capable of—all of my abilities—I had to learn through *Kala*, because nothing was given to me, unlike you. We had orders not to kill any Heroes unless provoked, so now, I'm *really* going to enjoy this. I would usually feel bad about killing another Golden, but it's about time we started fighting back against you fucks. It's a shame that the Headmaster sends you all to fight his battles for him, only to be slaughtered in the snow," the magic Rogue snarled as he dipped my head into the river.

My mouth filled with water as I screamed, trying to punch at him and break free from his grip, but I couldn't. My vision faded, my arms went limp, and I stopped fighting. My body became weightless as my heartbeat began to slow. I felt my consciousness and hold on reality start to slip.

"*Kaden!*" I heard Arissa's voice cry out to me. I couldn't tell if it was in my head or in real life, but it didn't matter because I still got the message loud and clear: she needed my help. I wasn't going to die in the snow—not like this.

An immense amount of energy flowed through me, giving me the strength to fight back. I grabbed his arms and began to levitate out of the water.

"No! You should be dead!" he yelled as I held onto him.

As I rose from the river, I could see my reflection in the water with my eyes glowing red and smoke pouring out of them from an overflow of energy.

"Please! I was just protecting *them*. We weren't hurting anybody!" he cried to me as we left the canyon and floated high above it in the clouds.

My head twitched and I thought, *Them?*

I focused my energy and passed it directly into his body which began to glow bright red, illuminating his internal organs. He began to twitch and convulse as the energy overwhelmed him.

"NO!" he screamed as his mouth and eye sockets filled with energy, shining out like a flashlight. In a burst of red light, most of his body disintegrated, and a mix of ash and blood fell to the bottom of the canyon, landing on the snow below us.

I flew back to the rest of my teammates and saw that they were losing the fight. Most of Theo's crystals that covered his body had shattered and were lying in various heaps around the battlefield. His bare skin was exposed to the elements, but he still tried to fight off the giant Rogue with the only thing he had left: a sharp point over his fist.

Arissa was helping where she could, acting as support for the team by redirecting attacks and getting teammates out of bad situations before they were killed, but she couldn't save everyone, and I could see her struggling to keep up with the action.

Dimitri was now completely wrapped in vines, screaming for help as his body was slowly being crushed under the tremendous pressure he was subjected to. His tentacles tried to fight back, but they were pinned next to his body, unable to move. His screams were muffled as a vine wrapped over his face and mouth and began to suffocate him.

Helio and the dagger wielding Rogue continued fighting in the sky, but she was obviously losing. She parried his dagger with her sword and disarmed him, but as she tried to slash at him, he did a 360 and threw another dagger, striking her in the shoulder. She screamed in pain and barreled toward the ground. Arissa threw out a portal that Helio passed through, getting her safely away from the battlefield.

Ezra was being pinned down with a torrent of ice and snow, extinguishing his flames and burying him.

"Arissa, get everyone and yourself out of here right now!" I yelled across the battlefield.

"What about you?" she yelled back.

I turned toward her, and the look of fear that I saw during the first mission crossed her face once again.

"Kaden…" she said, covering her mouth.

"Go," I said sternly. "NOW!"

She regained her composure and immediately started throwing out more portals. Dimitri managed to cut through the vines as a portal appeared below him. He dropped into it, and it closed behind him. Theo dodged a massive fist that was coming down on top of him and dove into another portal and escaped.

The snowpile Ezra was trapped under collapsed, and he appeared far away from the battlefield, safely reunited with the others. I watched as Arissa gave me one last fearful look before jumping through one of her own portals and disappearing.

My teammates were now safe, leaving only me and the

vermin that needed to be exterminated.

Thunk!

I felt a dagger get caught in the red glow that surrounded my body. It vibrated and shook, trying to pass through my energy field before I pulled the blade out, supercharged my arm, and launched it back toward him with tremendous speed, striking his fragile skull right between the eyes. His body went limp and dropped from the air face first into the snow. A small pool of blood formed around him.

"Jon, no!" the vine Rogue yelled before launching vines in my direction, wrapping me in them. He pulled me close to his face, squeezing me tighter. "That's it! You're not hurting anyone else!"

I focused my energy to expand outward from me, blasting the vines away. I floated a foot above the ground and saw fear in the Rogue's eyes.

"You should've turned yourself in when you had the chance," I said as I reached forward and grabbed his throat.

I directed energy into my hand and released it in one concentrated burst. All the vines dropped into the snow, and smoke rose from the area where his head used to be, but to my surprise, there was no blood. The wound was cauterized instantly. His decapitated body fell from my hand and crashed into the snow before I turned to the ice Rogue next.

"Get behind me!" he shouted to the giant Rogue.

He shot out a massive blast of ice that seemed to only tickle me. I pressed on further, floating closer and closer to him as his powers were unable to stop me. We were now face to face, and I raised my hands, unleashing a blast that forced him flat on his back. I kept on with the energy until nothing remained of the Rogue except a burn mark on the concrete where the snow had evaporated.

The last Rogue looked at me in horror, and I knew I was only moments away from accomplishing the mission and saving my friends.

He threw a punch at me, and I supercharged my fist, colliding with his. His giant arm exploded, sending bone and blood in every direction. He cried out in pain and grabbed at the stump that was now his arm. He yelled one last war cry and unloaded another punch toward me.

BOOM!

A shock wave blew past us as I caught it in my glowing, opened palm before lifting him into the air. I threw his pathetic body across the battlefield, sending him skidding through the snow.

His feet were slipping and sliding as he tried to find traction to stand up. He managed to get to his feet and limped away helplessly, holding his arm that was leaving a trail of blood in the snow behind him.

My body rotated in the air as I raised closed fists in front of me and launched at an incredible speed toward him. It felt as if I had passed through cardboard as organs, bones, and blood washed past me, creating an abstract, expressionist piece of art in the snow bank. I stared at it, floating motionless in the air. His body behind me now held a giant gaping hole, and his mouth hung wide open as if in a perpetual scream. He dropped to his knees and crumpled into the snow.

My friends were safe, the mission was accomplished, and the Rogues were exterminated, but the words of the magic Rogue kept playing over and over in my mind.

I was just protecting them!

Protecting them!

Them!

That had to mean there were more Rogues somewhere in the warehouse, which also meant the job *wasn't* finished.

A quick blast of energy cleared the warehouse debris, and that was when I saw *it*: a metal trap door that had been hidden under a rug—something we hadn't seen when we first came in. I floated over to it and ripped the door off its hinges, tossing the flimsy piece of metal to the side.

Hiding within were cowering children of different colors and sizes, no older than ten years. It appeared that they had just awakened and that their powers had developed in various ways. One had green horns sprouting from the top of his head; others had purple and yellow skin, multiple arms, and oversized limbs; and one girl had very thin, transparent scales covering her body as if they had just grown in.

A boy bravely stood in front them, facing me with his hands raised and a blue glow emitting from his palms. He shined the light brighter, attempting to push me back, but it didn't affect me at all. They didn't seem to be anything more than Class 2 rogues—*if* that—yet they were still old enough to remember everything that they had been taught and shown thus far. If we took them back to the Academy, they would grow up to hate us. They could also cause untold damage to the world if they happened to have Class 3 or 4 powers that I just wasn't seeing in this moment.

They must be neutralized.

I raised my hands, supercharging them as red light filled the entire area. I could see the light reflecting in the children's eyes as horror grew on their faces.

"Kaden, stop!" a familiar voice cried out from behind me, which slightly took me out of my trance. I kept one hand pointed directed at the children as I turned to see Arissa running toward me.

"We accomplished the mission, Kaden! Please stop! These Golden children are innocent! We can take them back to the Academy, and they can become Heroes!" She reached out a hand to mine, but the energy field burned her, causing her to jump back and cry out. "This isn't you! I know you, you wouldn't do this. We won, we can go home now—back to the Academy! Please just listen to me!"

I saw my reflection again on a shattered mirror that had been propped up on the debris. Blood dripped off of me, forming a small puddle below, and the smoke began to dissipate from my eyes as they started to flash intermittently as if two sides of myself were fighting for control over the same body.

"Neutralize the rogue Goldens, or you will fail your mission and never be a hero for the people of Earth or Gidoria!" Headmaster Fowler shouted in my earpiece. "No matter their age, we both know they are too dangerous to be left alive. They're Rogues, nothing more, nothing less. Finish the job!"

His words echoed in my mind as my eyes flashed violently.

"Listen to *me*, Kaden. If you love me, then stop this, and come back down here!" Arissa cried.

My mind raced at a million miles an hour, and it felt as if my head was going to explode.

"I will make you Champion of Gidoria and bring your teammates with you to the Golden planet!" Headmaster Fowler yelled desperately.

I saw the rest of my wounded team coming out of a

portal, staring at me in fear.

"Do it, right now. Make it quick. Make it painless. That is a *final* order."

My eyes exploded with bright red energy.

They must be neutralized.

"Kaden, no… Please, God, no…"

With a flash of red light, they were *gone*—reduced to ash. My body dropped, and I lay motionless in the debris as my vision left me.

CHAPTER THIRTEEN

A ONE WAY MISSION

"**N**O!" NOEL CRIED out. "Oh, god!" She dropped to the floor in front of the Council of the Sanctuary, tears streaming down her face.

"Noel! What is wrong?" Zahavi said as he ran over to her and held her in his arms. "Someone bring the healer! Now!"

She grabbed his arm, "No, it's not me. It's... the *children*." Zahavi looked at the other members of the Council in fear. "There's nothing left, there's... there's nothing left of them."

Silas and Donateo looked at each other with confusion.

"Noel, who are you talking about?" Silas asked, but she didn't respond. Donateo put a finger to his ear.

"This is Donateo transmitting on a secure line. Search and Rescue team #48, do you copy?" he asked. "Search and Rescue team #48, do you copy! This is Donateo, does anyone—" Donateo stood frozen before bringing his finger from his ear and dropping to his knees. "What have *they* done..."

Silas started to run out of the room, but Zahavi grabbed him by the arm.

"Silas, stop!" Zahavi pleaded. "It's too dangerous. They will be watching that area with every surveillance drone they have." Silas pulled his arm away from Zahavi and looked into his eyes with rage. "It's a trap, and you know it. They are trying to draw you out. Just stay here until we know what's going on."

"My daughter was among them, Zahavi. The rescue team, after all these years, finally found her. They were preparing to head this way…" Silas gritted his teeth. "I was finally going to see my—" He choked up.

"Silas, I know how you feel, but please don't do this," Zahavi begged.

"Just let me see her. Let me see my daughter, Zahavi."

"You know what will happen to you—what will happen to this place if you go."

"I don't care. *You* caused this," he said, putting a finger on Zahavi's chest. "I just hope her death was finally enough for you to see the truth that you have been ignoring for far too long."

He pushed past him and walked away across a bridge. Zahavi watched as a small ship took off and flew into the distance.

"Donateo, call all Golden Search and Rescue teams back to the Sanctuary," Zahavi said.

"Donateo to Search and Rescue teams, report back to the Sanctuary *immediately*," Donateo said with a finger on his earpiece as he exited the room.

"Leona, prepare all non-combatant Golden men, women, and children in the Sanctuary to move to the bunker at a moment's notice." She nodded to Zahavi and headed downstairs. "Noel, please take your time with your grief, but when you are ready, join us in the Battle Room," Zahavi said as he looked at the last person who hadn't gotten an assignment yet. "Arbor, with me."

They ran across the Council Room toward a zipline. Metal clips extended from beneath their sleeves, attaching them to the cable and sending them gliding across it. They jumped off the line and landed on an elevator platform which lifted them to the Battle Room—a room that was filled to the brim with computers and screens that monitored everything in the Sanctuary. Large windows provided a view to the vast ocean that stretched out endlessly before them. A hologram table was located in the center of the room, displaying the Sanctuary covered in a giant domed force field. Zahavi pressed a series of buttons on the table, and a holographic 100% appeared above the shield.

"Will it be enough to hold them?" Arbor asked.

"It will have to be. Once the remaining Goldens in the field return to the Sanctuary, prep them for battle procedures."

"What about the ones we have been training?"

"Prepare them too. We will need everyone we can get. Engage the defenses, and keep everyone on high alert. We won't know when the attack is coming, but I can assure you it will once they capture Silas. It is time we finally fight back," Zahavi paused as pain grew across his face, "but I'm afraid the end is near, Arbor."

"Of what?"

"All of this—one hundred years of work, everything I've built..." Zahavi looked out across his sanctuary. "Now, go!"

"Yes, Zahavi," he said as he made his way to the elevator and rode it back down.

Zahavi went over to a wall and stared at his family's crest: an infinity symbol held within a circle that stood for *power*. He pushed in the crest, and the wall split into two and opened, revealing a spiky black armored suit. The armor was organic in nature and seemed to move and shift around by itself. It pulsed yellow light as if it were breathing—begging to be worn.

Zahavi stuck out a hand and ran a finger across the chest plate. The armor held many memories for him— some good, others he would rather not revisit, as the last time he had worn it, he had nearly been killed in it. He had promised himself never to put it on again, for he hated what it represented, but he would need to for the coming conflict, and sometimes promises were meant to be broken.

"I know you have been patiently waiting. Please give me the strength I need when it is finally time to face him *again."*

Upon hearing these words, the suit hummed and glowed brighter, until it filled the entire room with yellow light.

• • •

Silas walked toward the destroyed warehouse while his ship sat in the distance behind him.

BOOM!

The ship exploded, sending debris and searing pieces of metal flying all around him. Silas knew how smart and thorough the Academy was, as it would only take a few seconds for Zo to scan the ship's computer systems and find the coordinates from which it had last departed. Silas knew that this was a one way mission.

As he got closer to the warehouse, he saw that nothing remained but debris and frozen blood in the snow. The DGC had already done their job of cleaning up the scene of the mission. All the bodies were taken away and incinerated, and the ones responsible for this massacre were back at the Academy relaxing in the sun.

The DGC had laid out motion sensors, immediately alerting the Academy of any movement that the devices detected, but Silas made no effort to avoid them.

He saw the trapdoor, ripped from its hinges and thrown off into a snowbank—the only line of defense his daughter had before her life was taken from her by a monster.

As he walked closer, he heard a familiar sound. Surveillance drones circled around him and inspected his every move. Silas saw the small hiding place where his daughter had spent her last moments. He picked up her remaining ashes—the one thing the DGC didn't care to clean up—holding them in the palms of his hands. Tears ran down his face and dropped into the snow.

"Isra, I failed you. I tried, but I couldn't find you in time. I shouldn't have let Zahavi take me back. I should've kept searching for you, but I *too* was a coward like him. When they told me that they found you, I couldn't believe it. I just wanted to hold you close in my arms—tell you I would never lose you again and that you would always be safe with me." Silas' head fell forward, tears streaming down his face. "You were the one thing I loved. I can't go on knowing you're not here with me."

He walked over to the destroyed cliff side, holding his daughter's ashes in his hands—the last time he would ever hold her. He threw her up into the air and watched the wind carry her away into the distance.

"You are now free from this never ending war. There is no more pain—no more suffering for you. I will be with you soon." He moved to step over the cliff, but a hand reached out and grabbed his shoulder, stopping him from jumping off.

"STOP!" a voice demanded from behind him.

"Release me!" Silas yelled as he spun around and drove a sharp scale straight through the face of Mark from Team #1. He saw the rest of the team rushing at him. "You will not take this away from me!"

"Mark!" Alex cried out. "NO!"

Silas pulled the scale from his face, blood dripping off the point. He turned and ran, diving off the edge of the cliff, but his foot was caught by Claire. She yanked him back from it and dragged him toward the ship. He fought and kicked, clawing at the dirt and snow, attempting to break free from her grasp.

"Please! You've already taken everything from me! Just let me be with her! Just let me finally be with my daughter!"

He kicked Claire away with his spiked foot, sending her flying backward. He desperately tried again to get to the edge of the cliff, but a massive bolt of electricity came down on top of him, shocking him as he screamed in pain.

"No, NO!!! LET ME BE WITH HER!"

He twitched and convulsed from the electricity as Jayson approached.

"No, Silas, that's not going to happen, not *yet* at least," Jayson said, keeping the electricity on him. "We still need our ticket to Gidoria, and we will get that once you give us the location of Zahavi and the Sanctuary. After we have that, then you have the Headmaster's permission to die."

Silas lay in the snow, crying out in pain as the electricity continued to engulf him.

"Isra!" he called out to the cliff as Claire dragged him through the snow. "Isra, wait for me!"

• • •

A hangar operator guided the Team #1 ship with two orange directional sticks. It landed in its designated spot, and a hatch opened from underneath the belly of the ship. Team #1 stepped out, carrying Mark's corpse while walking Silas down the steps with a muzzle and power cuffs on. Mark's body was concealed in a bag, and it floated on an antigravity stretcher across the hangar floor.

They took Silas to the Lock Up, passing many cells with Rogues lying in them—some badly injured, some starved, and some not moving at all. A beaten woman lying in her own excrement and blood was curled in a ball in the corner of her cell, next to the one Silas was thrown into. Jayson aggressively ripped the muzzle off, cutting Silas' face in the process, but he didn't flinch; he just sat there unmoving while staring at the blank wall.

"He will see you shortly, and for your sake, I suggest you give him what he wants," Jayson said with a smile as he exited the room.

The lights turned off, and Silas was left alone in a quiet, dark cell.

• • •

The Headmaster sat in his chamber watching a holographic television screen. A female news reporter stood in front of a parade with thousands of people celebrating in the background.

"As you can see behind me, the city of Los Angeles is throwing the largest Hero Parade that the North American Division has ever seen. This parade commemorates the valiant efforts of all of the Heroes of the Golden Academy for their work in keeping the world safe. Today marks the 100th day of uninterrupted world peace—the longest streak since the first Golden was discovered 300 years ago. Although the Heroes themselves could not be with us today to celebrate, as they are out saving the world, we would still like for them to hear this message: if you are watching, the non-Golden citizens of The Unity thank you for what you do each and every day to keep us safe. Continue saving the world, Heroes!"

The screen shut off, and the Headmaster rubbed the wrinkles on his forehead as Zo floated into his chamber.

"Sir, Team #1 has returned. They have successfully completed their mission."

A twisted smile appeared on Headmaster Fowler's face. "Wonderful."

• • •

The lights turned back on, and the door to the cell opened. Silas lay on the floor, unmoving.

"Oh, no, no, no, Silas. It is not time to die *yet*," the Headmaster said as he entered the cell.

Silas launched upward, driving a scale straight into the Headmaster's eye. The scale shattered to pieces the second it made contact, causing Silas to scream out in pain.

"Ah, you Rogues are all the same," he said. "So moronic and pitiful!" He kicked Silas into the wall, denting it and shattering more scales with ease. He picked him up by the throat and said, "I used what the Zaelzans taught me: honor, discipline, and control, and I conquered this planet with my bare hands!" He threw him down and shattered more scales. The Headmaster picked him up again and threw him into another wall, forming a giant dent. "I brought peace and order to Earth, the likes of which it has never seen before!"

Silas coughed up blood while he lay in his own shattered scales. Headmaster Fowler kneeled down and got face to face with him.

"You're weak, beneath me, and a *pathetic* excuse for a Golden. What you just tried to do to me was so insulting it deserves death, but no, I shall spare you. Right now, you are worth more to me alive, but if I could, I would rip your spine from your body and hang it in my study as a trophy. Now, this can all end—I'll even let you be with your daughter when I'm through with you—if you just tell me where Zahavi is."

Silas, nose broken and bleeding with a mouth full of blood, looked up at Headmaster Fowler.

"Go to hell," he said as he spat out the blood onto the Headmaster's face.

"Ah, you fool. Those were not the words I wanted to hear. You see, I already went there when they sent me to your planet. Living among you weak, pitiful people has been my own personal version of it." Headmaster Fowler slowly spun his own neck around and got a few audible pops and cracks out of it. "Unfortunately, I was afraid you were going to say something stupid like that. Now, Silas, what scale shall we start with first?"

He reached down and grabbed Silas' arm. Silas screamed as he slowly started to pull off a scale, eventually ripping it from his skin and tossing it aside.

"It wasn't that hard of a choice because that was the last one! I know they will grow back soon, and when they do, I hope you will have learned your lesson. I will only come back *once* to get what I need," the Headmaster said while wiping Silas' blood from his face, before placing a bloody hand print on the wall. "Use this as a reminder for what happened here today. I greatly look forward to speaking with you soon." He wiped his hands on his white toga and exited the cell, passing by Jayson. "You're up."

Jayson smiled and entered after him. Screams were heard echoing down the hall as the door closed, sealing Silas inside the soundproof room of torture.

CHAPTER FOURTEEN

THE RED DEMON

I T HAD BEEN months since I last spoke to Arissa, and whenever I tried to before, I would only make things worse.

"No! You know what you did! Don't come here anymore!" she yelled at me.

"Please just listen to me! I don't know what happened; it felt like something else took over. I was in my trance, Arissa. I'm sorry! I didn't know what I was doing!" I tried to explain, but I could see it on her face: the same fear she had when she saw me floating in the air with red energy pouring from my eyes.

"Why do you lie to me? Nothing took control of you. It was still you who followed those orders." There was a long pause as she looked down. "Where is that boy I once knew on the rooftop…"

"Arissa, please listen—"

"No." She looked at me with disgust. "You're not a hero, Kaden; you're a *monster*." The door slammed in my face, and that was that.

Anytime I saw her on campus, she would look away or ignore me—acting as if I didn't exist. I never got another chance to talk to her again.

The truth was: I did know what I was doing. Despite

what I had told her, nothing took control over me. I was still the one who released the energy upon the children. I was the one who watched them disintegrate and turn to ash, and although it had been harder to control my anger when I was in that trance, it was still *me* who had killed them.

I spent many nights alone training in the Power Dome or laying in the Library, staring up at the stars, replaying that memory over and over in my head. I could see everything as clear as day: my hands rising upward, the bright flash of red light, and then... ash falling to the ground in great heaps.

I didn't regret what I had done, because I had to do it. There was no other choice since we would have failed the mission and not graduated to Gidoria. I thought I was doing the right thing—protecting her and ensuring that we would all move on to the next place together, but I guess she didn't see it that way.

I eventually went to the Headmaster to talk about how I was feeling about what had happened. He seemed to always know best, and whenever we met, I left his chamber with a clear mind.

I knocked on the door and said, "Headmaster Fowler?"

"Yes, my boy?" he responded after looking up from a set of papers on his desk.

"Could I talk to you?"

"Of course, come, have a seat."

I made my way into the chamber and took my seat in front of him as I hung my head.

"Are you alright?" he asked.

"I've been better."

"Have you?" He looked at me intently. "What seems to

be troubling you?"

I took a deep breath and said, "*Arissa*... We haven't spoken in months, not since our last mission. Everything with her changed after I neutralized those...those..." I couldn't get the words out.

"It is truly a shame my boy, but some people will never understand why we must do the things we do here. Arissa is a sweet girl; I have known her for nearly all of her life, but she has always been misguided and rebellious. I had hoped your joining of her team would have set her on the right path for Gidoria, but it seems I was mistaken," he said. "I'm afraid she will not be graduating with you after all."

"No!" I shot forward in my seat. "Headmaster Fowler, please! I can try talking to her again, get her thinking straight. Maybe she will listen to me now that she has had some time to think things over. She has to graduate with us!" I begged. "I can't go there without her!"

The Headmaster just sighed while shaking his head and stroking his long beard.

"I can't sleep, Headmaster Fowler, so put me to work and give me more missions. Send me on my own, and I can neutralize the last remaining Rogues for you while everyone else sleeps. Just promise me that the points will go to my team, for *all* of us."

The Headmaster pondered this proposition for a moment, and finally said, "I suppose that could work."

"Thank you, Headmaster, thank you!" I said as I ran around the table and hugged him.

"Of course," he said while patting me on my back. "Now tell me, my boy, why can't you sleep?"

"I don't need to," I replied.

"Everyone needs sleep, Kaden. Even great Heroes such

as yourself."

"Not with my powers, I don't."

"Do you stay awake because you have the ability to… or because that is your only option?"

"Both, I guess. Every time I've tried to sleep, I've just found it easier to keep going—to stay awake rather than lying in my bed tossing and turning all night."

"I see, I see. Now I have to ask, what keeps your mind awake. Why are you unable to fully let go and relinquish yourself to sleep?"

I sat there thinking about the question, and trust me, I fully believed in the cause of the Academy, but something always nagged at me that I couldn't get out of my head. Every time I looked into the eyes of a Rogue—seconds before I neutralized them—I always saw fear.

I finally said, "Arissa, the girl I *thought* loved me, called me a…"

"A what?" he asked.

"A monster."

A singular tear rolled down my face, and he wiped it away.

"Can I show you something, my boy—something that I think will help ease your racing mind?" he asked.

I nodded, and a transparent, holographic screen appeared next to his desk. A news reporter stood in front of a large parade for the Heroes of the Academy. Earth and all of the Divisions that were under the rule of The Unity were experiencing the longest period of uninterrupted peace in human history. There was no crime, no murders, no destruction of cities, no pain, and no suffering. The planet was truly peaceful.

"If you were a monster, Kaden, and the things you were doing were bad—things only a *true* monster would do—

then how would you explain *that?*" he asked, pointing to the screen.

He was right, as he always was, and Arissa was wrong. She wouldn't understand these things because she never had. She never even carried her own weight on the team, always too afraid to hold up her end of the bargain. When the time came to neutralize a Rogue, she always hesitated, forcing me to step in and complete the mission.

I am a hero, and no one can tell me otherwise.

"Kaden, do as I say, and I promise you, you will one day be the Hero of Earth and Champion of Gidoria, just as you've always wanted. Now go, keep being the hero I know you are."

"Thank you, Headmaster Fowler. I promise, I won't let you down."

"You never have, Kaden, and I know you never will."

• • •

Weeks had passed since that conversation, and I had already gone on dozens of missions alone and neutralized hundreds of Rogues. Unless they were looking at The Wall, I doubted my team even knew what I was doing at night, and hell, it didn't even feel like I was a part of one anymore. I barely heard from them anyway.

After coming back from one of my missions, I saw Arissa walking across the courtyard and thought about talking to her again, thinking I could finally get through to her and explain what I had been doing at night, but I stopped myself.

She won't care, and if anything, she will hate me more for it.

Instead, I turned my attention to the hundreds of students gathered at the edge of the Academy for a funeral for Mark of Team #1. His body was marched through the center of campus in a levitating, closed casket, and I heard from other Heroes that his face was so unrecognizable and torn apart, they decided not to hold an open casket service for him.

As I stood in the crowd, it occurred to me that this was the first death of a Hero since I had been here. I saw death on a daily basis, and it didn't seem to faze me anymore, but this one was *different*.

All the Rogues I neutralized weren't people: they were enemies of the Academy and nothing more. Mark was someone I had seen walking around campus and heard so much about—one of the best at the Academy who had died on a routine mission—and his death made what we were doing here suddenly feel so real, like it could be any one of us in that casket.

The Headmaster took the stage and made his way to a podium in the center. He cleared his throat and raised the microphone to his mouth.

"Heroes of the Academy, today we are gathered here to honor one of our own who has fallen. Mark of Team #1 exemplified the Academy's values of strength, order, and peace, and he worked hard to uphold them every day. He always took his training and mission prep seriously and was a remarkable teammate. While fighting the evil and terrible Rogues who threaten this planet with their recklessness and selfishness, he laid down his life and made the ultimate sacrifice. He will be greatly missed by those who live on in his honor."

A few of his teammates at the front of the crowd began crying at the sound of this.

"One way or another, I still believe that *all* Heroes of

the Academy make it to Gidoria—even in death, as we carry his memory within each of us to the great place that comes next."

I looked up to the sky and pictured Mark's soul flying through space, heading to the Golden planet that lay somewhere out there among the stars.

"Goodbye, Hero Mark of Team #1, and thank you for everything you did to protect this planet and its people. You will never be forgotten."

We watched as the casket levitated through the crowd and made its way to the edge of the Academy. The force field opened, and the casket floated out into the open sea and ignited into a fiery blaze: *a Hero's farewell.*

We all joined in unison and said,

"High above the sea lies a Golden Hero's dream!
Together and forever, we stand as one team!
One team!
We fight for the Academy!
Never in battle shall we fall,
for we rise and crush them all!
Warriors unite!
Warriors unite!
To Gidoria, we go and fight!"

• • •

After the funeral, Theo and I sat on the steps in front of the building that held The Wall. I looked across the Academy filled with Heroes walking and milling about. A warm breeze moved through the campus, and the evening sun hung in the distance, casting a golden glow across the water.

"Remember your first day at the Academy?" Theo asked.

"When you were showing me around? Yeah, good times," I replied.

"Man, that feels like forever ago, doesn't it? I feel like so much has changed since then."

"What do you mean?"

"Well, I guess I just mean that we have—*us*. Remember when you didn't even know what your powers were? Now look at you, flying around, taking people's heads off, neutralizing Rogues, doing all the hard work for us. It's just crazy to think about how far we've come since then."

"Yeah... it is crazy."

I must've had a sad look on my face because Theo immediately picked up on it.

"Shit, man. I'm sorry. I didn't mean to say it like that. It's just... you've become so powerful out of nowhere. I just feel like you are kind of leaving the rest of us in the dust—like you don't really need us anymore."

"Well, it's not like I wanted this to happen! It's not my fault the rest of my team hasn't grown with me! Every day and night I was learning new things, practicing, trying to better myself, and where were all of you guys? Huh? All those late nights in the Power Dome or in the Library of Alexandria? You were nowhere to be found! Oh that's right, because you were asleep." There was a long pause. "I spent so much time *alone*... and not once did you ever check on me. You all abandoned me."

"I didn't mean to upset you by bringing that up," he said as he looked at me. "And I didn't know you were going through—"

"Whatever man. I don't care anymore. I'm going to get us to the Golden planet because I made that promise from the start, but once I'm there and become Champion of Gidoria, I hope I never see you again!" I yelled at him before taking off into the building.

The Wall towered over me, and I saw our team's points just below the cut off to graduate. After Mark's death, Team #1 had barely fallen *out* of the graduating teams, which I couldn't believe. I assumed the death of a Hero on your team would knock you down substantially, but I just never thought I would live to see this day. I had brought us off the bottom, and we were now so damn close to making it to Gidoria. All we needed was a final push.

• • •

The metallic silver ship flew silently through the sky as I sat alone at the controls, thinking about my earlier conversation with Theo. I knew I had overreacted, and I felt terrible for saying what I had said to him because he was right: I *had* grown distant from the team, and I felt it since the first mission. I never told anyone that because I didn't think it mattered. I didn't think anyone even cared because no one checked on me, and even if they had, I wouldn't have wanted to burden them by telling them how terrible I was feeling. It wasn't as if they could have fixed my problems anyway.

When I first came to the Academy, we were taught to use teamwork to get points and accomplish our missions, but as time went on, that part didn't really seem to matter anymore. In fact, the team was awarded more points the more *I* did, as if it were encouraged.

Headmaster Fowler never seemed to care that I took matters into my own hands, and, if anything, he only became prouder of me—trusting me with greater responsibility as I began to take complete control of the missions, becoming a one-man army. I didn't need anyone else because all they did was slow me down.

When I did go on the rare mission with them, they would cause collateral damage because of stupid mistakes they were making that they were never learning from. But when I caused it, it was different. Headmaster Fowler would tell me that collateral damage was the only way to get the job done, and I believed him. Still, I couldn't help but feel slightly guilty because of this, and my special and preferential treatment was obvious to my teammates.

And how could they not *notice?*

The Headmaster didn't exactly try to hide it, and no one else got called to his chamber to speak with him as much as I did—not even Jayson, who I thought was the literal *golden child* of the Academy.

The thing was, I knew we wouldn't have had any chance of making it to Gidoria without me taking control. I was the most disciplined one, I trained the hardest, and I never hesitated when it came to neutralizing the enemy. I couldn't say the same for the rest of my team. They always seemed to feel as if they were doing something wrong. No wonder they were at the bottom of The Wall before I showed up; they were *useless*.

"You have arrived at your mission zone," the operator reported, bringing me out of my thoughts.

"Powers on!" I yelled to the empty ship. I still did it everytime, but it never felt right not hearing it come from Ezra.

BEEP!

"Inhibitor Chip disabled," the operator said as I walked to the drop zone of the ship. "You are clear to engage the targets."

"Good luck out there, Kaden. I will be personally watching this mission for the Hero of Earth evaluation. Do not let me down," the Headmaster said over my earpiece.

No pressure right?

And with that, I dropped out of the ship and into the dark sky. I fell toward the Earth, flipping and spinning as I soared through the air. It had taken a while, but now I was used to being the only one doing tricks in the sky.

In the early days of these solo missions, I always landed and looked around for my teammates, and I would almost call out for a portal from Arissa before catching my words—a habit that took a long time to shake.

It doesn't matter, I'm better off without them, I tried telling myself, but I was never able to get past the feeling that something was missing.

Regardless, I couldn't get it back in this moment, so all I could do was focus on the mission at hand. I looked around at my dark surroundings and realized that I was somewhere outside of Tuscany in an area of rolling Italian hills filled with vineyards.

"The DGC has located Class 1 and 2 Rogues inside the villa. Stay alert."

I landed at the front door of the large villa that sat atop a hill. It had barrel clay tiles on the roof and a tan exterior. Drapes flapped softly in the open windows, and as I looked at it, I thought about how I always dreamed of spending some time in Italy but never like *this*.

The door to the villa creaked open as I pushed through, and I saw a fireplace in the center of the room that crackled and dimly lit the interior.

"Ah, I was wondering when you'd finally show up," an

older man in a leather chair said while closing a book and placing it in his lap.

My hands shot up and glowed with energy, turning the room red and forcing the man to cover his eyes from the bright light.

"So, you're the one I've been hearing about—the *Red Demon*," he chuckled.

"What are you talking about?" I responded.

"I must say, your powers give it away quite easily."

"Enough with the games, where are the Rogues!" I bluntly yelled.

"Oh, the *other* will be here shortly, especially once he knows you've arrived, but please relax a little bit; there's no need for anger—not now at least. Soon enough, you will get to do what you came here for, but before then, would you allow me to enjoy this last glass of wine?" He didn't wait for me to respond. He downed it, which was followed by an, "*Ahhhh.*"

"The DGC told me there would be *two* here. Are you hiding enemies of The Unity?"

"What do you mean?"

"You're not one of the Rogues I'm looking for. You're just a man," I said in a puzzled tone.

"Oh, but aren't we *all?* Indeed I am the 'Rogue' you are looking for. I am a Golden, but just a *man* all the same," he said as he got up and stoked the fire with an iron poker. "Not a god nor a deity as some Goldens might think of themselves—no, none of that; just a simple *man.* How could you blame the ones who think as such? Just par for the course when they gave god-like powers to mere mortals."

"What's your power then, because I can't see it, and

you've got about two seconds to explain yourself before I take you down with the others."

"Oh no, no. Power?" he said with a scoff. "I possess no such thing as *power*. The only thing that may set me apart from my fellow man is the ability to process and retain information at a faster rate. Sure I have a few PhD's, I've written dozens of books, and even recieved a Nobel Peace Prize; would you believe it? No, of course you wouldn't, because such a crime as that deserves death, according to you and your *enlightened* ones.

"Of course, I achieved all of that before they found out my true nature, and when I learned that they were coming for me, I fled to this lovely place, and I have been hiding here ever since, waiting in fear for this day to come. And you know what? Now that it's finally here, I'm not afraid anymore—not nearly as afraid as I thought I would be. Thankfully, I have made my peace, and that is why I've told my son to wait until I am gone before fighting you since I cannot live to see another ounce of Golden blood shed over such a silly conflict—*his* in particular. My poor son does not believe it, but you would kill him, as you have killed far more powerful men than he. I hope one day you will understand my words, but for now, how about we get it over with, shall—"

A red flash filled the room, and he was gone. All his memories, feelings, and emotions reduced to a pile of dust on the floor where he would forever remain. His voice was immediately replaced by a silence that hung in the air for a long moment.

"Dad?" a young man finally cried out from behind the wall. "Dad!" he yelled louder, but he was never going to get a response.

The wall leading into the other room blew open, and a teenager slightly older than I flew through it. He grabbed me, and we crashed through another wall before we were sent flying through the air. I managed to make a shield around me just before we crashed through another building, emerging on the other side of it.

We nose dived into the ground, and my body smashed through fences, tractors, farmhouses and everything I could possibly hit on a farm, until we went straight underground. He punched me as we went down, further and further, but I never fought back; I just stayed focused on the strength my shield, knowing I would soon have to complete my mission, one way or another.

I felt his pain, sorrow, and anger of losing his father with each punch that connected with my face. What his father had said to me echoed in my mind as he delivered blow after blow.

I hope, one day, you will understand my words.

We broke out of the ground once more and shot into the sky. He continued to hold on to me, punching me with tears streaking down his face. My shield was shattering, and pieces were flying off in every direction. I knew I couldn't keep this up for much longer. He was far too strong for me to be his punching bag forever, but at the same time, no part of me wanted to fight back against him. I *wanted* the punches that came to me, knowing I deserved every last one of them.

"You killed my father! How many more of your own will you kill before you finally stop!" he cried out.

I felt my eyes starting to smoke and saw the same look of fear that had previously appeared on Arissa's face.

"*The Red Demon...*" he muttered out as we collided with a mountain and sailed straight through it.

The end of *all* of this was near, and as we emerged from the other side of the mountain, I grabbed hold of his body.

"Neutralize the Rogue," Headmaster Fowler said over my earpiece as I looked into the Rogue's fearful eyes and saw that he knew what was coming next. He didn't fight back.

"I'm..." my voice choked up, "I'm sorry!" I finally yelled.

We took off into the sky and headed for the stars at supersonic speed. We burst through the clouds and kept going toward the black void of space where I saw the sun rising in the distance and the curvature of the Earth growing—a height I had never reached before. I looked in front of me and saw frost and icicles forming on his face while his body began freezing solid within my grip.

"Did... he... suffer..." he barely let out.

I gritted my teeth in anguish and whispered, "*No.*"

A tear froze on his face as I watched him close his eyes, his last cold breath leaving him.

"Well done, K... K... a...a..." the Headmaster's voice started breaking up as I was traveling beyond the transmission range. "Re... return... t...to..." It disconnected and was replaced by static.

I didn't know what I was doing or where I was going, but I kept flying. The glowing red shield I had formed around me kept me warm and breathing, but I didn't know how long that would last. I exited the Earth's atmosphere and filled his body with energy, disintegrating him as I watched golden ash drift off into the dark void, joining the stars. Seeing it from up here, the planet looked so beautiful; something I thought I'd never experience.

The pale blue dot.

The stars of the galaxy painted a mosaic in the distance—

Gidoria somewhere out there among them. As I started to lose focus, I felt my shield cracking, and I decided to extend my arms, releasing myself to the void. I closed my eyes and drifted away into the endless universe.

CHAPTER FIFTEEN

HERO OF EARTH

I AWOKE ON THE floor of my ship, gasping for air.

"Kaden? *Kaden!*" the Headmaster cried out over the intercom in a tone I had never heard from him before.

I held my throat, trying to catch my breath. I was freezing and tired as if my life force had been drained out of me. I focused, pulling the energy from the well inside me and re-energized, which brought me to myself again.

"What the hell were you thinking, my boy!"

"I was… completing the mission," I muttered.

"There are better ways to accomplish that without nearly dying! I almost lost you…" he said as his voice choked up. "The second we saw you leaving the atmosphere, we sent the ship up to get you, and thankfully we acted fast as it arrived moments after your shield cracked and dissolved. You were exposed to the vacuum of space for two minutes, and I'm not sure how you survived unharmed, but that's a question for another time," he said.

Two minutes? I don't know how I did either, because I definitely didn't keep myself alive, I thought.

"Since you've been thawing out, you've been on a direct flight path back to the Academy. Do not speak of what the Class 1 Rogue said to you. Is that understood?" I didn't say anything. "IS THAT UNDERSTOOD!"

"Yes, Headmaster Fowler, I understand," and with that I was once again alone in the ship.

• • •

The months at the Academy that followed that last mission were painful and isolating. I started losing motivation for everything, and each day seemed like a chore to get through. I never slept, not *once,* and even with the ability to re-energize myself, nothing seemed to get rid of the constant fatigue and apathy that loomed over me. I started to feel as if I were in a dream; each day was just a lifeless repeat of the last with no way to differentiate between them.

I would read or train all night instead of sleeping, and in the morning, I would head to the cafeteria to eat. A robot would deliver my food, and I ate alone, *always.* I would sometimes see my old teammates walk in, give me a side eye, and sit down on the opposite end of the cafeteria without saying a word to me. I heard them laughing and telling stories, but I never had the courage to join them— not like they wanted me to anyway.

I said "old" teammates because we had not been on a mission together since just before Mark's funeral—after I had killed those kids. I hadn't even spoken to anyone since the day I blew up at Theo, and the only social interactions I had came from Rogues begging me not to kill them before I did. Besides those rare occurrences, the only other place I ever talked to anyone was privately with the Headmaster in his chamber.

During this time, I still went on missions, but they were few and far between. Earth was nearing one full year of uninterrupted world peace, and it became harder and harder to find any more Rogues to neutralize. I wondered if they were going extinct because I had killed so many, but I knew the war against them would never truly be over since more were being born and Awakening every day.

We actually gained a lot of new Heroes during this time—more than any other time in the history of the Academy. The DGC was finding them quicker than ever before, and hundreds were being invited here every month. Headmaster Fowler had told me about a place called the Sanctuary where Goldens used to be taken against their will by Zahavi, but it seemed as if the competition between him and the Academy to find newly Awakened Goldens had all but ended.

When I wasn't on a mission, I continued to spend my time reading—and oftentimes re-reading—the scroll I had *borrowed* from the Headmaster's chamber since it was the most interesting one. It described the Great Gidorian War that was taking place on the Golden planet between the evil Royal Gidorian Family and the mighty and strong Generals of the Zaelzan Empire.

Of course, Headmaster Fowler—the former Champion of Gidoria—was front and center of every story, leading his brothers and uncles in battles around the planet, gaining new territory and killing Royal Gidorians as they went. I read the stories over and over again, trying to picture myself as Champion of Gidoria, but I just couldn't, as it never seemed right to me. That wasn't who I was, and I couldn't see myself in that role—leading those alien armies—no matter how much I tried to force it. It was hard for me to accept, but with each re-read, it only became clearer that that *wasn't* me.

One day, I was out on a mission and had just finished

hearing a Rogue plead for his life before I neutralized him, when I realized that I was in the city where I grew up. The streets were familiar, the buildings were instantly recognizable, and I saw that my old apartment was only a few blocks away.

I couldn't help myself from going back to it even though every instinct I had was telling me I would be punished severely for it. Yet, I felt as if I was losing my mind, and I probably wouldn't last much longer at the Academy anyway.

I have to go home.

The only person in the world that could help me was my mother. She would set me on the right path and help me deal with how I was feeling about everything that had happened on the missions so far. I would finally be excited for graduation to Gidoria again and come to terms with the idea of one day being the *Champion.*

I knew doing this was breaking every rule in the book, and it would land me in some pretty deep shit with the Headmaster when I got back—keeping me from graduating or potentially being expelled...

But, I don't care, I just want to see my mom.

I waited until the surveillance drones had flown back toward the ship before flying straight over to my old apartment. The first thing I noticed was that the blue tarp was still flapping in the wind like it had been the day I left. My heart began to race, and my eyes filled with tears.

"Mom!" I called out as I burst through the tarp, *"I'm home!"* But the apartment was *empty.* It had been completely gutted, and nothing I remembered remained.

It was virtually unrecognizable, and for a second, I even wondered if I was in the right apartment, but the familiar marks on the floor that the wheels of my mother's oxygen tank had left told me that this was it. I started to panic, wondering where my mother was, and if she was OK.

"Mom! Where are you!" I frantically called out again.

Silence.

Seeing my old home like this broke my heart, and the living room where we used to sit on the couch and watch Christmas movies now sat empty and desolate. The table where I had my last birthday was also gone and nowhere to be found. My mother's bedroom—the place a young child felt safest in a world full of chaos and Goldens—was now completely bare. As I looked around the apartment, a terrible feeling washed over me as I realized: *I no longer had a home.*

"Your mission is complete. Report back to the Academy, *immediately*," an operator demanded… "When you return, meet Headmaster Fowler in his chamber."

My eyes squeezed shut as I clenched my teeth and banged my fist hard against the wall, smashing through it. The entire apartment shook, and a ceiling tile dropped down, revealing a yellow crystal necklace that my mother always used to wear. I picked it up and blew off the dust, remembering how much it had meant to her. She had probably put it in the ceiling for safe keeping as we didn't live in the best part of town. I held it up to the sun, and a beam of light shone through the crystal making it *glow*. I tucked it underneath the chest plate of my armor before walking to the edge of the opening in the wall. The tarp flapped in the wind next to me, and effortlessly, I floated into the air and took off into the sky.

• • •

Headmaster Fowler sat in his chamber reading a book. I

knocked on the large door and peered in.

"Ah, Kaden, my boy. Come in, come in," he said, waving me over as I took my seat in front of him. "I must say, you have been doing exceptionally well on your missions these past few months."

"Thank you, Headmaster."

"And have you still been reading?"

"Of course," I replied.

One of the only things I could do here.

"How have you liked my stories from Gidoria?"

My stomach dropped, and my heartbeat picked up.

I tried playing dumb and said, "What stories? If they're in the library, I haven't found them yet. That does sound really interesting though—"

"Kaden, I want you to be honest with me. Have you enjoyed reading through the scroll that you took from my study?" he asked again.

"How did you..." my voice trailed off as I tried to think about how he would've known.

Laser tripwire? Motion detectors? Pressure sensors? Cameras?

"Funnily enough, I discovered it was missing when I went to read it myself. The stories that it holds are some of my favorites, so you can imagine my fear and shock when I noticed it was gone. Had I misplaced it? No, not possible, as I never move it from my study. I was very worried, as I couldn't bear to lose it, but then I thought to myself: who do I know who is a curious person by nature and an avid reader who would want to take a dusty old scroll? Then it *clicked,* and there was only one person who fit the bill," he said, staring intently at me.

"Headmaster, I'm sorry. I don't know what to say. I got here early one day and was looking through some of your books on the shelf when I accidentally pulled the one that opened the door to your study. I shouldn't have gone in or taken your scroll, but I just couldn't help myself. I *had* to read it," I pleaded.

"You worry far too much, my boy."

"You're not mad?"

"Now why would I be? Did I not already tell you that what is mine is yours?"

"Yes sir, you did."

"And have I *ever* lied to you?"

"No sir."

"Then you should already know that you're not in any trouble at all."

A massive weight was lifted off my shoulders, and I could finally breathe again.

"As a matter of fact, how about we go down there together?"

"Right now?" I asked in disbelief.

Headmaster Fowler nodded, stood up from his seat, and signaled me to follow him. Going down into a creepy dungeon with Headmaster Fowler was not something I expected to do today.

What's the worst that could happen?

At this point, I didn't have anything to lose, so I said, "Sure," and followed him over to the book shelf. He pulled a book in the middle of the shelf, and the large door swung open toward us.

We passed through it and descended the staircase into what he called his "study," but I still felt like the name "dungeon" fit better. The purple amethyst crystals lit up as we passed them, finally entering the large crystal cavern.

"Why all the crystals?" I asked.

"It reminds me of a *special* place on Gidoria. You will understand soon enough when you see it."

I saw a touchscreen with a radar dish attached to the top of it, sitting on a desk.

"What's that over there?" I asked.

"A communicator."

"Who does it communicate with?"

"I've never used it, so does it matter?"

I shrugged and continued on through the study, seeing the same set of damaged, white and gold armor from before with a massive hole in the center of the chest plate.

"Where'd you get this?" I asked, pointing toward it. "No way anyone who had been wearing it could have survived a hit *that* big."

I ran my fingers across the raised gold engravings before trying to lift the armor off the rack of wood, but it felt like a million pounds, and I actually thought it was. Headmaster Fowler walked over to it and casually picked it up with one hand. I caught my jaw before it dropped too low and tried to hide my reaction.

"Ah, this old thing," he said, inspecting the broken and mangled metal. He placed it over himself and fed his arms through the shoulder pieces. "I probably wouldn't be here right now without it."

"Wait, *you* wore that?"

"Of course I did. I wasn't able to put up much of a fight against the great beast who damaged it, but I owe my life to it," he responded.

"What is it?"

"Zaelzan Battle Armor."

"'Zale-Zahn'? I was wondering how you pronounced it. I read about the Zaelzans in that scroll. Who are they?"

"Your thirst for knowledge can never be quenched it seems," he said with a chuckle.

"I'm sorry, I just can't help it. Anytime I hear about something that I don't know, I have to learn about it. It's like an itch that never goes away until I do, and then another question forms in its place."

"There are worse things to be addicted to than knowledge, my boy. As for the Zaelzans, they are my family, and the ones who make up the intergalactic Zaelzan Empire. This armor was crafted by the Dwarves of Azarath in the Forge of the Core."

Dwarves are real? Whoa.

"It's not like I *need* it anyway, but it is bestowed to any and every Champion of Gidoria as a ceremonial right of passage. Since I see you one day wearing a set of your own, how about you try it on?"

"But isn't it *yours?* I feel like that wouldn't be right to wear it."

"Nonsense. This is no longer mine, as it now belongs to the battlefield. Truthfully, I should've buried it out there after the damage occurred, but it holds too many memories from commanding the war."

"The Earth Civil War, First Golden War, or Great Gidorian War?"

Headmaster Fowler smiled and said, "You are quite intuitive, my boy. No one can deny that."

"Well, which one?"

"All of them." My eyes grew wide. "Now, *that* armor over there is one you cannot wear." I looked over at the other armor set, the purple crystals reflecting off the breastplate.

"Did you get that from the Dwarves as well?"

"Indeed. All Champions receive two sets in case *that*

happens," signaling to the hole. "Now, if I damage the second set, we will have a problem," he said which made me laugh.

Before I could realize what was happening, he raised the damaged armor above my head.

"Wait!"

My head easily slipped through the head hole for the chest plate, and my arms felt like toothpicks in it, which of course they were. He held it lightly over my body so that it didn't crush me.

"I can already see the ceremony now, Kaden. I cannot wait to be there when you get your own," he said as he slowly started to hold less and less of it. The weight pushed down on top of me like a heavy squat, crushing my spine underneath it.

"Headmaster, I can't…" I barely mumbled, trying to fight through the pain.

"Yes you *can*. Zo, disable Kaden's inhibitor chip," he called out.

BEEP!

The familiar noise of my powers coming back to me sounded from my neck.

"Focus your energy, Kaden," he said in a stern voice. I tried to, but my legs began to buckle under the weight. It felt like my entire spine began to crack and break away as more weight came down. "Use it to strengthen yourself to carry it atop your shoulders!"

"No, it's too much! Take it off!" I yelled, nearly screaming at this point.

"Focus! Or I will drop the full weight and crush you!" he yelled back. Smoke began to pour from my eyes.

"I… said… *TAKE IT OFF!*"

A beam of energy shot out from my hands and collided with him, sending him skidding backward across the study. I faced him as my eyes plumed red energy and smoke while I breathed heavily. I wanted to blast him again for hurting me like that, but I watched as a twisted smile formed on his face.

"There you are," he said, raising his arms out in front of him. "The future *Champion of Gidoria*."

I saw myself in a mirror glowing bright red, wearing the armor without any strain on my body. In fact, it felt weightless. I wanted to rip his stupid armor off and throw it at him, but I kept staring at myself in the mirror and loved what I saw because... I felt *powerful*.

"Wearing that armor is no easy feat, my boy. Many men before you have tried, and it cost them their lives, but *you*..." he said as he looked at me, "were born to wear it as it is your destiny."

My destiny?

I pulled the armor off and placed it back on the rack as the light slowly faded from my eyes and a tired feeling grew over me.

"Headmaster Fowler, I have to tell you something, and you have to promise me you won't get angry," I said as I looked up at him.

"I promise to hear you out before I react," he said with a nod.

I took a deep breath and said, "I went by my apartment while out on my mission today, hoping to find my mom." Fowler's brow furrowed as I took a seat on a nearby chair. "I know you said we weren't allowed to speak with our families, but ever since everything happened with my team and Arissa, I've felt so lost and *alone*, as if I've been losing my mind." I had to fight back tears to get through the rest. "I just wanted to talk to her, because I knew she would tell me what I needed to hear—to help me climb out of this hole that I feel trapped in."

"Are you still feeling this way?"

"I *was*… up until I put on your Battle Armor," I explained.

He pondered this and nodded, before a worried look appeared on his face.

"Did you *find* anything while you were there?" he asked.

I thought about it for a second, feeling the crystal necklace against my skin hidden underneath my shirt, and said, "*No*. The whole place was empty."

"Well… that would make sense."

"Why?"

"Your mother said she was moving somewhere safer away from a Rogue hotspot like your old city was. The DGC agreed to cover the cost of the relocation since her part of the building was heavily damaged in that Rogue attack a year ago. From what I understand, the building wasn't safe to live in any longer, and she had no choice."

"Really? You talked to her?"

He hesitated and replied, "Of course, many times."

"Please, Headmaster Fowler, I don't ask for much. Is there any way I could talk to her?" I pleaded.

He ran his fingers through his beard and paced around the room.

"That's all I want! *Please!*"

Finally, he said, "Of course, my boy."

"Really!" I jumped up and hugged him and said, "Thank you! Headmaster, thank you!"

"On one condition," he said, interrupting my celebration. "There is something I need from you first. As you know, the deadline for graduation to Gidoria as a Warrior is coming up, and although you have made considerable progress on your independent missions, you are still *not* past the graduation threshold. And don't worry, I made sure that every last point went to your old team as you requested."

"*Thank you,*" I said with relief.

"Unfortunately, Team #1 is in the same predicament, and as you already know, only a certain number of teams can graduate to Gidoria every year. Something big is coming—I can feel it. We are on the precipice of finally winning the Second Golden War. I know you've seen it and felt it, as it has been harder than ever to find Rogues to neutralize, and it seems that our enemy has all but given up at this point."

"*Zahavi...*" I said as I balled up my fists.

"Yes," he said with a wide smile. "I am very close to finding the location of the illegal Rogue Sanctuary, and when I do, we will launch a full scale attack." He looked deep into my eyes. "I need *you* to lead it, Kaden."

The words repeated in my head, and my heartbeat picked up again.

"You want *me* to lead the final attack on the Sanctuary?"

"Yes, who else here possibly could? I wouldn't trust anyone else with such a role, and if you succeed, you will be able to speak to your mother and graduate at the top of your class, sending you well on your way to Gidoria to become the Champion."

I couldn't believe what I was hearing. He wanted me— Kaden Collins, who only Awakened a year ago—to end the Second Golden War, once and for all. My heart raced faster as my mind filled with worry.

"What if I'm not ready to lead the Academy's Heroes?" I asked.

The Headmaster just shook his head and laughed to himself. He looked over at the armor on the rack as my eyes followed.

"*That* just told me everything I needed to know, Kaden."

I looked at my reflection in the armor and pictured myself leading our Heroes to victory.

I gave the Headmaster another big hug, and although I never had a father, Headmaster Fowler felt like the closest thing I would ever get to one.

I started to head up the stairs, but Headmaster Fowler called out, "Oh, Kaden, I almost forgot," he said as he lifted a cover from a silver platter, revealing a birthday cake. "Happy Birthday, my boy." He patted me on the back as I blew out my big #1 and #7 candles. We each took a piece with a fork and made a toast.

"To the *newest* Hero of Earth and *future* Champion of Gidoria."

CHAPTER SIXTEEN

THE FINAL VISION

HEADMASTER FOWLER WATCHED as a shadow moved across the floor of his study.

"I was wondering when you would return," he called out to the shadow as he finished cleaning up the cake. He placed the silver cover on the platter, sealing the remnants of the cake inside. He wiped his hands on his toga as the cloaked woman rose from the shadow and stared at him.

"Is there no such thing as privacy where you're from?"

"You must appear before the High Lords, immediately," she said.

"So be it," the Headmaster said with a sigh, walking over to her. "Let's get on with it then."

The cloaked woman grabbed him and *focused*. Their eyes went black, and the study fell silent as they dropped into the shadows and disappeared.

• • •

Dark gray storms swirled overhead, rustling the leaves of the tall trees that surrounded the stone castle. A flash of lightning lit up the sky as flying creatures infected with black blights roared out into the night. Inside the castle, a shadow swept across the floor. Headmaster Fowler and the cloaked woman emerged from it and found themselves in the oversized living room of the giant High Lords. Headmaster Fowler grabbed the edge of a table, attempting to steady himself.

"How do you do that with such ease? I can't even see in there," he said as he shook his head, trying to get rid of the nausea that persisted.

"Only the unworthy see it as darkness. To the worthy, it is merely a path to our destinations," she said. "The High Lords are waiting," and with that she was gone.

The Headmaster looked around at the room filled with oversized chairs, tables, and books. He had been in this castle many times before and always seemed to leave with bad news. The visions were never aligned, and one of the High Lords always seemed to disagree with the others. But when all of them agreed on the same vision, that was a time to worry as it indicated that the prophecy they had foreseen was set in stone.

When the Headmaster first arrived on Earth, the High Lords had given him a split vision: two saw him succeeding and two saw him dying in his conquest of the planet. He secretly knew that his exile was meant to be a death sentence, and it would only come true *if* he did not succeed.

As the wars continued, the shadow woman brought him back here, time and time again. Their visions constantly changed: three High Lords would see his victory; one would see his demise. One would see his victory; three would see his demise. He came close to dying many times during the wars, but he always managed to find the strength to keep going, and even the Headmaster himself didn't fully know how he did it.

The High Lords went back and forth with their visions

for two hundred years before he finally conquered the planet, ended the First Golden War, and founded the Golden Academy. Through sheer will and determination, Headmaster Fowler had prevented his death prophecy from coming to fruition.

When he finally returned to them with news of his victory on Earth, they *rewarded* him with a unanimous vision of his ultimate fate: even though he had survived, all four still saw his eventual death in battle during the Great Gidorian War.

"We have all foreseen the same vision, Headmaster Fowler. There is no changing it now," High Lord Ristottem said.

"What if," Headmaster Fowler gritted his teeth and said, "the visions you speak of were *wrong*."

High Lord Risottem banged his fist on his throne, shaking the entire room.

"Sacrilege of the highest order!" he called out as he pointed a giant finger at the Headmaster. "You dare speak against the High Lords' visions—the prophecies of the Infinity Tree! If it were up to me, I would kill you for speaking as such."

"In the 600 years that we have been on Gidoria, when all four visions align, we have never been wrong," High Lord Avan said. "The prophecies of death weigh greatly on the shoulders of the foretold—a burden they shall carry for the rest of their lives. This is the price one must pay for a glimpse into the future."

"I am a Zaelzan with the power of the Core. I thought I was now immortal? Should I not live forever?"

The High Lords looked at each other and shook their heads in disappointment.

"You may now be immortal, Fowler, but as much as you

believe otherwise, you are not invincible. Your death in battle is inexorable."

Headmaster Fowler shook the memories out of his head and found himself standing in front of the Doors of Judgement. He placed his hands on the smooth stone and mustered up the courage to enter. His muscles flexed as the doors groaned and rumbled before opening.

Only those who were strong enough to open them were deemed worthy of carrying the heavy burden of prophecy until the end of time.

"Fowler Zaelzan of the first blood, Headmaster of the Golden Academy... welcome," High Lord Ristottem's voice shook the room.

"High Lords Ristottem, Avan, Orion, and Thedeus, thank you for giving me the honor to be among you."

"We bring you good news, Headmaster," High Lord Thedeus called out.

The words took immense weight off of his shoulders as he breathed a sigh of relief.

"Never in all of my years would I expect to hear something such as that," Headmaster Fowler said, which made the High Lords smile.

"Moments ago, Avan's vision aligned with the visions of Thedeus and Orion, signifying a near guarantee of victory in the Great War for the Empire. Mine has still not changed, making it now a three-to-one alignment."

"That is wonderful news, High Lords."

"The Zaelzan Empire has been very pleased with your delicate handling of the prophesied boy so far, and if he is even half as powerful as we have foreseen, I can imagine it has been no easy task to tame him. With the third vision finally aligning, Emperor Ozul has personally requested to speak with you," High Lord Ristottem said with a nod.

The Headmaster froze, wondering if he had heard him correctly.

"My fa-" he stopped, unable to bring himself to call him that name after the same man had exiled him. "Emperor Ozul would like to speak with me?" he asked, his voice quavering.

They all nodded in unison as a shadow crept across the room behind the Headmaster.

"The third vision aligning means we are nearing a guaranteed victory, but be forewarned, Headmaster Fowler, it still does not mean that the vision is fully aligned. Your job with the Red Demon and exile on Earth is not yet finished. Do not fail the Empire when you are so close to restoring your honor."

"I will not, I promise you, I will not," he said as he bowed before them. "When do I speak with him?"

The cloaked woman rose from the shadow and grabbed the Headmaster.

"Now."

Their eyes went black, and they disappeared into the shadows.

CHAPTER SEVENTEEN

THE GOLDEN PLANET

H EADMASTER FOWLER ROSE from a shadow and collapsed forward onto a soft gold carpet. He pressed his face into it to take a long sniff and immediately recognized where he was: *home*.

He heard a voice before him, "Thank you for retrieving him, Thorne. I will call for you when we are finished here."

Thorne bowed behind the Headmaster and disappeared into the shadow beneath her feet.

In the massive white and gold throne room, hundreds of shirtless Zaelzan Empire soldiers wearing gold gauntlets were organized into perfect rows on either side of him.

Headmaster Fowler's eyes tracked upward as he exhaled slowly, seeing a man's bare feet before him. He looked further, seeing gold rings on jagged knuckles and strong hands. Gold bracelets adorned his vascular forearms, and gold upper arm cuffs rested on biceps bigger than the Headmaster's head. A white toga that covered half of his incredibly muscular physique hung down between his legs and rested on the white marble floor beneath his feet. Eventually, Headmaster Fowler's eyes focused on an instantly recognizable face.

"Emperor Ozul…" Headmaster Fowler said, noticing that he had not aged a day during the three centuries that he had been gone. His face was bare, without a blemish, scar, or wrinkle tainting it. His curly, black hair sat perfectly atop his head.

"It is good to see you again, my dear Fowler," Emperor Ozul responded as he got up from his white marble throne. He reached out and felt the Headmaster's beard, rubbing the coarse hairs with his thumb and index finger. "It seems as if you could use a dip in the Pools of Rejuvenation, no doubt." Emperor Ozul looked at him intently. "You look tired, Fowler. Earth has not been kind to you, has it?"

"No, Emperor, no it has not," he said as pain grew on his face. A small tear ran parallel along a scar that traveled down his left cheek. His father wiped it away and smiled.

"A light punishment for what you did to your own brother," he said as he shook his head.

"Emperor Ozul, I—"

"Silence! This is no court to justify your actions. Not here, not now. What has been done is done, and the time for that has long since passed. All that is left for you now is to make things right."

"I understand."

"Walk with me," Emperor Ozul said, signaling Fowler to follow.

Ozul and Fowler moved through the sleek marble halls of the Zaelzan Tower before emerging onto a balcony that overlooked a utopian city. White and gold futuristic buildings with greenery intertwined stretched out as far as the eye could see. Goldens flew between the buildings and into the sky above them, carrying objects and building materials. Trains carrying citizens of the Empire floated silently around the edges of the city.

The city itself was built upon a large mesa, surrounded by a ring of beautiful pools of water. The pools formed into waterfalls that flowed endlessly off the edges to an unknown world below covered in mist. A golden sky sat above them, and a large planet loomed with a detached moon and twin suns to the right.

Fowler stared at all of this in complete and utter awe. Gidoria was even more beautiful than he remembered, and he wondered if he only felt this way as a result of the time he had spent on the hell hole that was Earth— surrounded by the vermin.

"As you can see, much has changed since you've been gone, my boy. The City of the Eternal Falls has been fully constructed now that the Royal Gidorians are no longer attacking it. Those wretched imbeciles..." Emperor Ozul shook his head with disgust. "The Royal Gidorian family has nearly been eradicated, and the planet is now under the control of the Zaelzan Empire. Gidoria is *thriving*— more so than it ever had in ten thousand years of their rule.

With the help of the Dwarves, construction is currently taking place, and we are building more and more advanced cities across the planet, bringing all the inhabitants up to speed with the greatest technology and medical care that the Empire can provide them. They have never been happier in all of Gidorian history!" he said while gazing across the city.

"Incredible, truly incredible. I wish I had been here to see this great transformation," Fowler said as he looked down in shame.

Emperor Ozul didn't seem to notice or care and said,

"They lived in squalor before we got here, Fowler. I call that *salvation*... but from what Thorne tells me, the Earth is also basking in the glory of the Zaelzan Empire, no?"

"Yes, it is, all thanks to the advancements the Empire has brought to it through the Academy. We crossed over a year of uninterrupted peace, the most the planet has ever seen since the Seeding—perhaps even in all of its history."

"That is truly remarkable. Maybe Gidoria could learn a thing or two from the planet you now call home."

"I assume that means the Great Gidorian War has not drawn to a close then?" Fowler asked.

Emperor Ozul looked into Fowler's eyes and grabbed him by the shoulder, feeling the immense strength of his father's grip.

"No, no it has not; however, we are winning!" Hearing those words made all of the years he had spent fighting and wasting away on that vile planet worth it. "And I believe that we are finally nearing the end of this great conflict that has claimed so many of our own."

"So it has, so it has; however, that is great to hear indeed. Perhaps we may find our own peace soon enough."

"Perhaps we shall, but, our victories thus far in the war would not have been possible without you and all you have done for us on Gidoria."

Fowler wondered if someone had replaced Emperor Ozul during his exile with someone more compassionate and caring.

"Thank you."

"I believe your exile has made you into a better man after all—just as the High Lords had foreseen. You have grown and matured much since we last talked. I barely even recognize you now. Look at you," he said as he ran his hands down Fowler's muscular arms. "The Earth, with its never-ending wars, made you *stronger*—the greatest gift a Zaelzan could ask for."

"It has, great Emperor, it has. I nearly gave up on myself, and I had very dark days alone on that planet. I didn't know if I had the strength to continue on and accomplish my mission, but I found it deep within me because I pictured this moment right here," Fowler said.

"But your job is not yet done, is it?"

"No, no it is not."

"Tell me about the Red Demon. How is he coming along?"

The Headmaster imagined Kaden fighting alongside the Zaelzans while wearing his own Champion of Gidoria Battle Armor.

"I believe I have found my successor, the next true Champion of Gidoria—the one who will kill the remaining Royal Gidorians and end the Great War, once and for all."

Emperor Ozul pondered this for a moment.

"Those are big promises that the High Lords have foreseen as well, but are *you* truly sure? You're the only one who has seen him since his Awakening. I can only dream of what he is like. He's strong, isn't he?" Emperor Ozul asked as he looked into the sky, picturing Kaden floating above him.

"Yes, Father, he is the strongest Hero at the Academy— maybe even the strongest Golden of *all*. I know he will fulfill the prophecy as, only hours ago, I witnessed something beautiful."

"What did you see?" Emperor Ozul asked, leaning in closer.

In his mind, Fowler saw Kaden standing tall in his Battle

Armor, eyes glowing bright red with power bleeding off of him.

"He wore my Battle Armor."

"He WHAT?!" Emperor Ozul shouted.

"My *damaged* Battle Armor," he corrected himself. Emperor Ozul calmed down after hearing this and nodded. "It should have killed him—crushed his pathetic, weak earthborn bones—but instead, he stood tall while wearing it with no sign of strain."

Emperor Ozul was nearly salivating while listening to this, and he stared in absolute fascination and astonishment.

"That is very good news, my boy, but there is another matter, isn't there?"

"Yes, the Royal Gidorian on *Earth,*"

Emperor Ozul's grip tightened on the gold railing, slowly crushing it within his palms as he said, "I thought you killed him…"

"As did I, but he survived our battle and has been in hiding for the past 100 years. He has only recently shown himself, threatening my Academy and our operation every day."

"Have you done anything to stop him?"

"Of course, I have done everything in my power. My Heroes have hunted his allies to near extinction, but we have still been unable to find him thus far. I believe we are closing in after capturing one of his own. We are now torturing the location of Zahavi out of him."

"Ah, the Zaelzan way, you learned from the best," Emperor Ozul said as he patted Fowler on the back, making him wince. "When you find him, I want you to kill him and burn his home to the ground, leaving nothing remaining but ash. We cannot afford to have any loose ends with the Red Demon prophecy.

"When that is complete, bring him to me immediately. He will start his training to become the Champion of Gidoria here under my personal supervision. Once he is ready, we will begin our final assault on the last Royal Gidorians and Heaven, eliminating them once and for all. If you succeed at both of these things, then I shall sanctify you and remove you from your duties on Earth, effectively ending your exile and allowing you to return home."

Through the boy, Fowler had a chance to set things right with the Zaelzan Empire, to find his successor for the Champion of Gidoria, and subsequently end his exile. He knew what was at stake here, and he couldn't let anything or anyone stop him, especially not Zahavi.

"I will not fail you, *Father.*"

"No, no, you will not, my *child.*" Emperor Ozul whistled, and a shadow washed over Fowler, casting him in darkness.

CHAPTER EIGHTEEN

CEREMONY FOR THE HERO

THROUGHOUT HIS ENTIRE life, Jayson had never felt what it was like to not be in first place. He had always been told he was the best—the greatest Hero that the Academy had ever seen.

All Jayson could remember when he thought back to his childhood was the Academy. He had begun his training and mission prep, been assigned to a Team, and neutralized his first Rogue earlier than any other Hero in its history. His team only consisted of four Heroes instead of the standard six, as anyone more than that just got in his way.

For many years, he led Team #1 as the top team at the Academy, even before it was his year to graduate. His mission IQ was top-notch, and his ability to follow orders and perform successful missions was unparalleled. He was the *perfect* Hero in the eyes of Zo and Headmaster Fowler, and Jayson was always reminded of that during their numerous conversations in the Headmaster's chamber.

Jayson had been well on his way to claiming the undisputed title of Hero of Earth, and once he graduated to the Golden planet as a Warrior, he would eventually be crowned Champion of Gidoria… until Kaden Collins showed up.

Jayson didn't know much about Kaden other than the fact that everything had changed since the day he first got there. The previously routine meetings with the Headmaster became less and less frequent, until months had passed since he had last spoken with him.

Jayson obsessively monitored The Wall and watched as Kaden slowly pulled his team up from the bottom, bringing them closer and closer to graduating as Warriors. Rumors had begun to spread around the Academy that Kaden started going on solo missions without his old team slowing him down—a privilege that only a few Heroes had ever been given since the Academy's founding, something Jayson had never been allowed to do despite his impeccable track record.

Jayson didn't know how or why, but his team started to falter and make more mistakes than ever before during this time. He could only summise that it had something to do with their first failure during their encounter with Zahavi. After that, they became sloppy and uncoordinated, ultimately resulting in the death of his former teammate Mark, who broke formation and impulsively engaged a dangerous Rogue alone. Team #1 had begun a downward spiral and slowly started to slip from the top spot on The Wall, point by point.

Jayson bottled up all of his anger and refused to blame anyone but himself for his team's shortcomings, but despite his perceived stoicism, Jayson didn't know how to handle failure. Internalizing his emotions and frustrations as he had been doing for the past few months was not good for his health, and he started to feel the effects of it.

Jayson was sleeping less and less, sometimes staying up

all night staring blankly at the wall of his room until the sun came up. In mission prep, the sound of the professor's voice was drowned out by a constant and never ending ringing that played loudly in his ears at all hours of the day.

His eyes become bloodshot, and he had a persistent nagging headache that he attempted to fix by pounding his head against any wall that he could find. He wasn't eating, and he was rapidly losing weight which made him feel even worse. His teammates worried about him, but he never told them what he was going through behind closed doors.

How could I? Who would follow a broken, lost, and hurting leader?

Even though they claimed they were there for him, he knew the second he showed weakness would be his last second as leader of Team #1. Losing that position would *surely* kill him.

Every day that passed, his mind slipped further and further from him as he descended into madness. He had lost all sense of time and purpose, and he found it increasingly harder to get out of bed in the morning.

Whenever he did find the motivation to get up and face the meaningless world, he would spend his time in the Power Dome punching a wall over and over and *over* again until his knuckles were black and blue and covered in blood. He dropped onto the floor and pressed his hands into his face, smearing the blood all over it while tearing out his hair and rocking back and forth.

His teammates didn't know how to help him when they found him like this—not even his professors. When they tried, he sent out a bolt of electricity, shocking them all while they screamed in pain. He only stopped once he no longer enjoyed watching them helplessly convulse on the floor.

Despite this, Jayson didn't seem to get in trouble for his actions since the Headmaster never called him to his chamber to reprimand or punish him for any of his terrible acts. It was almost like Headmaster Fowler was distracted by something or someone else, and he couldn't give a rat's ass about Jayson or what he was doing.

The only person who even seemed to pay attention to Jayson during this time was Zo, who would observe him silently in the Power Dome while pushing buttons on his touchscreen device. The further Jayson slipped into madness and delusion, the more Zo would mark down on his screen—perhaps noting the changes in his personality and actions.

• • •

Jayson stood in the crowd for the Hero of Earth ceremony which was held every year for the top Hero in the graduating class. His other teammates stood a few feet away from him, almost afraid of his presence. Jayson's bloodshot eyes peered out across the stage and watched as Kaden was called up to it.

Kaden rose from the crowd and took the stage, waving to the Heroes that stood before him. They cheered madly, pushing past each other in an attempt to get closer as he walked by. After all, he was a bit of a celebrity since he was the only Hero to pull a team off the bottom of The Wall while also achieving the record for collecting the most points in one year by any Hero or team. Everyone either wanted to be him or date him, but it didn't quite appear that he himself knew that.

Truthfully, he looked as tired and exhausted as Jayson did. His hair was disheveled, and he carried dark bags under his eyes as if he hadn't slept in days. When he finally made his way to the podium where Headmaster Fowler was standing, he looked across the crowd with a nervous stare as if he didn't want to be up there.

"Today, we honor the greatest Hero the Academy has ever seen," the Headmaster said as he nodded toward Kaden.

Jayson's eyes twitched at the sound of these words.

"Ever since Kaden Collins got here one year ago, the world has been a better place. He has shown all of us what it truly means to be a hero by upholding the Academy's values while proving himself to be a phenomenal leader to Team #22. When he first arrived, they were at the bottom of The Wall and are now only one spot away from graduating in the top half of the class as Warriors!"

The crowd erupted in cheers, but Jayson only continued to blankly stare without blinking as the sunlight burned his eyes.

"He is living proof of how you can achieve any goal at the Academy with enough hard work and discipline. It is my greatest honor to award Kaden Collins with the title, 'Hero of Earth' for his never-ending fight to protect and save this world." A statue draped in fabric was uncovered, revealing Kaden standing in his armored suit with his gauntlets crossed over each other. "Well done, *my boy.*"

Jayson's ear's rang violently now, and his world began to spin. Electricity crackled in his hands before he turned around and pushed through the crowd while Kaden was getting his Hero of Earth medal placed around his neck.

Jayson burst out of the back of the crowd and looked

around frantically. His heart felt like it was going to beat out of his chest. He ran straight toward the edge of the campus and dove over the railing, but instead of crashing into the water, he collided with the force field and bounced off of it, landing hard on the ground again. He curled up into a ball and rocked back and forth while dry heaving as the words:

My boy.

My boy.

My boy… played endlessly in his head.

• • •

Later that night, Headmaster Fowler was sorting through papers on his desk. He heard a creak and looked up to see blood shot eyes staring back at him in the middle of the dark room.

"Jayson? What are you doing here? I have not called for you," Headmaster Fowler said.

"I really need to speak with you," he said, his voice trembling with every word.

Headmaster Fowler shook his head while putting his papers into a neat stack.

"Very well. What is it you would like to discuss?"

"We have not spoken here in over a year. It used to be nearly every day…" Jayson remained still as his head craned around the room, "but it's been so long that I nearly forgot what your chamber looked like."

"Jayson, tell me what has been going on."

"No, *YOU* tell me what has been going on! Did I do something wrong? Please tell me what I did wrong!" Jayson yelled as he stepped closer into the light, revealing his malnourished physique and sleep-deprived face.

Headmaster Fowler reacted with disgust as he got up from his chair and walked to the large windows that overlooked the Academy.

"No, Jayson, you have not done anything wrong."

"Then what the fuck happened! You told me *I* would be the Hero of Earth and the Champion of Gidoria one day, not Kaden! You can't do this to me! You can't, you can't, you CAN'T!"

"SILENCE!" Headmaster Fowler yelled at Jayson, his voice shaking the room which caused dust to fall from the ceiling. "You do not raise your voice at me, is that understood?"

Jayson didn't respond; he only continued to stare with blank, bloodshot eyes—never blinking.

"I take back what I said earlier. You *did* do something wrong. You've become weak, and Kaden is stronger and better than you in every way! In spite of what Zo thinks, Kaden possesses an inherent gift—something that cannot be designed, cannot be built, and cannot be taught! You listen to me now, *very* carefully, and understand every word that is about to come from my mouth. You are a failure, a mistake—an abomination of a Golden—but I choose to spare you, despite what you said to me, because I still see potential in you. You should be grateful that I am still giving you a chance to go to Gidoria."

"Why did you lie to me…"

"Things and circumstances change, Jayson, as I could have never foreseen Kaden coming into the mix as he has, but one day, you will realize that nothing is set in stone, and the universe has a way of giving you things you never expected. For instance, I never expected you to fail at the one job I had assigned to you while also losing an outstanding student—"

"Mark's death wasn't my fault! He broke formation and—"

"ENOUGH!" Headmaster Fowler shouted, shaking the room so violently that the windows rattled, and the Headmaster's desk finally broke in half. "I am giving you one last chance to kill Zahavi in order to still graduate as a Warrior, and I call that mercy. Do not fail me."

Jayson's hands flexed hard into fists as his face changed from a blank stare into one that was filled with immense rage. He looked up and saw a red light blinking in the dark corner of the room before facing the Headmaster again. "I won't," Jayson said as he turned and stormed out with electricity crackling all around him.

"Headmaster Fowler," Zo said as he floated into the room, "I greatly apologize for what has become of Jayson. Perhaps I did something wrong with his—"

"Do not speak of that failure of a Hero ever again."

"Understood."

"Now, what did you come to discuss?"

"We have made a breakthrough with Silas, and I believe you should hear what he is saying for yourself."

A crooked smile grew on the Headmaster's face as they left his chamber.

• • •

Headmaster Fowler walked down the long hallways of the Lock Up while Zo floated close behind. He passed many Rogues—some cowering in fear, others dead. He glanced at the curled up, broken woman before stopping in front of Silas' cell. He typed in a code on a number pad, and the cell door slid open.

"9.67142," Silas said while shivering and stuttering. His body was beaten and burned, and he lay in a pile of broken scales and a pool of blood. "-84.66907." He repeated the two sets of numbers, over and over again.

"What is he saying?" the Headmaster asked Zo.

"The numbers appear to be a set of coordinates that correspond to a cliffside in Costa Rica. I believe he is telling us where the Sanctuary is."

The Headmaster nodded and smiled as Silas' bruised and swollen face angled upward to meet his eyes.

"You made a promise... if I told you... I would finally get to see my daughter," he said as blood spilled from his open mouth.

The Headmaster placed his wrist on Silas' bloody, scaleless shoulder. His hand gently wrapped around the back of Silas' head, caressing it softly.

"Yes, of course, I remember, and I *always* make good on my promises. No more pain now, go on and be with her. You earned it."

CRACK!

The sound of his neck snapping echoed through the halls of the Lock Up. As the Headmaster left, he dragged his hand along the transparent cell doors, smearing a trail of blood across them.

"Prep the teams, Zo."

"Which ones?" he asked.

"All of them. It is time to end this war."

CHAPTER NINETEEN

LEADER OF THE ACADEMY

AFTER MY LAST meeting with Headmaster Fowler, I felt much better about everything. Wearing the Battle Armor and picturing myself as the Champion of Gidoria made me realize that I had a greater purpose than all of this.

I could care less if Arissa didn't like me, or if I had no friends, as none of these Earth-bound things mattered to me anymore. My destiny was out there—somewhere among the stars on the Golden planet of Gidoria.

I never felt at home at the Academy, or even on Earth, for that matter. All my life, I had desired something bigger than this, and I surely wasn't going to find what I was looking for on a floating pad in the middle of the ocean, helping out teams that couldn't even help themselves.

Although I had been nervous to accept my award as the new Hero of Earth, I felt proud the moment the medal was placed over my head. Wearing it immediately cemented my belief that I was the best Hero of the Academy... and the world.

There was no one who was better than me and no one who could stand against me. All of the missions I had been on only reminded me that I had quickly outgrown this world, and it was time to move on to the next one where I would finally be able to reach my true potential as the Champion.

After I had finished signing autographs on T-Shirts and water bottles, getting kisses on the cheek from cute girls, and taking polaroid pictures with other Heroes of the Academy, I walked down the center of the campus alone with the medal around my neck.

"Hey, Kaden," a familiar voice called out behind me.

I turned around to see Ezra slipping his fingers into his pockets with his thumbs resting outside of them.

"Oh… hey," I replied. The awkwardness in the air was palpable.

"You got a second to talk?" he asked.

I thought about it for a moment.

Why not?

• • •

We sat on the platform at the top of the Power Dome, legs dangling over the edge—the place where I made my first true leap into anything, the place where it all started. I remembered seeing the smiling faces of my friends around me, laughing as they watched me fail over and over while learning how to fly.

If only they could've seen me flying in space.

In a weird way, I probably wouldn't have even been here—been alive for that matter—if Arissa hadn't saved me from an almost certain death that day. Maybe one day, after I've become the Champion, I would try to find her again and thank her.

"I'm surprised you agreed to talk," Ezra said with a

chuckle. "Last time any of us tried, we didn't see you again for months."

"I was busy; that's all," I replied as my legs swung back and forth.

"You know, I always wanted to ask you: where'd all the points come from?" All of the terrified faces of the Rogues I had neutralized flashed endlessly in my mind. "After all, we never were assigned any more big missions after that last one at the warehouse, yet somehow our team still kept climbing The Wall."

"I worked something out with the Headmaster."

"Really? Like what?"

"If you don't mind, I don't really want to talk about it."

"Fair enough. You met with him a lot, didn't you?"

"Yeah."

"Lucky. You know, after ten years of being here, I never once met with him."

I looked at him with surprise as it never dawned on me how *special* my treatment really was. Headmaster Fowler meant so much to me and was someone I looked up to greatly, so it was hard to picture my life without him at this point. I couldn't imagine how lost some of these kids must have been without that guidance.

"Don't worry about it, Ezra. It wasn't that great anyway. Honestly, it was just a lot of reading of dusty ass scrolls and more work to be done. Be grateful you didn't have to do all that."

"Man, that *does* sound shitty," he said, which made us both laugh. "So... what's next for the newest *Hero of Earth?*" he asked with a nudge of his elbow.

I sighed and thought about it as I drummed the tips of my fingers on the platform.

"Well, I guess I'm graduating to Gidoria," I finally said.

"Damn, bro, I'm proud of you. After all that work you did, you deserve it—probably more than anyone else at the Academy."

"Thanks, Ezra. I appreciate that, but the funny thing is… you're coming with me."

"What? Me?"

"Yep, and the rest of Team #22."

"But we don't have enough points? I thought that maybe the Headmaster had worked out something special just for you but… Really? All of us? How?"

"I *did* work something out, not just for me but for all of us. I'm getting us there, just like I promised."

"Wow, I can't believe it. For these past few months, none of us thought we were graduating. We had no idea what waited for us after this." Ezra took a moment to process it all. "You're a good guy, Kaden. *Thank you.*" He gave me a fist bump. "So once we get to Gidoria with the Hero of Earth, what happens next?"

"Honestly, I'm not sure. Something about me being the Champion?"

"What? You?"

"That's just what Headmaster Fowler told me," I said with a shrug.

"I remember thinking *I* was going to be the Champion." He laughed to himself. "Man those were the days… He used to hold that so far over all of our heads—telling us that any of us could be the Champion one day, and for a time, I really did believe it. Funnily enough, ever since you got here, I haven't heard that mentioned again. I guess he really did find his Champion after all."

There was a long silence after that.

"Ezra, there's another thing I need to talk to you about: the *way* we're going to get the final points we need to graduate."

"And what's that?"

"Something big is happening, like, the biggest mission that the Academy has ever attempted since it was founded."

"Holy shit. When is it happening?"

"I'm not sure, but I'm assuming any day now."

"How do you know about it? The rest of us haven't heard anything."

"I know about it because the Headmaster asked me to lead it."

Ezra rolled backward on the platform and then forward again with wide eyes.

"Whoa... well, that's a big responsibility," he said while raising his eyebrows and rubbing the back of his head.

"Trust me, I know, and if I actually could sleep, it would probably have still kept me up at night," I said, which made him laugh until the seriousness of the situation returned.

"Are you nervous?" he asked.

"You really can't tell?"

"Of course I can, I just wanted to see if you would lie about it. It's written all over your face."

"*Thanks*, that makes me feel better," I said while rolling my eyes.

"But I'm not worried about your ability to lead us. There isn't anyone else I'd want to charge into battle with than you."

"Appreciate that," I said as we stared out across the Power Dome. "Hey, Ezra?"

"Yeah?"

"Can you tell the rest of Team #22 that..." I took a deep

breath, "I'm sorry for abandoning them."

"You didn't—"

"Can you just tell that to them? Please? To Theo and everyone else in case I don't see them again before the final mission? Can you tell Arissa that everything I did... I did for her."

He patted me on the back and gripped my shoulder.

"I think you'll get a chance to say whatever you need to say, but if you don't, I promise I will, Hero of Earth."

• • •

I stood under the stream of water from the shower and watched as it poured over my face, down my chin, and off my body. A ball of red energy formed in my hand, and I directed it around me in circles and figure eights. Headmaster Fowler must've forgotten to turn my inhibitor chip back on after I had worn his armor, and I even wondered if he had disabled it permanently, showing his complete trust in me.

There was a window in the shower that faced the open ocean, and I watched as the waves passed underneath the Academy, picturing each one as if it were a memory of my time here.

When I first got to the Academy, I thought I would have all the time in the world to get used to this "Hero" stuff, but now I was only days away from graduating to an alien planet and departing from the Earth forever.

Yet, despite everything that had transpired here, I still felt like that same kid who had unknowingly left his apartment and his mom for the last time—*lost and alone.*

My time at the Golden Academy had gone by quicker than I ever thought it would, and I wondered if I should have tried to enjoy it more instead of always looking toward the future. If I had slowed down a little bit and paid attention to the *actual* world around me instead of always dreaming of the one that was quickly coming over the horizon, maybe I could have been happier.

Maybe I wouldn't have lost the only person I cared about.

The entire platform jolted, pulling me out of my thoughts and indicating that we were on the move again. It almost felt as if we were going *to* something which meant the final mission was even closer.

"All Heroes, report to the Nîmes auditorium for mission prep. All heroes, report to Nîmes auditorium for mission prep," Zo said, blasting over the intercom, and just like that, it was time to get to work.

I threw on a blue TGA, skin-tight, t-shirt from my closet, and before I left, I saw my mom's yellow crystal necklace hanging on my wall. I raised it in front of me, holding three fingers through the silver loop, and admired its beauty one last time before I slung it over my head for good luck and protection as I exited the room.

I had hoped Theo would be in our room while I was there which would have given me a chance to say something to him before we started mission prep, but he was nowhere to be found. Ezra had promised I would get a chance to talk to the rest of my old teammates before we all parted ways for good, but I didn't know if I fully believed him even though I wanted to.

I heard static come from a speaker above me, "Kaden Collins," Zo said, "report to Headmaster Fowler's chamber immediately with your suit on."

• • •

The metal pieces of my suit clanged and clunked

together as I walked toward the Headmaster's chamber.

This was it, I thought to myself. *No turning back now. It's time to be the leader that the Academy needs.*

I entered and immediately stopped in my tracks as I saw Headmaster Fowler wearing his full Champion of Gidoria Battle Armor. The overhead lights reflected off the white and gold color scheme which created an almost blinding effect, but at the same time, it was mesmerizing to look at. I walked up to him, and we clasped hands. I felt his immense strength and grip within mine.

"Are you ready?" he asked. "To finally destroy Zahavi and the Sanctuary?"

My legs wanted to shake out of my armored suit right then and there, but I just kept remembering what Ezra had said to me: *There isn't anyone else I'd want to charge into battle with than you*, and I just hoped the rest of the Academy thought the same thing.

"I'm ready to lead the Academy to victory—to finally end this war," I said confidently.

"Good," he said with a smile, putting his armored hand on my shoulder plate. "I'm fully trusting you with this, Kaden. Do not look to me for guidance on any matter. This is *your* battle to lead, and you make the calls. Show me how much I trust you." I held up a ball of red energy, and we both watched it swirl in my hand as he nodded in approval. "Now, show them the leader that Kaden Collins truly is."

I placed my shaking hands on the door leading to the auditorium. It was my last chance to turn back—to give this all up and run out of the building, take off into the sky, and head to space where I would be out of signal range before anyone could ask what the hell I was doing. I could find a new planet somewhere out there in the void—one that I could call home and finally leave this world behind forever... but *no*.

I am the Hero of Earth.

I pushed through the doors and walked across the stage, trying not to look at the massive crowd of Heroes that sat before me. I could *feel* how many people were in the room—easily a thousand of them, as anyone over the age of thirteen who had mission experience was there.

I finally made my way to the center of the massive auditorium and saw that teams were placed in numerical order, starting with Team #1 at the front of the auditorium, leading all the way up to #168.

Jayson sat in the front row, glaring at me with bloodshot eyes which sent a shiver down my spine, but I ignored him and scanned the rest of the room, immediately making eye contact with my old teammates—my friends. Theo gave me two thumbs up with a big ear-to-ear smile.

My eyes instantly locked with Arissa's, and she mouthed, *You got this*.

After seeing that, I was locked in.

"Heroes!" I yelled to the auditorium, not a single nervous cell in my body. "For far too long, Zahavi, the leader of the Rogue Sanctuary—the one who has fought against the Golden Academy for the past one hundred years, the man responsible for countless innocent non-Golden and Hero deaths alike—has remained at large and has not answered for his reprehensible crimes that he has committed upon this world. He has been in hiding since the First Golden War ended, attempting to destroy the peace, safety, and order of Earth that this Academy has worked so hard to achieve. We are now in our Second Golden War against the same enemy once again, and this war and his reign of terror will never end as long as he is alive. Today, we neutralize *THE* rogue Golden, once and for all."

The Heroes in the crowd looked at each other as I heard whispering amongst them. No one said anything, and I felt like a complete failure standing up here in my ridiculous suit thinking I was some kind of leader... but then, Theo stood up in the middle of the crowd.

"High above the sea lies a Golden Hero's dream!" he yelled as others stood up to join him.

"Together and forever, we stand as one team!
One team!"

The rest of the Heroes joined in unison.

"We fight for the Academy!
Never in battle shall we fall,
for we rise and crush them all!
Warriors unite!
Warriors unite!
To Gidoria, we go and fight!"

Underneath my suit, my arms filled with goosebumps, and I knew that these Heroes would follow me into battle and fight by my side. I turned to Headmaster Fowler who gave me an approving nod, before signaling to Zo who floated silently next to him.

"Zo, pull up a map of the Sanctuary," I said as Zo pressed a few buttons on his chair, illuminating a glass table in the middle of the stage. A hologram Earth appeared above it as Zo continued to press buttons, creating a red dot which pinpointed the Sanctuary on the globe. The Earth expanded as the hologram zoomed in on the dot, revealing a cliff face that overlooked the ocean with a forest behind it.

It's just a bunch of trees? I thought to myself.

We must've been given incorrect information because there was nothing there, but then I realized that's exactly what he would want us to believe.

From what I read about the First Golden War, Zahavi was a master strategist while also being extremely elusive, and that was the only way he was able to survive as long as he did.

"Zo, give me a thermal imaging scan of the tree line."

"Certainly."

Zo pressed some more buttons, and a thermal overlay appeared on the hologram. A massive heat signature appeared in the trees as if an entire city was in there. I looked over and saw the Headmaster nodding while running his right hand repeatedly down his beard.

"And there it is, the Sanctuary."

"Well done, Kaden," he said as he started clapping. The rest of the auditorium joined in, shaking the room with cheering.

Time for a plan of attack.

"As we can see from the multiple, independent heat signatures that run along the ridgeline, the base is well defended by what can only be presumed as cannons, which makes sense as Zahavi has had one hundred years to fortify his base, waiting for the day we attack. The second layer of defense that we have to get through is the base's shield." A holographic shield appeared over the trees. "Looking at this now, it seems that the way he has been able to avoid detection for so long has been through the use of an advanced bubble shield, which not only protected them, but also hid them from... our satellite imaging?" I asked as Zo nodded. "Zo, how strong do you suspect that shield to be?"

"Very," he replied. "It would take hours to break through it with the on board weapon systems that our ships are equipped with."

"And by that time, our ships would already have been blown out of the sky…" My mind raced as I devised a plan—all of the puzzle pieces perfectly clicking into place. "Therefore, the first phase will be led by me and any other Heroes who can fly," I said as Zo looked at me with surprise. "Those of you who are apart of this first phase will need to watch out for potential fire from the cannons as we make our approach. Once in range, Arissa, who will be carried by Helio of Team #22, will throw out a portal behind the shield, giving us access inside. We will all fly straight through the portal and make our way *here*," I said, pointing to a large heat signature toward the roof of the bubble.

"The heat signature at this location is off the charts, indicating that something big is drawing a lot of power. We will then destroy it, which I hope will bring down the shield and disable the cannon defense system."

The hologram table created an explosion within the bubble, causing the shield to collapse, revealing a simulated village within the forest.

"As we move toward phase two, all flying Heroes in the immediate area will take to the skies. It is imperative that you get out of the city as soon as possible because phase two consists of our ships raining down hell upon Zahavi's base. Unfortunately, as history tells us, this won't be enough to kill him, and it will probably only piss him off." The Heroes laughed among themselves. "Focus!" I yelled which stopped the laughter. "This is no time for laughter; this is war!" The Heroes sat up further in their seats as Headmaster Fowler smiled even bigger.

"Once phase two is complete, and we have turned the Sanctuary to rubble, we will move into phase three. The flying Heroes will return from the sky and set up a perimeter around the base, ensuring no Rogues escape during this time. The rest of the Heroes without flying abilities will be on the ground looking for survivors to neutralize. The shelling during phase two should take out any Class 1 Rogues hiding there, but there will be many more Class 2 and 3 Rogues who will survive the attack and need to be taken care of.

"As you're moving through the rubble, leave no piece unturned as you look for any Rogues who may still be alive. All Rogues must be neutralized, and you have my full discretion to eliminate any you find on sight. They are the enemy, and this war is ending with zero prisoners… and no survivors." The Heroes looked at each other again with determination. "Now, let's end this war!" I yelled as I raised a fist into the air. "For the Academy!"

"For the Academy!" a Hero yelled from the crowd, which erupted into loud cheers with fists raised in the air.

I looked across the crowd, nodding at the cheering Heroes before seeing Arissa in the center of it, smiling and clapping.

"*HERO OF EARTH! HERO OF EARTH! HERO OF EARTH!*" the crowd chanted as an immense and overwhelming feeling of *power* washed over me. I raised my hands to the crowd and basked in the glory of the moment.

• • •

Headmaster Fowler and I stood in his chamber, peering out the large windows that overlooked the Academy. Droves of Heroes moved across the campus wearing their suits—some armored, some not—and I watched as Team #22 emerged from Power Dome #1 and headed underground to the hangar.

"Exceptional job during mission prep, Kaden. You are a true leader, and I could not have picked a better Hero of Earth," he said as he patted me on my armored back.

"Thank you, Headmaster Fowler."

"Therefore, I would like to give you *this*." The Headmaster brought out a small, wooden box from behind his back. He opened it, revealing two large omega symbols: one gold, one red.

"These are crests of the Zaelzan Empire," he said as it shimmered in the light. He picked up the gold one and placed it in the center of his chest plate. It fused into the white armor.

"What does it mean?" I asked.

"*Strength*," he replied, which sent goosebumps up and down my arms. "Go ahead, take yours."

"Mine?"

"Yes, it belongs to you now."

"Why?"

He grabbed the crest from the case, placing it onto my chest plate as it clicked and secured into my armor.

"Because, you are now an honorary General of the Zaelzan Empire and future Champion of Gidoria."

I looked at the crest in the reflection of the window and felt a great sense of pride carrying it.

"We will forge your ceremonial Battle Armor when we arrive in Gidoria after this war," he said.

"But I thought you told me that I needed to win the war in order to graduate?" I asked.

"After seeing how you conducted the mission prep as

the leader of the Academy, I would say that you have already won the war since everyone believes in you just as much as I do. You will make a fine Champion and General of the Empire, Kaden," he said with a smile.

I wrapped my arms around him and hugged him tight as the metal of our armor clanged together.

"*I love you, Headmaster Fowler.*"

He hesitated and then slowly put his arms around me.

"*I... love you too... my son.* I am very proud of you and the hero you've become."

I stayed in his arms for a long time, never wanting to leave.

"Now, go. Win this war for everyone on Earth and Gidoria."

• • •

Heroes ran past, chanting my name and slapping the back of my suit as I walked through the hangar. My mind was only focused on one thing: *Arissa.* I looked around trying desperately to find her but had no luck. She must have already boarded a ship by now and was strapped into her seat waiting to take off.

I barely missed her, and now I'm never going to see her again.

"Are you looking for someone?" a familiar voice called out from behind me.

I turned around to see Arissa smiling as she walked up to me. The first thing she noticed was the Zaelzan crest in the center of my chest plate. She brought her finger to it and ran it across the smooth metal.

"It means strength," I said.

"Fitting," she responded, which made my face red.

I was more nervous standing face to face with her than I

had been standing on the stage, and I almost felt like that kid on the roof again… *almost.*

"Arissa… I've been meaning to tell you," I hesitated, my voice trembling. "Everything I did—" She pulled me into a kiss.

We kissed for a long moment until she pulled back and said, "I know why you did it, and I've always understood. Thank you for everything, Kaden. No matter what happens today, I want you to know that I loved you, the whole time. Now go save the world, hero."

She pushed me away and ran off.

Me too, I thought to myself as the hatch to the ship she boarded closed behind her, and just like that, she was gone, and I was alone again.

CHAPTER TWENTY

CALM BEFORE THE STORM

IT HAD BEEN months since Silas had gone missing, and Zahavi hadn't heard a word from him. Noel told him that Silas was still alive somewhere over the ocean, but at this point, he expected the worst and didn't believe that Silas would ever return to the Sanctuary.

"Zahavi!" Noel cried out as she came running into the council room, collapsing in front of him with tears streaking down her face. "They killed Silas! He's… He's gone."

Zahavi held Noel as she cried.

"His life force disappeared, I can't sense him anymore. He's really gone, Zahavi." Noel looked up at Zahavi. "Does this mean…"

Zahavi nodded and replied, "You should get some rest, my dear Noel. This may be your last chance to." Noel wanted to protest, but she could see that Zahavi wasn't asking.

"I understand," Noel said as she wiped the tears from her eyes and got to her feet again.

"I'm sorry about Silas, Noel. I know you loved him," Zahavi said. "We all did."

"Thank you," she said before turning to exit the room. "You should sleep too."

After Noel had turned in for the night, Zahavi sat alone in the council room and stared out across the ocean. He had done everything he could to try to stop Silas before he left, and Silas knew the consequences of leaving the Sanctuary—not only knowing that he himself would never return, but, more importantly, what it would mean for everyone else still living in it. Death and destruction would soon follow if it were located, yet he didn't care.

The Sanctuary had successfully stayed hidden for the past 100 years, and it had served as a safe haven for Goldens who managed to escape before the Golden Academy captured them. What it stood for—what it represented— would soon be destroyed.

For years, Zahavi had sent out countless Search and Rescue teams to find Goldens in need of shelter away from the DGC. Silas was the boots on the ground leader for those teams and was responsible for saving the lives of many Goldens seeking refuge from the evils of The Unity and Golden Academy.

Zahavi wondered if he had truly been responsible for the death of the one person that Silas could not save—his own daughter.

Had I made a mistake? Did my cowardice cause the death of an innocent child? Zahavi thought to himself. Her blood was now on his hands.

Silas greatly disagreed with Zahavi's beliefs which were formed after the First Golden War. He realized he would never be able to defeat the Headmaster if he were to face him again, and therefore, he only had one move left: to build the Sanctuary and rescue as many Goldens as he could without the use of force or violence.

For years, his pacifistic approach seemed to be working. The Academy's Heroes steadily declined as more and more were shipped off to Gidoria to fight in another meaningless war. By rescuing Goldens, Zahavi was winning the war without fighting in it, but, of course, that victory was short-lived.

Many of the Goldens who were living inside the Sanctuary had grown restless and sought a means to end the war themselves. For the ones who went rogue and left to go fight, Zahavi never heard from them again, proving his point that violence was still not the answer to winning the war—not yet at least.

He was only waiting for the right time to fight back. Zahavi remembered the vision he had been given from his mother Gora. It had been the last time he had spoken to her before he left Gidoria, and she told him that all he had to do was wait for the vision to come to fruition. Sadly, he was unable to convince the restless Goldens to stay hidden in safety until that time came.

Zahavi saw the painful memories flash in his mind.

"We can't stay here and let our brothers and sisters die out there! You keep telling us to wait—to stay here until he comes, but how much longer can we wait for someone or something to save us when we could be fighting back and saving ourselves!" Silas yelled to Zahavi during a council meeting.

But Zahavi had no answers for him, for even he did not know how long it would take for the vision to be realized.

"Promise me that you will never lose hope, Zahavi. If you lose hope and give up, he will never show. Only one who fully relinquishes control to the Infinity Tree can receive the

fruits of prophecy and life that it provides," Gora said as she held Zahavi's hand under the twinkling golden glow of the Infinity Tree.

She was about seven feet tall and ancient—old as life itself. She wore a white, shimmering dress over her gold skin, and she swayed with the limbs of the Tree as if they were blowing in the wind. Everytime she took a deep breath, so did the branches, glowing brighter as she breathed in, and dimming as she breathed out. After seeing this, there was no denying that Gora and the Infinity Tree were connected.

"*No matter how hard it becomes, you must stay strong. In time, everything I have foreseen will come to you in the least expected way,*" Gora said, releasing his hands and dissolving into the Tree in a beautiful display of twinkling golden lights.

Hundreds of years had passed since that conversation, and he never lost hope—not once.

• • •

The next morning, Zahavi looked out across the Sanctuary, studying the hundreds of Goldens moving about, who had returned from the outside world to give their lives to protect their home—*his* home. They were running war exercises in the training area as electricity, smoke, fire, and energy shot into the air in random bursts. Hand-to-hand and weapon combat was taking place between different swordsmen and combatants who leapt and lunged across the training area, sparring with each other. Arbor watched over them, calling out different commands and moves that they followed with perfect form and tempo. Flying Goldens swooped through the trees, diving in and out while dodging branches.

One Golden grew rock across his skin and told the others, "Give me everything you've got!" in an attempt to pierce through his outer layer, but no one was able to, and everyone cheered with him.

A sad look grew on Zahavi's face. He was afraid to accept it himself, but he secretly knew that the Sanctuary would not survive the attack unless the vision from Gora arrived before it happened. As each day passed and nothing changed, Zahavi realized that the inevitable death and destruction he foresaw was upon them. Although he had never given up hope, he knew this was the last time he would look out across the Sanctuary, as he would soon lose his home... and many of the people he loved along with it.

• • •

Zahavi entered the Battle Room of the Sanctuary and inspected the hologram of the shield. It would have to hold for as long as possible—at least until they were able to take out the Academy's ships—or even more Goldens would perish in the conflict. It was their only chance of winning the war.

A Golden flew by his window, waved, and dove out of sight, disappearing into the tree line as Noel came up the elevator platform into the Battle Room.

"Zahavi, it's time. The Golden Academy is coming," she said, looking toward the horizon.

Zahavi nodded and pressed a button on a command terminal, sending out a siren across the Sanctuary. Every Golden willing to fight ran to the cliff side and stood behind the bubble shield ready for the attack. All the other noncombative Goldens—older and injured men, women, and children—ran to a bunker entrance that led underneath the Sanctuary.

"Go, go, go!" Leona yelled, waving them inside. She welded the doors shut from the outside with laser beams from her eyes.

Zahavi pressed the infinity crest once more, and the wall that held his armor opened.

"It is time," he said as he extended his hand to the slithering, black, organic suit.

It shot out of the wall and formed a suit of armor around him. Spikes on his shoulders, knees, forearms, fingers, and elbows extended into sharp points, and the yellow energy contained within the suit breathed as he did.

Zahavi walked to the front window of the Battle Room where Noel was standing and peered out to the horizon. In the far distance, he could see hundreds of Academy ships coming directly at them. His eyes narrowed, his brow furrowed, and his teeth gritted together.

"This is the end of all of this. I'm not hiding anymore."

CHAPTER TWENTY-ONE

THE SECOND GOLDEN WAR

I LOOKED OUT THE front window of my ship toward the open water, and in the distance, I could see the faint shimmering effect of the sunlight bouncing off the bubble shield that covered the Sanctuary. Whatever was hidden beneath it was completely invisible, and it looked as if only a jungle sat there. Headmaster Fowler stood next to me with his metal gauntlets crossed over each other.

"It is time to begin phase one," I said as we inched closer to the Sanctuary.

"Good luck, Kaden. I will see you when this war is finally over," he said with a nod, stepping back from the drop hatch.

I pressed a button on the side of my earpiece, activating it.

"Heroes! Initiate phase one!"

Suddenly, the floor below me dropped, and I fell through the sky toward the ocean. To my left and right, hundreds of Heroes began dropping from the hatches underneath their ships, plummeting toward the Earth and using whatever abilities they had to soar through the air. The ships stayed far behind us to ensure they were out of the range of the

Sanctuary's defenses. We flew through the air in a 'V' formation, and as we approached, the cliff face began to shake. Large cannons emerged from the rock, locking onto us before unloading a volley of explosive projectiles.

"Evasive maneuvers!" I yelled.

We dove, dodged, and barrel rolled as explosions filled the sky and blocked out the sun with smoke. I formed an energy shield around me just as I was hit by one of the rounds and blown backward. My body plummeted toward the ocean, and seconds before impact, I regained my bearings and blasted energy from my hands and feet, turning the water below me into vapor and sending me back into the sky.

Other Heroes—who couldn't project shields—were getting blown out of the sky left and right, but there was virtually nothing we could do to stop the cannons. We were too far to disable them, and we were only moments away from being completely destroyed. My mind and heart began to race as I pictured losing the war and all of the Heroes of the Academy with it.

You're not going to win this by thinking like that, idiot.

My mind refocused as I locked onto the cannons far in front of me and unleashed a massive beam of energy toward them. My aim was slightly off, and it bounced off the bubble shield.

"Come on!" I yelled as I redirected it toward the cannons, cutting trees in half in the process.

A massive explosion erupted in the distance and blasted the top of a cannon far into the air.

"Nice hit, Kaden! Oh, shit!" Ezra yelled as a flaming streak of fire did a barrel roll in front of me, just before a cannon projectile exploded next to him.

I saw another projectile coming straight for a group of Heroes below me. I focused as hard as I could, projecting a shield in front of them just as the projectile collided with it, causing the shield to explode and shatter into a million pieces of energy and smoke.

"Arissa! Are you in range?" I yelled. "We need to shut down those cannons NOW!"

"Almost!" Arissa threw out a portal with her right hand, but it was just short of the bubble, not making it inside. Helio flapped her metal covered wings as hard as she could, trying to get Arissa closer. "Almost... there!"

I saw her hand move in a throwing motion, but before she could release a portal, a cannon projectile beelined straight for them.

"Look out!" I yelled as I projected a shield in front of them, but I didn't have enough time to strengthen it.

It shattered to pieces upon impact with the projectile, and the resulting explosion filled the sky, completely engulfing the area where they had been flying. When the smoke finally cleared, they were *gone*.

"NO!" I cried out, stopping in mid air, and looking everywhere for them, but they were nowhere to be found—disintegrated into nothingness. "ARISSA! HELIO! DO YOU COPY?"

Ezra flew down beside me. "Oh, no..."

I stood frozen as explosions filled my vision. My ears rang, drowning out the noise around me.

I faintly heard Ezra yell, "Kaden! Come on! We need to finish the mission!"

All around me, more and more Heroes were getting knocked out of the sky and blown to pieces. A flash of smoke would appear, then body parts and blood would rain down into the water below, turning the sea red. Heroes cried out, screaming and yelling—trying to escape higher into the sky, only to get obliterated by the cannons.

Rage flooded my mind, and the sounds of dying Heroes filled my ears from every direction. Arissa's death replayed over and over again in front of me. She had risked her life to save the planet, only to be blown apart by Zahavi.

Red energy exploded out of me.

"Kaden!" Ezra yelled before I turned my head to face him. He immediately saw the smoke pouring from my eyes and knew what it meant.

"Get everyone back," I called out over the explosions as I pooled up all the energy I could around me. "NOW!" I screamed, trying to contain it all.

"Everyone, fall back! Fall back now! Retreat to the ships!" Ezra yelled to the remaining Heroes who hadn't yet been killed by the cannons.

I focused harder, drawing in everything I could, forming a solid shield of glowing red energy that encompassed my entire body. I shot off into the sky and burst through the clouds in a bright flash of light.

Higher!

My body became a solid missile of red energy as I exited the upper atmosphere.

Faster!

The planet faded in the distance behind me as I soared through space.

FASTER!

I did a long back flip, keeping my speed as I aimed myself straight back down to the planet in a nose dive. The Earth's atmosphere ignited around me as I directed myself toward the battlefield. The bubble shield reappeared, and

I was right on target, flying parallel to the water.

Goodbye, Mom, I love you. Arissa... I'll see you soon.

The ocean split in two as I raced along the surface, sending giant walls of water up on either side of me. The bubble shield quickly approached, and my body collided with it.

BOOOOOOOOOOOOOOOOOOMMMMMM!!!!!!!!

I sailed straight through it like it was a piece of glass, sending out a shockwave and mushroom cloud as big as a nuclear bomb. A flash of yellow light appeared in front of me as I tore through the top of a tower and crashed into the ground far behind the Sanctuary.

● ● ●

Over the ocean, the Academy's ships drew closer, but one remained at the back of the pack. Headmaster Fowler stood inside it with a hand on his beard, overlooking the battlefield before him. The wind began to clear away the mushroom cloud over the Sanctuary, revealing a pitiful village in the trees, connected by bridges and ziplines. He shook his head in disgust.

"Headmaster Fowler," Zo's voice came through his earpiece, "the shield has fallen, and the Academy ships are now within striking distance. Kaden is not responding." A worried look grew on Fowler's face. "Should we begin phase two and commence the attack?"

"Make sure Kaden is safely out of striking distance, and then rain hell upon the Sanctuary, Zo."

"Certainly."

Within the War Room at the Academy, Zo floated in the center of the command ring. He saw Kaden's location away from the Sanctuary and signaled to the War Room operators.

"*FIRE!*" he screamed. All at once, the operators locked onto targets and pressed red buttons on their keypads.

Headmaster Fowler watched as the ships' cannons extended from their sleek underbellies and rained hell upon the Sanctuary.

BOOM! BOOM! BOOM! BOOM! BOOM! BOOM!

Thousands of explosions erupted in the distance, fires rose, and the Sanctuary was reduced to rubble. Headmaster Fowler smiled.

"We have located Kaden," Zo said through the earpiece. "He is in the jungle behind the Sanctuary and appears to be unconscious. Should we retrieve him?"

"*No!*" snapped Headmaster Fowler. "He will wake up eventually. For now, let him rest for the battle that is upon him."

• • •

Ash fell from the sky and landed on my face, causing my eyes to flutter open. I awoke in a deep crater in the dirt with a trail of trees vaporized along my flight path.

"Hello?" I said as I held my head in pain. "Does anyone copy?" In the distance, I could see smoke and fire rising.

"Kaden! You're still alive?" Theo called out through the earpiece.

I was in fact, *still alive*—to my surprise—but I didn't feel great as my energy was drained and everything ached. I wiped the blood that had pooled under my nose across my metal gauntlet.

"Yeah… I'm still kicking."

My legs were weak and shaky as I attempted to stand, only to fall back down to my knees. My armored suit was heavily damaged, and the only thing that seemed to be untouched was the symbol of strength that sat in the center of my chest plate.

I focused, pulling energy from deep within me, trying to gather any that I had regained after that risky maneuver. My body slowly healed, sealing my wounds and eliminating the trickle of blood that dropped to the dirt below me.

"Kaden, I'm glad you're finally awake. You slept through phase two, and we're now in phase—" Ezra's voice cut out before he could say anything else.

If they were in phase three, that meant my plan had worked and the shield was down. The Academy's ships would've already leveled the Sanctuary, explaining the fire and smoke in front of me.

I tried to focus my vision into the distance, but it was too blurry to identify anything. All I could see were faint flashes of yellow light through the trees. I stood up and formed just enough energy to protect myself before I shot into the sky, flying straight back toward the battlefield.

Below me, I saw a thousand Heroes and Rogues fighting in the ruins of the Sanctuary. Heads were being cut off as blood sprayed from the fresh wounds, while other Heroes were being torn in half by Rogues with super strength.

I saw Theo running across the battlefield as he lunged forward and jabbed a sharp point through a Rogue's face. He quickly pulled it out and sliced sideways, removing two more Rogue's heads in one move. I landed in the ruins next to him and began fighting, sending out energy beams in every direction. A Rogue ran toward me, and I charged up my fist.

"For the Sanctuary!" he yelled as my charged fist collided with his body, sailing straight through his stomach before exiting out the other side with what was left of his internal organs.

I tossed his body away and saw Dimitri cutting through hordes of Rogues with sharp tentacles as they came at him—body parts and blood flying in every direction.

Ezra descended from the sky and sent out a wave of fire, torching a crowd of Rogues. They screamed and jumped off the cliff, hoping to land in the water below. Flying Heroes swooped down and sliced them in half before they reached it. Their remains fell, painting the rocks below in blood.

Just then, a large sword swung over me, and I narrowly dodged it. I turned to face the one wielding it and saw he was wearing silver armor. He looked deep into my eyes and pointed his sword at me with rage growing on his face.

"You, the Red Demon, you caused all of this. You destroyed my home, my passion, and my pride! I'm going to enjoy killing you now, very, very MUCH!" he said as he swung down his sword again.

I caught it with an energy blade and began dueling him as he swung at me repeatedly with high intensity and strength. My weak energy sword cracked with every blow before completely shattering as I stumbled, landing flat on my back. He rammed his sword down into my chest, but the tip of the blade was caught in the shield that encompassed my body. My fingers—glowing solid red—wrapped around the face of the blade as I slowly pried it from his grasp, flipping it around so the hilt was in *my* hands now. I shot up off the ground.

"Oh, fuck," he said as I flew straight toward him, piercing directly through his feeble armor and impaling him into a large tree. He screamed out in pain and stared at me with hatred. "Why… Why did you do this?"

Life drained from his eyes, and his head slumped forward. I stumbled backward from his corpse and watched as blood trickled from his wound and ran down his armor.

"Kaden! Someone is taking out our ships, and we're losing Heroes before they can even arrive," Dimitri yelled through the earpiece before I could dwell on what he had said any longer.

I gazed into the sky and could see countless ships being destroyed by a flying ball of yellow energy. Within the ball of energy, I could see a spiky black suit.

Zahavi…

I timed it as best as I could and accelerated from the ground, directing energy out of my hands and feet. I crashed into the glowing figure in the sky and sent us on a collision course with the shoreline further down the coast. I formed a shield around me just before colliding with everything possible: rocks, trees, sand, and dirt. We eventually disconnected from each other, skidding across the ground and coming to a halt on the beach.

A wake of destruction was left far behind us leading back toward the Sanctuary. Then, I got my first true glimpse of the glowing yellow man in the spiky black armor that moved organically around his body. He was the one responsible for all of this—the cause of the war. Killing him would be the only way to truly end it.

I watched as Zahavi barely managed to get to his feet, stumbling while trying to hold his balance. I painfully rose to my own, not once breaking eye contact with him.

"You murderer!" I yelled as I flew toward him.

We collided once more and sailed through trees and hills. I took him into the sky, punching him the entire time.

"You killed my friends!

CRACK!

"My heroes!"

CRUNCH!

"You killed *her!*"

I pummeled him over and over again, but didn't realize that energy had begun swirling around his fist until it was too late.

Fuck.

BOOM!

He blasted me backward, sending me flipping through the air. His body collided with mine, taking us straight down toward the ocean. Yellow and red streaks of energy swirled around us as we crashed hard into the water which felt like concrete from that height. We dove deeper and deeper until we struck the ocean floor. My back scraped along it, crashing into every rock and reef it could possibly hit. I tried punching him under water, but nothing seemed to work. I couldn't focus, I couldn't strike him hard enough… I couldn't do *anything*. I felt terrified as we went over a sandbar and plunged deeper into the depths below.

The shield around my body began flickering, and I felt cold water rushing in all around me. As we descended into a ravine, the light of the sun dwindled, leaving us in complete darkness aside from the glow of our shields. My entire body felt like it was in shock. Everything was shutting down, and my vision became blurry. Water rapidly filled my mouth, and I began to drown.

The pressure in my ears felt like my head was going to explode, and soon after, I felt my eardrums rupture. The light emitting from my eyes began to flicker, the air bubbles from the vaporized water began to decrease, and I felt his grip loosen until he fully let go of me. The glow from his body faded into the distance as he propelled himself to the surface. Fish swam around me as I lay motionless in the dark void of nothingness.

"Hey, Kaden," Arissa said to me on the rooftop of the Villas as we looked up to the galaxy above us. She wrapped herself around me and squeezed tight as I looked over and stared into her pink and purple eyes. "I love you."

"I love you too. Can we just stay here, forever? I don't have to go back to that, do I?"

"No, you don't. You don't have to do anything, Kaden, as you don't owe them a thing. We can stay here together... forever. It's your choice."

Then I saw her back in the hangar, ships flying all around us.

"I want you to know that I loved you, the whole time. Now go save the world...

"Hero."

Red energy swirled around me, creating a cocoon over my body. I felt cold water being expunged from my lungs, my fractures healing, and my mind becoming clear again as my energy began to return. Red light shot out of my eyes, mouth, hands and legs until...

BOOM!

Suddenly, I was standing in a dome of air with the ocean expanding outward in all directions. Anger grew inside me as I screamed and shot out of the ocean. I hovered over the water, red light pouring from my eyes and swirling around me as I looked out to the destroyed Sanctuary in the distance. I launched toward it, air ripping past me, but I didn't feel *anything*—no pain, no sensations, only pure energy, pure power, and pure rage.

Theo, Dimitri, and Ezra continued to fight their own battles against various Rogues. Theo cutting and stabbing with his crystal arms, Dimitri slicing and slashing with his tentacles, and Ezra providing air support by raining down more fire into the crowds. I floated down to the center of the Sanctuary, which was now reduced to ash and rubble. Everyone stopped fighting and froze in their tracks as they turned toward me.

"ZAHAVI!" I yelled out, looking for him. "It is time to end this!"

Zahavi descended from the sky and floated in front of the crowds of Rogues and Heroes, facing me. The glow of energy swirling around my body nearly blinded him.

"If this is how it ends…" Zahavi said as he looked around at the carnage before clenching his fists. "Then so be it."

We flew forward and crashed into each other.

BOOOOOOOOOMMMM!!!

An explosion of energy erupted around us. Red and yellow beams of light shot out in every direction, and Heroes and Rogues screamed as they were melted by them. We dished out a barrage of lightning fast punches, headbutts, and kicks—each one creating sonic booms that leveled trees and sent Heroes and Rogues flying backward. I grabbed his arm and flipped him over my shoulder before slamming him into the ground. He barely managed to form a shield in front of him that I easily broke through with a charged punch.

"YOU'RE WEAK!"

I punched him repeatedly, his face becoming more bloody and swollen with each hit.

"FIGHT BACK!"

I swung left and right, sending blood, spit, and teeth flying in every direction. All the pain, all the suffering, all the needless deaths he had caused… all of it at the hands of this *monster.*

"THIS IS HOW THE GREAT ZAHAVI DIES?!"

Anger poured out of me with each punch until he was barely recognizable. I wound up the finishing blow behind me, my fist glowing solid red as I stared down at his mangled body and face.

"*Then so be it.*"

I rammed my fist toward him.

"Kaden! Stop!"

I stopped my fist at the last second, inches from his bloody face.

"Arissa?"

I turned to see Arissa limping out of a portal.

"Don't do this. Please, Kaden, be the hero that I know you are. Don't kill him."

I looked back down at the broken man in front of me, beaten to near death. My clenched fist hung in the air, blood dripping off my knuckles as it shook violently, wanting to come down and deal the finishing blow.

If I killed him, I could end the war and go to Gidoria as the Hero of Earth and become the Champion and General of the Zaelzan Empire. All of this could be achieved with one punch, right here, right now.

"The Kaden I know is still in there somewhere behind those red eyes. Please, for *me,*" she said, covering her face from the bright glow of my body with her opened hand as she drew closer.

The two sides of me fought for control.

Kaden Collins vs. the Red Demon.

I looked down at Zahavi as he coughed up blood. He stared back—not with horror, not with fear, not with anger but with *acceptance.* He closed his eyes in defeat, preparing for what was to come next.

I bent backward and yelled as a beam of energy shot straight into the sky. Everyone cowered in fear, covering their eyes from the blinding light. The energy formed a bridge to the heavens and shot deep into space. The body of Zahavi—beaten, broken, and bloody—lay underneath me. My vision started to fade, and weakness and pain returned as the light and smoke in my eyes *extinguished.*

"Arissa?" I called out, nearly blind as I stumbled backward.

"I'm right here, Kaden, I'm right—" A massive bolt of electricity struck me and sent me flying to the side, rolling across the dirt.

I twitched and convulsed helplessly. The attack was a direct hit to my back with no shield to protect me. Excruciating pain coursed through my body.

"*I'm* going to Gidoria to become the Champion, not YOU!" Jayson stood over me, his eyes expelling electricity as he sent another volley into my body. I screamed in pain as my body spasmed violently while surveillance orbs circled our position. "See, Headmaster Fowler? Do you finally *see?* He's the weak one, not me! I've always been the strongest! I did everything right! I won't let Kaden take this away from me! *I* shall win the war! *For the Academy!*"

"Jayson, NO!" Arissa yelled.

Jayson unleashed a torrent of electricity toward helpless Zahavi, but Arissa redirected it into the sky with a portal.

Jayson stood frozen, nearly in shock. He looked between Zahavi and Arissa multiple times.

"You're protecting the enemy? You're protecting HIM!" Jayson sent out another bolt toward her, faster than she could redirect it. It struck her, sending her flying backward before coming to a halt in the dirt. "That makes you a Rogue, and as Kaden said... *all* Rogues must be NEUTRALIZED!"

He electrocuted her, causing her to scream and cry out in pain.

"A... Arissa..." I groaned as I reached out an arm to her while writhing in pain in the dirt.

She screamed louder as red light began to flicker in my eyes. I sheepishly rose from the dirt, barely able to stand.

"YES! Show me you're not weak, Kaden Collins! Show me why you believe you deserve to be the Hero of this planet!"

I brought my hands together and gathered a faint ball of energy within them as Arissa's screams filled my ears. I yelled, light and smoke exploding from my eyes, as I unleashed a beam of energy toward him. He shot out a bolt of lightning, and the two opposing forces met, sending out a shockwave across the surrounding area.

My eyes glowed brighter as I released more energy from my hands, pushing his electricity back toward him, but I could feel my life force draining, my body growing skinnier, and the light from my eyes beginning to putter out. My emergency energy reserves were fully depleted, and I was *dying*.

"It was a respectable effort, Kaden, but we both know you can't keep this up." His electricity started to overpower the beam and it pressed further toward me. "I'll make sure to collect your Hero of Earth medal off your corpse once this is done."

In a bright flash of light, Ezra landed next to me and released a wave of fire from his hands. Jayson kept one hand toward me while using the other to send out another bolt to meet Ezra's fire before it torched his body.

Dimitri swooped in with black wings and wrapped around Jayson's legs with tentacles just as a portal appeared next to him. Theo and Helio launched out of the portal, spearing through Jayson's back with a sharp crystal point and sword. They dove for cover, and all at once, the electricity stopped, and fire and energy engulfed his body, incinerating him instantly, leaving nothing in his place.

Helio collapsed, bleeding and badly injured. Half of her body was burned, and she was missing one of her wings.

"Helio? Helio!" Arissa said as she crawled over to her and began to cry while holding her in her arms.

"I see… the endless freedom of the sky," she said as life faded from her eyes. Dimitri ran over to her and slid down next to them, putting a hand on Helio's face.

"No, NO! Please, Helio! Please wake up!"

He hung his head, tears streaming down his face. Ezra and Theo joined them and wrapped their arms around the group as I limped over to Zahavi's bloody body and looked down at him. A single finger rose from the dirt and pointed at me as I quickly raised my fists in case he tried to attack.

"Where… Where did you get *that?*" Zahavi asked, coughing up more blood and pointing to my chest.

I looked down and saw my mother's crystal necklace, hanging in front of the Zaelzan crest.

"That is my wife's necklace. I gave that to her… a gift

from Gidoria." My friends turned toward him at the sound of this, looking at each other in disbelief and then at me. "Did you kill her and take it from her corpse?"

I froze, unmoving as I couldn't comprehend what he was saying.

"This is my mother's necklace," I said, barely able to get the words out.

My fingers reached the crystal, and I held it up to the sunlight. It glowed bright yellow. My eyes tracked downward, and I saw the yellow glow fade from Zahavi's body. My hands puttered out a faint amount of energy as I held them over him.

"Your *mother...*"

"What are you saying!" I yelled. "ANSWER ME!"

"Amanda Collins."

"Don't listen to him!" Headmaster Fowler yelled. "He's ly—" I ripped my earpiece out and threw it to the side before he could finish.

"That's her name... This was hers."

"I know, *Kaden.* Gora's vision... It was you. It has always been you," he said, gripping his side in pain.

The energy from my hands began to fade as my brain worked to put the pieces together.

"*Dad,*" I said, before he raised a hand out to me.

I reached for it, our fingers almost touching.

His lips trembled as he said, "*My—*"

BEEP!

I collapsed onto the floor. My powers were gone, and I was left lying in the dirt—helpless and in agony.

What happened to my... The inhibitor chip.

"No," I muttered.

A ship landed next to us in the ruins of the Sanctuary.

The drop hatch opened, and Headmaster Fowler emerged from it, walking toward us in a full set of white and gold Battle Armor that glistened in the sun.

"NO!" I screamed.

"Stay away from him!" Theo yelled, running toward the Headmaster.

He swatted Theo away like he was nothing more than a pest, sending him crashing into a tree with ease. Theo's crystals shattered around him, and his face dropped into the dirt.

"Stop!" Ezra yelled, holding up his hands.

He unleashed a blast of orange fire that turned white. It was brighter and hotter than the sun, engulfing Headmaster Fowler in flames. We all covered our eyes, the immense heat ignited everything behind the blast. The Headmaster raised his hands and pushed through the fire, eventually grabbing Ezra's arms and throwing him far into the distance toward the sea. Headmaster Fowler's armor now glowed bright red and steam rose from it, but he was unscathed with not a burn on him.

"Kaden! Run!" Arissa said, but I was unable to move, and with the little strength she had, she sent out a portal below Headmaster Fowler. He quickly side-stepped it, not falling in.

Dimitri slashed him with a tentacle, but he grabbed it and threw him into Arissa, knocking them both aside.

Finally, Headmaster Fowler stood over Zahavi and I, looking at what was left of the Sanctuary around him. Huts and trees were engulfed in flames, and mangled corpses lay across the floor of the jungle as death hung in the air like a thick fog.

"So, this is where the great Zahavi has been hiding all

these years…" he said, picking up a piece of rubble off the ground, inspecting it, and flicking it aside. "As your *son* said, you're weak. You've been pathetically cowering in fear, letting your loved ones fight your battles for you, leading them to their deaths, all because you were too afraid to face me again."

Headmaster Fowler put an armored boot on Zahavi's chest, slowly pushing down as Zahavi screamed in pain.

"Stop!" I yelled. "You're killing him!"

Headmaster Fowler smiled as Zahavi's bones cracked and crunched under the enormous weight of his boot. Blood gushed from Zahavi's mouth, but a conflicted look grew on Headmaster Fowler's face just before he stopped the pressure and lifted his boot from him.

"But I'm not here for a weak and useless Royal Gidorian, no, I'm here for the strong and powerful one: my future Champion," he said as he walked toward me.

He grabbed me by the neck of my armor and dragged me across the dirt. I tried to fight back, but I had *nothing*— no energy to fight with, only my torn apart, bare hands. The skin across my knuckles cracked and broke open, trying to punch my way out.

"LET GO OF ME!" I yelled as I fought, but there was no way I was getting out of his grip.

"My exile and mission here on Earth is done, Zahavi, and I choose to spare you now, not because I *can't* kill you, but because I want you to see this moment. I want you to watch this time as I take your son away from you," he said, raising me into the air next to him. "Goodbye, old friend. I'm truly sorry it had to end this way." He wrapped his hand around the crystal necklace and tore it from my neck before tossing it at the feet of my father. "You should have stayed dead."

"You're not taking my son, Fowler." Yellow light flickered within Zahavi's eyes. "You're not taking him from me again!" He launched straight at the Headmaster, who reacted quicker than the speed of sound, grabbing Zahavi by the neck which sent out a sonic boom.

"I won't... let you take... my—" The Headmaster slammed him so hard into the Earth that his body created a tunnel through it, disappearing from sight.

"Dad!" I called out, fighting and screaming. "Dad! Please come back!" He dragged me into the ship, and the drop hatch began to close behind us.

"Dad!"

CHAPTER TWENTY-TWO

RETURN
OF THE HERO

"**I** LOVED YOU LIKE my own son," Headmaster Fowler said as I painfully limped down the hallway of the Lock Up. My hands were bound in magnetic cuffs, my inhibitor chip was still activated, and my injuries were not healing.

"I gave you *everything*—everything I knew, everything I learned, and most importantly, I offered you salvation—a new life beyond this pathetic, worthless planet and existence. We could've conquered the universe, Kaden, and yet, you still chose this path? This is how you repaid me? Choosing someone who never even loved you? Someone who never loved you as *I* did? He left you—*abandoned* you, and now he has killed your teammate and hundreds of other Heroes, all for what? To bring an end to the most peaceful time in human history. But it doesn't matter now; nothing does. Earth and this chapter of both of our lives has closed. We will put this all behind us; I know we will. The dark vision—the Red Demon prophecy—has yet to be fulfilled. There is still hope for the Zaelzan Empire."

"Where are we going?" I weakly asked.

"I always make good on my promises."

A door slid open, and lying before me, crumpled in a

ball of blood and broken bones, was my mother. Her face resembled that of my father's: beaten and bruised.

"No, no! Stay away, please! What more could you want from me? I told you everything! Just let me die," she groaned.

Her eyes were swollen shut, and I wondered if she could even see me.

"Mom! Oh God, Mom! What did he do to you?" I cried as I dropped down and held her hand in mine, unable to hug her as my arms were bound by cuffs.

"K... Kaden? Is that... you?"

"Mom, I'm right here, OK? I'm right here. You're going to be okay. I'm going to get you out of here," but I didn't know how.

My powers were gone, Headmaster Fowler was much stronger than me, and I couldn't even carry her. Truthfully, there was *nothing* I could do, and we both knew it. Tears ran down my face as I saw bloodshot eyes barely crack through her swollen eyelids.

"Oh, Kaden, my sweet boy. You came back to me. You finally came back to me like I always knew you would, but... why did you leave me?"

"I didn't leave you! They took me away! I tried to come home, but they didn't let me, Mom! I really tried to come home!"

A tear from one of her swollen eyes rolled down her cheek.

"Did... Did you become a hero? What you always wanted to be?"

My hands trembled, holding hers, as tears dripped onto the cold floor and nearly froze the second they touched it. I looked at her skin and saw that it was black from frostbite.

"No, Mom, no, I didn't... *He* took everything from me."

"I'm sorry, Kaden."

"It's not your—"

"I'm sorry that you still don't see."

Her swollen, busted lip dripped blood onto the same tattered clothes that she was wearing the day I left the apartment for the last time.

"See what?" I asked.

"That you were *always* a hero... and my hero came back for me."

The pain on her face faded as she went limp and slumped against the cold wall.

"Mom?" I said as I shook her. "Mom, please don't leave me. Please don't leave me here alone! I don't want to be alone again, Mom, PLEASE!" I called out, but she was gone, and there was no bringing her back.

"It is time to go," Headmaster Fowler said as he grabbed my armor once more.

"All that time... you *lied* to me. You took me away and *killed* her..."

My entire body began to fill with more energy than it could contain—a power that I had never felt before. Headmaster Fowler grabbed me by the throat and lifted me to face him.

"I did what had to be done for this planet and for Gidoria! How can you still not see! One pathetic, worthless life for billions across both planets!" he yelled as my feet dangled in the air.

"*YOU KILLED MY MOTHER!*" I screamed.

BEEP! BEEP! BEEP! BEEP! BEEP! BEEP!

The inhibitor chip in my neck melted underneath my skin. My eyes expelled energy, and I became a being of solid red light as my cuffs snapped apart.

"How did you—"

My hand shot to his neck, and I squeezed tight, feeling his spine crack within my palm. The glow from my body filled the room as energy swirled faster and faster until…

BOOOOOOOOOOOOOOOOOOOOOOOOOOOOOOO OOOOOOOOOM!!!!!!!!!!!!!!!!!!!

I flew into the sky, and a massive plume of smoke rose behind me where the Academy once floated. The energy around my body carried me through the air, and I wasn't sure where it was taking me, but I felt like I was going in the right direction. I ended up in space, high above the planet, with stars and galaxies far off in the distance. I wanted to fly to them, leaving all of these Earth and Gidorian problems behind me.

I can start a new life somewhere out there in the cosmos. Just go! There are endless worlds, possibilities, and lives to be lived!

But, instead, I just floated—suspended in space for what felt like an eternity, until a voice called out, telling me my work was not finished as the Hero of Earth. Energy blasted out of me toward the stars, and I began falling down to the pale blue dot.

• • •

I hovered above the rubble while a drenching rain poured down on top of me, extinguishing the remaining fires in the trees. Rain drops bounced off my glowing red shield and evaporated instantly. The only thing that was left of the Sanctuary was smoke and ash. Energy began to fade from my body, dissipating into the air as I raised my head to the person before me.

"Welcome home, my son."

AFTERWORD

A ND THAT CONCLUDES *The Golden Academy*, book one in the first trilogy of The Gidorian Saga, with many more books to come. I hope you enjoyed reading it as much as I enjoyed writing it, as this book means so much to me and has allowed me to rediscover a passion that I so greatly missed.

I first began writing stories when I was thirteen years old, and my understanding of grammar, vocabulary, and the art of story-telling and structure was very limited. Despite these things, I still gave it my best and attempted to tell the stories that I wanted to tell.

The two novellas I wrote were called *Inferno* and *Trapped and Alone*. The former is a superhero story, and the latter is a survival story. Both of these stories were too big for me at the time, but I still finished them and read them to whoever would listen. I never published either one, but *The Golden Academy* heavily draws elements from both of those stories. Little did thirteen-year-old Eric Bowden know at the time, he would one day help write twenty-two year old Eric's first novel.

Many years after writing those first novellas, I found screenwriting, which I greatly embraced, and began writing comedy scripts in my free time just for the joy and satisfaction it gave me. To me, writing is as fun as any of my other favorite hobbies. Although it can be difficult at times, there is usually nothing else I would rather be doing than writing, and that feeling has not left me a decade since first trying it.

After many years of writing scripts, I decided that I wanted to pursue screenwriting in college. I attended the University of Utah as a film major, and for four years, I religiously studied story and character in an attempt to hone my skills as an aspiring screenwriter.

In the spring semester of my senior year, I was talking to my screenwriter friend, and he mentioned that he was wanting to write a book. I encouraged him to do it and gave him a few tips, remembering the days when I used to write short stories and novellas myself.

As the days passed following this conversation, I couldn't help but wonder if I should try to write a book too. It had been almost ten years since I last tried to write one, and I wondered what it would be like now that I had many more years of schooling under my belt and a better understanding of storytelling itself.

The original idea that came to me was *Super Hero High School*, and it was the first note that I had ever put down in my phone while brainstorming for this novel. It is still there to this day. The galactic story that has blossomed from that original idea has been nothing short of incredible. Soon after, the title for that "High School" came to me as the "Golden Academy," which ended up being the title of this book.

When you start to dream about a school filled with superheroes, you must ask yourself many questions: Who runs it? Who populates this school? How did they get their powers? Who is the specific student you want to follow?

What makes him special? And from there, the story begins to unravel itself in ways you never expected.

It became hard to focus on anything but the story, as I found myself daydreaming when I was awake and dreaming about it when I was asleep. When I finally sat down to write it, I had the beginning up until "The First Mission" and the ending planned out, but that was it. I had a lot of ideas that I wanted to incorporate: scenes I wanted to create, ideas and themes I wanted to explore, and experiences that I've personally lived through in my own life that I wanted to share with the world, but they hadn't all come to me yet, so I was nervous to start.

I finally sat down and went for it, and I finished the first draft in exactly seven days. It was 51,000 words, just over novel length, and I achieved this by working nonstop, doing three, four-hour sessions a day for a week straight, and finishing it on Sunday night a few minutes before the clock struck midnight.

Almost ten years after writing my first superhero novella, I finally finished my first full-length super hero, sci-fi, fantasy novel. I was able to do this by setting a goal of 50,000 words and not stopping until I accomplished it. It took over a year to fully rewrite and edit it multiple times, but finally, it was finished.

Most of the story revealed itself during the writing of the first draft, as I hadn't outlined much. During this time, I also discovered I was a pantser, not a plotter, which means I am the type of writer who likes to fly by the seat of my pants and come up with the story as I go. I know this may make some of my readers fearful for the ending to this series, but fret not, as I have never stopped thinking about it since the day I started, and I have already written drafts for books two, three, and four, as well as the eventual end of the entire Gidorian Saga.

Just as Gora spoke of, sometimes things in our lives come back to us in the most unexpected ways—as writing books has now come full circle for me. I have rediscovered my love for novel writing, and I plan on continuing to write books until the end of my days. As I continue pursuing a Master's of Screenwriting at Loyola Marymount University, I plan on utilizing both crafts side by side in order to tell all my stories through any medium I can.

Thank you for joining me on this journey so far, and I can't wait to show you what the rest of this universe has in store as we venture deeper into it, unraveling the mysteries and secrets as we go along.

—ERIC BOWDEN,
LOS ANGELES, MAY 19, 2024